BEING HERE

Jaime P. Espiritu

PETRADOME ENTERPRISES
Virginia

Library of Congress Catalog Number 96-70904

ISBN Number 1-57087-290-2

Petradome Enterprises
P.O. Box 4471
Alexandria, Virginia 22303

Manufactured in the United States of America
00 99 98 97 96   10 9 8 7 6 5 4 3 2 1

To all my American friends, past,
To all my ***fellow*** *American friends, present;*
And to all the immigrants to America today and in the future,
I dedicate this work.

-jpe

CONTENTS

📖

📖

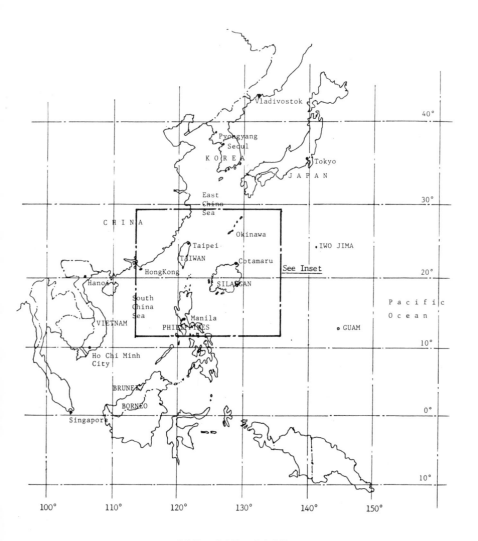

THE   FAR   EAST

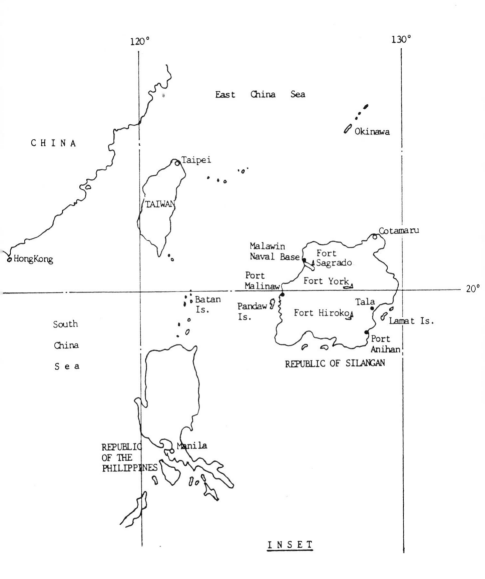

120°   130°

East China Sea

CHINA   Okinawa

Taipei

TAIWAN

Cotamaru

Malawin   Fort
Naval Base   Sagrado

Port   Fort York
Malinaw

HongKong   20°

Batan   Pandaw   Tala
Is.   Is.   Fort Hiroko   Lamat Is.

South   Port
China   Anihan
Sea   REPUBLIC OF SILANGAN

REPUBLIC   Manila
OF THE
PHILIPPINES

INSET

▥ 1 ▥

THE MAN WHO WOULD BE PRESIDENT

T he end of summer was only a week past and already, it seemed far behind. The past days in Washington had been rather uncomfortably below normal. Very windy, even now as Nicholas Harrison Gabriel fought the evening rush-hour on 15th Street bound for Virginia.

But he didn't mind any of these: the weather or the traffic. This was all part of life inside the Capital Beltway. You get used to it after seven consecutive years in the area. As a matter of fact, he thought as he drove past the classic edifice of the Main Treasury building, that's what makes this town what it is: its own sets of knowns and unknowns.

For instance, the hordes of civil servants that implement or enforce the government bureaucracy daily upon the newborn and the social security recipients alike: there

1

wouldn't be much need for keeping them on the government payroll if they all knew what they were doing and then maybe learned how to do them better later so they wouldn't have to do them again. Most of them have to be kept in the dark, some sort of the netherworld of the unknown, so they could justify keeping their jobs.

On the other hand, there were the givens, the known events before they happen such as an evening logjam on a cold and windy late September workday, the government holidays, the blooming of the cherry blossoms around the Tidal Basin, the July Fourth parade and other such Washington things.

Nicholas Gabriel was on his way home from work just like these hordes of civil servants he was on the road with heading south towards the Potomac. Unlike them, though, he didn't work for the U.S. government. Work was for Hunt, Ingram and Kimura Partnership, PC, Consulting Engineers, up 18th Street between M and L Northwest. And home was a two-bedroom condo in Alexandria near the beltway at Duke and Telegraph. But he wasn't heading straight home either. He was on his way to the Ellipse, a stopover he had made on a few other occasions, to see a friend, a man who introduced himself to him some six months ago at a construction site as Edward McKenny.

Edward McKenny was a bum. A real bum. One of several thousand homeless in the city. But before he was a bum, he was a member of the working class society. Middle class. Family. Wife and two kids (a boy and a girl). He was a man. And he had friends. At least he thought he did.

Everything was fine: the marriage, the job, the kids, the wife. For twenty years. The kids were grown and off to college. There was some talk of a renewal of marriage vows, a second honeymoon. Then he made some decisions which sometimes cost people their credibility at work when they didn't work out, and sometimes cost them their jobs. When the job went, so did the money savings, the house, and so did the wife. But what hurt the most was the loss of respect especially those of his kids, not to mention that of his wife and everybody else's.

All of that happened in the next four years, followed by the next three of trying to bounce back, getting into another relationship, and another, and another, a process which brought him to the conclusion that women aren't trustworthy people and perhaps colder than men. Not much happened, in terms of employment and personal economics, and human relationships, to regain the respect and dignity he lost in life.

Thus, it came to be that as far as he was concerned, he might as well have lost his life. In the two years that followed which led to this day on a bench at the Ellipse, he descended rapidly into a state of gloomy alienation, relinquished all his cares in the world, what little self-respect he had left and any hope of adding to it.

He turned into a bum. Not a wino, though, which he refused to be called as Nicholas once inadvertently did. He wasn't the drinking type. Beer was the only alcoholic beverage he cared to dull his senses with when he could afford it. But he was a regular bum just like any other seen at the Farragut Square, McPherson Square, Lafayette Park, the Ellipse, the DuPont Circle.

His alienation from humanity ran so deep within him that even among his (present) kind, he was an outcast. He gave no quarters and asked none of his fellow bums. He refused to share a grate with anyone once he had claimed it for the night. Very rarely would he remain on a park bench when someone else came to occupy it.

Of all people, bums or regular humans, it seemed very unlikely as he felt then - six months ago at that construction site up 14th and L - that a fellow like Nicholas, a foreigner... well, a naturalized American citizen, might gain his confidence. He wasn't particularly fond of any foreign nationals with their many accents and alien ways coming over to take over American jobs and everything else that goes with them - housing, schools, the whole neighborhood. At the same time, however, he admired how they virtuously manage to overcome anything that tries to put them down especially some people's attitudes toward them, and make something out of themselves in America.

This was basically what fueled his curiosity about the man and caused him to open up to Nicholas, besides the fact that Nicholas helped him get a few days of temporary work at the construction site. He was scavenging at the site for some scrap pieces of plywood or drywall he could use as a lean-to for when it rained (it was late April and it poured frequently then). The carpenter foreman caught an eye of him and was about to have him thrown out to the other side of L Street when Nicholas, a professional engineer who could toss any ordinary foreman about the jobsite at the flick of a finger, intervened.

Nicholas offered to give him a chance to work for what he needed, and then some. He stayed for four days clearing up finished rooms and floor areas of construction remnants, picking up trash piles and carrying them to the trash bins. When he left, he had his lean-to parts, plus eighty-five dollars in his pocket, more money than he had seen at one time in almost three years. He also carried Nicholas' phone number on a piece of paper which Nicholas had offered for him to use to get in touch, for anything.

Whatever form of relationship now existed between the two of them came as a result of human curiosity. The help

Nicholas extended to Edward at the construction site was a purely humanitarian act, not at all personal. But later, when he looked into the bum's eyes, he saw a man with a human dignity that still stood out but somehow lacking in the spirit to defend it, pursue it. The man, in other words, simply didn't care as he would frequently mumble on every single occasion of Nicholas' presence.

"I don't give a damn," he would say under his breath, looking at the Washington monument at a distance across Constitution Avenue or the rush of humanity around Farragut Square. "I don't give a damn anymore," he would say again with absolute indifference to all that existed around him.

He wasn't mad or angry, Nicholas had observed. He was just totally uncaring. Empty. Devoid of any desire for any form of recognition or the basic human respects from anyone.

He meant what he said everytime he said it: He didn't give a damn; he didn't care. It was the simple truth about him, the single, most meaningful thing he stood for. He was a bum.

There was no escaping his curiosity when Nicholas learned that this social derelict was once a middle-class wage-earner. And not only that: a husband and a father. A family man.

What happened? How could this be - in America?

People from all over the world would do anything - risk their whole life-savings, even their lives, sell the clothes off their backs if they have to - to come to America. And then start from nothing once they're over.

My parents did the same thing twenty years ago, he thought. They didn't have to sell the clothes off their backs, and they didn't exactly have to start from nothing. But they came, uprooted the whole family from the old country, brought me over when I was twelve, and my sister, two years older, and bettered themselves, their lives. Our lives.

But this - this abysmal human existence. This bum's life. This bum! How could anyone possibly allow this to happen to himself? In America?

What could possibly bring a man to this point of uncaring in life? Here, in America?

Nicholas finally squeezed himself out of the tangle on 15th Street, made the right turn to Constitution and pulled in quickly to the Ellipse where he had no trouble at all finding a space at the perimeter parking.

Edward was waiting for him on a bench facing the White House. He wore a spring coat that must have fitted him nicely ten, twelve years ago when he belonged to the working class and before he lost that middle-class weight, without which now the coat and even the rotting corduroy jacket under it looked one or two sizes too big. He sat with arms folded over his chest, legs stretched out one over the other on a heel, contemplating the mud-stained tip of his beat-up shoes and hardly took notice of the man who stood beside him.

"Wake up, you bum!" said Nicholas abruptly.

"Huh?" Edward muttered, stirring. "Oh, it's you. Hey, don't call me that. I'm no bum," he said, mocking a reprimand of Nicholas. "I might look like a bum, but I'm no bum."

"What the hell are you? Who the hell are you - the Secretary of State? White House Chief of Staff?"

"I'm a human being just like you and the man who lives in that house and everybody else in this stinkin' world. I didn't think you'd show up. Welcome to my bench. Have a seat."

"I got your message," Nicholas said, sitting down while Edward inched away to his half of the bench and straightened up a bit. "The secretary couldn't wait to give it to me as soon as she found me. 'A call from the White House' she said."

"That wasn't exactly a lie. I made the call form that telephone over there," Edward said, pointing to a public telephone several yards away clockwise of the Ellipse with a good view of the White House. "I have to make reference to a specific location I'm calling from -"

"Cut the crap, Edward. What's up?" Nicholas asked, turning serious. "You've finally decided to contact your family and let them get you out of this waste?"

"What family?" the bum muttered. "I don't have any family. I never had any family. Don't talk to me about that."

"If that isn't it, then I know what it is. I know what it is. You bought a house in McLean, Virginia!"

"Get outa here."

"Potomac, Maryland?"

Edward didn't even open his mouth that time. He just stared at Nicholas looking somewhere between irritated and seriously desperate to communicate something to another human being.

"I know," Nicholas went on, hoping perhaps to cheer the man up even for one moment of his wretched situation in life or to actually succeed in conning him out of his honest reason for wanting to see him. "You went and got yourself a job out there. A full-time job."

"Please don't insult me. Quit making fun of me."

"Alright, I'm sorry."

"Don't say you're sorry," said Edward, shooting up from his half of the bench, stomping a shoe in a half-step on the ground toward Nicholas. "If you're going to do something for which you're going to be sorry, then don't do it. But once you did it anyway, don't apologize for it. Stick to it.

If you made an ass of yourself, then be an ass." And walking a few steps away while gathering the loose coat and hugging it around him against the early fall chill, added: "Just be a goddamn ass just like everybody else out there."

"Alright, alright," Nicholas cajoled, unable to reconcile with the idea that he just admitted being an ass to a street man. "So, can we talk straight now? Is there anything I can do for you? Anything you'd like me to do for you, Edward?"

"No. Nothing," said the homeless man without turning.

"C'mon, Edward. What did you get me out here for?"

"Nothing, I said."

"Then why did you call?" Nicholas now half-yelled. "You must have a reason for it."

"Maybe I do, but why do I have to tell you? Why do you have to ask?"

"Look, man, I haven't got all night. And it's getting darker, and colder. You're used to this kind of life. I'm not."

"Then go home," Edward replied, still not turning, talking to the wind, watching the mist coming out of his mouth and letting Nicholas talk to his back. "Don't let me hold you up."

"Darn right I won't," said Nicholas, getting up quick and walking towards the car.

Halfway there, he heard Edward call: "Got anything to eat?"

Nicholas hadn't intended to leave. He just wanted to see how long it took Edward to drop his cover. To open up. And when, a minute later, the two of them were sitting on the bench again, he knew that asking for food wasn't itself Edward's act of opening up. It was just another cover. Maybe he did need the food alright. But that wasn't it. He needed to unload some inner burden. He was lonely, in his mind, and in his heart.

Why do you have to ask? Nicholas knew he really didn't have to. And the food he brought - a chicken sandwich - which he had in his overcoat lining pocket all along was secondary to bringing himself as company on the bench, or anywhere else around the Ellipse the two of them might wander off to. He sat quietly on the bench while the bum ate, both hands buried deep in his overcoat side pockets, one of them holding two packs of cigarettes he would hand out in the next appropriate moment.

"How's work today?" Edward asked unexpectedly when the chicken sandwich was down to approximately two bites.

"Not bad, thanks. Very kind of you to ask."

"Say, what kind of money do you make working as a -"

"That's not very kind of you to ask," Nicholas rebuffed.

"What the hell does it matter? I don't care."

"That's right. However, I might say that working as a structural engineer for these guys, the partnership firm I'm with, I do okay. I pay the mortgage, and the bills, pretty much on time."

Silence. Then, finally, Edward did open up, saying: "I want you to tell me something, Nicholas. What is important to you?"

"What do you mean important?" Nicholas asked after two seconds of tossing it around in his head.

"I mean - is that it? Paying the mortgage and the bills? Is that all that's important to you?"

Nicholas suddenly felt insulted but laughed at himself for having let himself feel that way because he underestimated the depth of a bum's question. He must not forget that Edward had as much and perhaps more experience in life as a regular person or member of society than he did at this point of their lives. And especially now that the man had joined the lowest of the American socio-economic class - the scum stratum of society, and learned to live on the streets, to do without. He had seen both sides. If nothing else, this one human being, this one bum, had depth.

"No, that's not it. Of course not," he said to the street man, beaming with belligerence. "Don't be fucking smart with me now!"

"Well, then tell me."

"For one thing, if paying the mortgage and the bills are all that's important to me, you wouldn't be eating that sandwich, and I wouldn't be sitting here with you right now."

Edward held from taking the last bite while he regarded Nicholas through the corners of his eyes. The few moments of silence that followed spoke to each of them the words that neither one had to say to the other. Nicholas knew that Edward understood his answer. And Edward knew that Nicholas knew that he understood. He finished up the sandwich and began searching meticulously for something in his coat pockets with both hands to make sure Nicholas noticed.

"What else," he said, "do you consider important? For yourself. Money? Women? Fast cars?"

"You think I'm a shallow person, don't you?"

"Not at all, my friend. Not at all."

"Of course I'd like to have money, women and I don't know about fast cars. But I'd also like to be good, very good at what I do, if not the best, but better than most. And I'd like to be recognized for it. Have some respect. That's what's important to me, too. What are you doing? What - you got fleas all over?" Nicholas asked as Edward continued frisking himself.

"No," Edward said. "I'm looking for my cigarette. I thought I had one I saved earlier." And before he could say another word, an unopened pack of Marlboro dropped on the bench beside him so suddenly he thought at first it fell from heaven. He stared at it a moment in disbelief. A whole pack! Then he picked it up, broke the seal on the flip-top box and took out a stick. He found a book of matches in his hip pocket and lit up. While he did so, Nicholas said: "That stuff's eventually going to kill you."

"Is that what you're trying to do?" asked the street man, exhaling the cigarette smoke in satisfaction. "Kill me?"

"I'm not kidding you."

"What's there to kill? You can't kill a dead man. I don't think that's what you bother with me for. I think the reason you're sitting here with me now instead of being in bed at home getting laid with some woman is because one, you're a natural-born soft-hearted sucker and two, I remind you that things could be worse than it is now in your own life. This helps give you strength. And this is one other thing that's important to you but which you're not saying, you liar: to know that though there may be others up there above you, spittin' down on your face, there are others here below you that you could do the same thing to. So if you think I'm gettin' a chicken sandwich and a pack of cigarettes free, look again. I have to be a homeless person, a street man, a total failure, for you to know that you're not doing so bad for yourself after all."

"You're sicker than I thought you were, you know that?"

"But I don't care," Edward continued, ignoring Nicholas. "You can do anything you want. Here, you want to spit on my face too? Spit on my face! Everybody else in the world has done it."

"That's not what I'm doing. That's not what I want to do, and you know that, so cut it out!" Nicholas looked at the homeless man sideways and added: "You want to know what I see when I look at you? You really want to know?"

"Yeah, I want to know. What?"

"I see a defeated American. And I just can't accept that. Or I refuse to believe that. Not after a whole life back in the old country of seeing all those western heroes, all those John Waynes and other American characters, tall men of virtue, strong in body and spirit. I just can't believe you!"

"You've been a victim of American commercial propaganda. Maybe that's one good thing you came to this country. To learn the truth."

"Okay, then let's forget that. Maybe I was too young. Too naive and impressionable. What about all those people, including me and my family, immigrants who flock to this country past and present and make something out of themselves, some of them practically from nothing? Some of them totally hopeless in their own country, rejects, bums, and they come to America and rebuild their lives. A rags-to-riches story in many cases. You're already here. You were born and raised here. And what happens? You go from a comfortable suburban living to a bench in a city park!"

"They have a different story to tell!" Edward yelled, giving Nicholas a start. "Everybody has a different story. In their case, and in your case and all the rest of you foreigners, you have an America to go to. I don't! I'm already here!"

They backed off for about a half a minute, a long half-minute during which Edward sucked and enjoyed the Marlboro while some resentment gnawed inside of Nicholas for being referred to as a foreigner. He expressed this to Edward when he spoke again, especially, he said, when this year is a special year for him being his twentieth anniversary of coming to the United States of America. Also, that he had been a citizen, an American, for the last fourteen years. "Congratulations," Edward said with little interest. "May you live a long and happy life in America. Enjoy." Nicholas' reaction turned from resentment to irritation. "Isn't there anything at all that means something to you?" he asked and immediately felt stupid for having done so for he almost read the answer on Edward's lips even before it came out of them.

"No," said the homeless man, "nothing at all. Not a damn thing."

"I'm getting pissed," said Nicholas matter-of-factly. "I think I'm getting pissed."

Edward turned his head slowly to look at him.

"You shouldn't let me do that to you," Edward said.

"I know. I shouldn't."

"There used to be a lot of things that mean something to me. Like those things you said are important to you now. Credit and recognition, respect, competitiveness, winning." Edward paused, contemplated the south view of the White House. "Not anymore. They're not important to me anymore."

Now Nicholas felt sad, and afraid. Afraid that if a single human being could come to such a state of hollowness, so could he. It's alright if the man was ninety-eight years old, he thought, half blind, half deaf and bedridden twenty-four hours a day. But the man was in his mid-fifties, able-bodied and alert as a thirty-two-year old man as he was.

"One comes to a point in life when -" Edward continued, now gazing uncaringly at the silhouettes of the coming night above the trees around the Ellipse. "- after having done so much for some of those things, and then some, and then some more, they just lose their importance to him. You... you just don't care anymore. Somehow it doesn't matter if you lose or win. It seems, with the passing of time, everything becomes less important, less valuable, less exciting, less of whatever the hell it was before, until.... " A last puff of the Marlboro before it was tossed away on the grass. "...until it means no more to you than a warm potful of piss, or even a cold one." He switched his eyes to Nicholas and looked at him defiantly.

Nicholas inched subtly away to his end of the bench. He was trying to decide whether he must pity this man or be angry with him. Is this man mentally unbalanced? he asked himself, but somehow the more drastic question that came to him was: Is the man right, or wrong?

These he must tell Emil in the old country. The whole scene: everything since he came to sit on this bench. If what Edward just said was true, he wondered what had really become to this point in time, of Emil's lifetime ambition to do the same thing he and his family did: come to America? He wondered, too what sort of true awareness, and maturing - ideological, cultural, and everything else that comes with growing up and getting older - he might have come to now at his age of twenty seven years which might have made that ambition less important while living all his life in the old country. Back there, beyond the west coast, across the Pacific Ocean in that ancient island melting pot of a country.

They had been writing to each other for years. It hadn't stopped for more than two months on a stretch. They were good friends, and remained so. All those twenty years since he left when he was twelve, and Emil seven.

He loved that boy, like the younger brother he never had. Took care of him, looked after him since he was two or three. To this day, it was never clear to him if their families were any blood relations at all. But they were neighbors, close neighbors, and in the old country, that was as good as being blood related.

By now, Nicholas thought, he must know just about as much as he does what it's like living in America with all the things he'd read from the letters through the years. What it's like being here.

He must. Just about, before today.

Nicholas decided to listen to what Edward told him a minute ago - that he shouldn't let Edward piss him off or he simply should not be pissed at Edward. And on his own, he also decided that he shouldn't pity him or be angry with him. The things they understood at this point that one represented to the other did not, and should not, provoke any kind of reaction on a personal basis. Each of them must realize - and he assumed Edward did all along (you shouldn't let me do that to you) - that the basis of their human relationship was out of pure curiosity.

"Looks like it's going to be another cold winter soon, much like last year," Nicholas said to lead them off to a different course, the weather, traffic, anything, scanning the gray firmament above Washington. "That was a terrible winter. Worse than I've ever seen here. What did you do to get through it? You went to the shelter, I hope?"

"What does it matter what I did or how I did it? The point is I survived. I'm here, aren't I? No, I did not go to the shelter. I don't like it there. I hate it there. I told you that." Once again, Edward caught himself looking straight at the White House. He noticed the light in a couple of second-floor windows just turn on. "You want to know something?" he said partly to himself. "The man who lives in that house and I are the same age."

"Is that so? Interesting," said Nicholas, looking at the mansion too. "So what?"

"I could've been the one living in there now."

"You're right. What would you do if you were president?"

Edward spoke without interruption for the next several minutes during which Nicholas questioned off and on what he was really doing sitting in a park bench in the cold listening to a bum talk about economics, life's philosophy and running the U.S. government?

"On foreign relations and policies," Edward said with determination, "the first thing I would do is invade Cuba and re-indoctrinate the population with our ideologies and way of life. It's a question of culture over there, basically, you understand: Anglo versus Hispanic, that is. That's why you never hear Castro speak a word of English, even if he went to Harvard. Next, I'd straighten out that mess in Central America good. Clean up this whole side of the world first. Land the Marines. Then the Army. Re-activate the draft if needed. Then I'd go back to Southeast Asia and get even with those gooks over there.

"On the question of the economy, I'd go protectionism. That's really the same thing everybody else is doing, especially the Japanese. It doesn't matter who's doing it - the government or the people. If they don't want to buy our goods, then let's not buy theirs. Simple as that. Keep 'em out of the country. That would cut down the unemployment. That's one way, anyway. Another is to put them in the military - the unemployed - and send them out to fight in Cuba and all over the world. War is good for this country. It creates work. Generates economy. Keeps everybody busy and out of trouble."

Nicholas nearly broke out laughing at that.

"On the social and domestic front, I would work hard to emphasize the role of the family to maintain law and order in the American society. Parents who don't discipline their children to the minimum legal standard of social conduct, work and study habits would be subject to prosecution. The same thing goes for schools all the way up to college. Teenagers who become pregnant get sent to farms supported mostly with fines levied on their parents and their boyfriends' parents.

"Children of senior citizens would be held not only morally but legally responsible for the maintenance of their parents' mental and physical well-being. Anybody who shows any kind of disrespect to the elderly would pay dearly with time and money.

"All drunk drivers are to be executed right at the site of a fatal accident in the event of one. The same goes for drug dealers and pushers caught in action. Finally, I would establish a national funeral kitty, some kind of a presidential commission that obligates every taxpayer to contribute to, so everybody is assured of a decent funeral. That would eliminate rip-off undertakers. Get rid of the funeral industry altogether. That's right. We'll let the government take care of its dead and the living of themselves and one another."

This part about the funeral kitty understandably must, Nicholas thought, have come out of an immediate personal concern the bum had at the possibility of one day finding himself dying on a city street or park or in a trash bin.

He couldn't wait to write to Emil about all these. He could probably start tonight after dinner.

"Election is coming up in a few weeks," Nicholas said after Edward ended his presidential platform speech. "Who are you going to vote for?"

"Nobody," Edward replied coldly. He was back to his usual mood of indifference to the world. "Although I'd like to see somebody else live in that house instead of that nincompoop sissy in there right now."

"Me, too. He let just about everybody kick his butt around. The Russians, Castro, the Jews, the Arabs, the Vietnamese, the Iranians. It's sickening."

"I don't care. Who gives a shit?"

"Listen, I got to go. It's getting late."

"Go, go, go," said the homeless man with which Nicholas understood he really meant 'yes, go and continue to live your life in pursuit of those things that are important, or are *still* important to you.' In that, Nicholas also heard a farewell with some undertone of gratitude although he could not expect the man to mouth it.

But he was wrong. The man found the words to mouth it with. As Nicholas rose to head to the car, Edward said boldly: "Chicken sandwich was good. Thanks."

"You're welcome."

These last words they spoke without looking at each other. In fact, Nicholas was already making the slow steps to his car while Edward remained on the bench looking at the shadows of the cold night at his feet. When Nicholas fished for his car keys while still a few yards from the car, he felt the other pack of Marlboros in his coat pocket.

"Hey!" he called back to the man on the bench who turned around and got up slowly. "I almost forgot. Catch!" And he tossed the pack which Edward caught with both hands.

As he turned away to get into the car, he waved to acknowledge a hand the street man raised weakly with the pack of cigarettes.

📖 2 📖

THE LETTERS

It was a pain plowing down I-95 in the middle of the evening rush-hour. But then I-95 was always a pain morning or evening. It was bad enough getting there through the Memorial Bridge over the Potomac and Washington Boulevard right by the Pentagon with its sea of cars pouring onto the roads, just to get stranded for a half hour along the four miles of the expressway to Seminary Road where he got off to go home to George Washington's boyhood hometown of Alexandria.

It was a quarter past six when he walked into his two-bedroom third-and-top floor condo apartment. He found Gail Phillips in the kitchen putting away the dishes she just snacked on.   Gail worked less than a mile away at a government office complex off Telegraph Road for the Department of the Army and got home before four-thirty. But her home was not his home.   Hers was two buildings away in the same two-hundred-unit condo complex.

She went up to him after hurrying to wipe her hands with a kitchen towel, threw her arms around him and gave him a long passionate kiss on the mouth.

"Why, thank you very much," he sighed after regaining his breath. "Now, just what do I have to do for that?"

"Make love to me," she said naturally.   "I haven't got much time.   I told mother I'll be over before eight tonight. It's now almost six-thirty and it takes me forty-five minutes to drive to Chevy Chase.   You know that.   You've been there with me enough times."

"Let's see now.   That leaves us forty-five minutes to..."

"I came over after Nancy got home.   I wanted us to have plenty enough time.   Howcome you're late?"

"I had to stop by someplace to see Edward McKenny after work."

"Who's Edward McKenny?"

"A friend I hadn't seen in a while.   He called at work."

"I got hungry waiting for you so I had a snack.   You hungry? I can make you a -"

"No, I'm okay. I'll survive."

She led him by the hand to the bedroom and they made love twice in forty-five minutes.   Actually, less than that for she had to take a few minutes off of that to spend in the bathroom afterwards and to   put her clothes on and everything else to get ready to go visit her seventy-five-year old wheelchair-bound mother in Chevy Chase, Maryland.

After two years of this part-time live-in relationship, sex hadn't lost its place as a vital ingredient in it.   They got together between two to three nights a week mostly in his place because it was simply more convenient not to have Nancy, her daughter just turned fourteen, around during intimate moments which happened when it happened anywhere in the apartment. She always went home before too late at night, though, and occasionally he went with her to spend the night.

Nobody complained about anything in this arrangement. When somebody wasn't in a good mood, the person went to stay where he or she found it more convenient at the time. This was true for Nancy as well as had happened when she had a fight with her mother and sought refuge for a day or two at Nicholas' place.

The question of how long this arrangement would last never got center attention long enough for the adults to seriously think about it. Gail was thirty-seven, divorced five years, separated a year and a half before that and the way Nicholas saw it had no thought of getting married any time soon, if at all.

And him - he could very well say the same for himself, mainly because after several committed relationships, which for one reason or another didn't make it, since coming out of college eight years ago, he needed to take a break from it, take things lightly for now. He didn't think he could handle the stresses of a committed involvement right now, and sustain it for an unknown length of time.

Not at this time. Maybe sometime later, when he's the wiser. How much later, he had no idea presently.

Each of them sensed an awareness of the things they value in each other, the most important of which being their belief in family ties. Gail didn't have to spend as much time or do as much for her mother. She had four siblings: an older sister and brother, and two younger brothers, who could all help take care of their mother as well. And they did. But she wanted to do her part. So decent of her, Nicholas thought on many occasions.

But there was more to it than decency on her part as he understood later. She did it as an act of gratitude to her mother who raised them, all five of them, took care of them and made strong, stable human beings out of them in spite of all the odds she faced when her marriage ended in divorce and the family broke up, well, partially.

That's why she had always tried to be a thoughtful mother in raising her own child but also quite firm with discipline. Nancy seldom needed reminding of her place at home and everywhere else. But even so, today's sub-culture of Rock, drugs and sex never rest from trying to pull down the young.

She had a thirteen-year old girlfriend come over to spend the weekend one time. It turned out the girl just got through an abortion and had to recuperate before going back home. Gail was furious and grounded her own daughter for several weeks. This was one of those occasions when Nancy sought refuge in Nicholas' place.

Nicholas explained to Gail long ago that family ties where he came from were not only never broken but in most cases grew even firmer through the years. The umbilical cord was never cut off. In his case, even that connecting him to the old country remained uncut, as was proven by his continuing exchange of letters with Emil back home. 'Back home', he caught himself a few times, was really a misnomer in that. Because home to him was California where his parents and Melissa, his sister, had been living for the past nine years and where he spent most of the year's holidays.

Gail knew about Emil to the point that Nicholas shared freely some of Emil's letters with her now and then. After all, Emil knew about her as well. As a result, Gail too had on occasions received letters from Emil to which she responded without delay.

Emil had written her such things as:

> You're very fortunate for having been born in America. You must always remember to be thankful for this.

> I hope to be able to go there too, someday. Like my dear old friend Nicholas.

And this, only several months ago:

> There is so much that needs to be done in our country. Sometimes, when I think about it, it almost drowns my desire to go to America. My brother, he's thirty-six years old, married and has a three-year old child - a very sweet baby. He and his family I see as part of the masses who are continuously becoming materially deprived as the political and economic conditions here worsen. He's not doing too bad right now, as a lawyer. But he's not doing too well either. Just enough to support his family daily.

> Someday, if it ever happened that my time to go to America came, I would be thinking about them and many others like them. I'd want to take them with me and I can't. And I'd feel bad. How bad I don't know. Perhaps bad enough not to leave.

An hour after Gail left, he had taken a shower, eaten dinner and gone through most of the day's mail. Near the

bottom of the remaining pieces, he came upon a letter from
Emil, the first in a little over a month.

Dear Nicky,
    There are a few things I'm anxious to tell you
all at once but first I must tell you about what's
been happening with my family. Greg Inomura
Carson, a college school friend of mine (I don't
know if you can recall, you met him once) had
been accused by the government as one of the
high-ranking officers of the rebel movement
operating here in the capital area.
    He had gone underground for fear of political
persecution. The judicial system here is rapidly
being overshadowed by the military courts.
People have been jailed for months in army
camps before they get to hear from anybody
what they're in for.
    Last week, they caught him on his way out of
the city at one of the highway checkpoints. He
was lucky he was allowed to make one
telephone call. He contacted one of our former
university professors whom he asked to contact
me for the purpose of asking my brother Arthur
for his legal services. So I told the professor I
will ask Arthur if he'd take on the case as the
defense attorney for Greg Carson.
    Arthur agreed right away. He knows Greg
personally himself. They're close too, enough
for Arthur to do for Greg what he would for me.
    They didn't give us much time to get an
answer back to the professor. Two days later, a
man came to see Arthur to make sure, perhaps

by some measure which was not necessary, to get a positive answer.

So my brother and I went to visit Greg that same day in the city prison. In a way, he was lucky he was caught before he got out of the city because if they'd caught him in one of the bordering provinces instead, he might not have been able to make that phone call for a long time.

Incidentally, you might have guessed already what the professor had to do with the underground. He's one of the regional commanders of the rebel movement. And in case you're worried about anybody tampering with this letter, not a chance. I'm having it picked up by the professor's intelligence courier. He has a secure foreign mailing route via Hong Kong. He's doing this not only as a favor but as a precaution after I made him realize that government intelligence might already be on to my personal correspondence as well as Arthur's.

He stopped reading for a while, suddenly becoming concerned about the content of the letter. Emil shouldn't have written as much about the professor, he thought, and hoped there wouldn't be any more such material in the rest of the letter. He turned to the next page.

On the lighter side, I hope to be able to move out of my parents' house by the end of the year. That raise I've been waiting for is finally coming. It's a promotion from purchasing officer to project controller. I'll be managing schedules of construction work, tracking the flow of activities

between purchasing, delivery and the project site.
Work has picked up in the construction company. We've won biddings on several big projects.
My girlfriend just found a full-time job. About time. She's been out of college two years. Now she's talking about - you know what. Come to think of it, there's a real possibility we might. Tell you more about this later.
Let me hear from you soon.

He sat back for a few minutes to let things sink in. Whenever he learned something of significance in the life of Emil, he always remembered him as that boy not even ten years old when he left. It's hard to imagine him as a man taking a woman for his wife and perhaps having a family although the last time he saw him - three years ago during a two-week vacation in the old country - Emil had firmly impressed in his mind the image of a physically grown man. An adult, who after they'd spent many hours, days together, proved to be some step ahead, for one newly graduated from college, in the maturing of the mind.

Emil spoke with the eagerness and thirst of youth then. But he spoke with conviction. And he spoke not of the superficiality of youth but of his social awareness, of the ideological beliefs that were developing in him, from what he saw with the poor and the rich in the country, the powerful and the powerless among the people, and lately, he said then, the government and the rebel movement.

Nicholas wondered how involved Emil really was with Greg Carson's situation to this point. He and his brother evidently would do as much as possible to help the man personally. But how sympathetic was Emil with the man's cause? With the anti-government movement? Was he a part of it now? Had he been absorbed?

He reached with some urgency for the desk drawer that contained the stationery but pulled the wrong drawer. He pulled the one where he kept all of Emil's letters through the years as well as copies of his own he always made before putting the letter in the mail.

He looked at the stacks of letters only for just a moment before closing the drawer and pulling out the one with the stationery. He took out several sheets of typing papers and began composing a letter to Emil in longhand.

> Congratulations on your job promotion. So you think you might get married soon. Best of luck when it happens. Just make sure that's what you want before you make it happen.

He stopped abruptly and thought after a second: "That doesn't sound good. It's not too bad, but why say it altogether?"

Then he knew why. He knew why that thought formed in his mind and he got as far as actually writing it down. He completely overlooked the fact that he was writing it to someone outside the United States, someone who lived in a different society with a different way of life.

He crumpled the paper and trashed it.

He had no idea what kind of a relationship Emil and his girlfriend had. But chances are it had more potential for becoming a lasting and meaningful one over there than the many he had seen here including a few of his own. And, yes, including his relationship with Gail.

Make sure that's what you want - something like that you'd say to a fellow like Brian Cooper. Brian Cooper was a friend who was first a college classmate then a co-worker and now a former co-worker who seemed not able to hold a job longer than six months, and a relationship in even less time.

He envied Emil for having lived in only one culture and known only one way of life. He wished he hadn't broken away from it as far as he had. In it, life seemed more in order. And this was because of its many limitations. One learned to accept the inevitable more easily, and go on with the next stages of life.

Here, in America, one had so many choices, so many possibilities before one classified a particular situation as inevitable. One could simply run away to Boise, Idaho or to Dallas, Texas and start over again. Or he could just hang on and make do with what's at hand. What job, possessions, and relationships he had. Or he could give it all up, simply don't give a damn, and maybe even turn into a bum.

He tried to imagine what it would have been like if his parents had not immigrated to the United States. He wondered how life would have turned out for him back in the old country. How similar or any different his may have been to that of Emil's.

He recalled the experience of his visit to the old country three years ago: its people, its culture and way of life. The sight, sound and smell of Silangan, an island country of one hundred thirty thousand square miles east of Taiwan and the Philippines with resources in gold, minerals, fertile agricultural soil, precious hardwood forestry and oil enough to support even twice its population of twenty-five million Silanganese for centuries. And there was Cotamaru, the capital city, jewel of the Far East. A most alluring city where East truly meets West, which he still missed even after Detroit, Washington, D.C., Los Angeles and the other cities he'd been to in America.

In a minute, he had re-opened the drawer containing the letters and begun poring over several of them. One he re-read practically sentence by sentence was Emil's letter from eight years ago addressed to him at his parents' house in Brentwood Park, California, where he then lived. The family had just relocated west the year before from Virginia. For years, since they arrived as immigrants to the United States, both his parents had suffered from allergies of one type or another which they blamed on the regional climates of the midwest and the northeast.

First, there were the five years in Warren, Michigan where their body systems initially had to undergo the adjustments from the temperate climate of the old country to the bitter-cold winter of the Great Lakes region, its hot and humid summer and what's left in between those two extreme seasons. Then his father one day succeeded with his plan to move a little to the south, where they might find the weather a little more tolerable, when he received a job offer from the U.S. Department of Agriculture in Washington, D.C.

The weather was nicer, less cruel in terms of the elements but it didn't do much for their running noses and allergies. It took his father six years to spot a similar USDA position in southern California. When they moved, Nicholas was caught in the middle of his last school year at GW and had to stay behind for five months to finish his last term.

Come time to go west, however, he realized how he had taken some root in the Washington capital area. The midwest he didn't mind leaving permanently to the past, but this area - after six years, and owing perhaps to the fact that those were the years he passed from youth to manhood, it wasn't as easy to leave. He had gotten to like the area so much he planned to come back, get a job, his own place and be on his own at last once he had saved enough money.

The time Emil wrote the letter, Melissa, Nicholas' sister, recently got married.

In case they didn't get my card - you know how bad mailhandling here gets sometimes, both ways - please give my best wishes to Melissa. I wish I could have gone to her wedding. I wanted to see what a beautiful bride she makes. But of course you're going to send me a picture in your next letter. I'm counting on it.

Once again, I want to tell you how happy I feel for you that you're finally out of college. I can't begin to imagine what a relief that would be for me, how good it must feel when I graduate. I'm only in the second semester second year of a five-year curriculum. I'm still carrying a couple of subjects from the first-year semesters I left behind.

I haven't given up on my dream to go to America one day, just thought I'd mention it here again in case you're beginning to wonder. If I must do it on my own, and I don't see any other way since my family aren't as rich as I would have liked us to be (sometimes I suspect that we are actually poor), then I must finish college first.

You've now lived your life there for as long as you have here. I've lived all my life here. All nineteen years. I'm sure you know as much of America now, more than you've told me, and perhaps more than you know or care to know now of our native country. Time brings many changes in everything. Very true. But I'm not discouraged. I won't ever be.

You see, a dream, if it must come true, must
first be a dream.

Through the years, one of the changes time had brought
about upon Emil himself and which Nicholas had noticed
was Emil's steady progress in his ability with language, both
in their native tongue and American English. Nearly every
word they had ever written one another was in English,
except for a few words with which their native language lent
more intimacy or fondness of memory, perhaps, on certain
occasions. Earlier, Emil's letters sounded very academic, basic
English. A few years later, they began to read like
colloquial American, the type of language not much
different from that heard in an educated neighborhood in
Michigan or Virginia but not quite the colloquial out in the
streets yet. One of his letters where he wrote of his steady
diet of American culture - paperback novels (at least one
every two or three weeks), a Hollywood movie almost once
a week and, of course, the television - gave Nicholas
sufficient explanation.

But Nicholas had some concern about this then, as he
had now after re-reading that part of the letter. And he
knew he was as responsible for it as hot dog and Coca-Cola
and all the American heroes from McArthur to Gary
Cooper. He came to America as a child and found it pretty
much - from behind the cloak of innocence - what he had
imagined, if not exactly. Then he grew out of that
childhood, out of that innocence, and learned what was real
and what was imaginary about America, about being here.

Emil would be coming as an adult, not an innocent child.
If his dream to come to America ever came true (and it
could in two or three years: the word about his two-year old
application for an immigrant visa was that the INS had

pretty much caught up with the application backlog from Silangan and was now processing the three-year old applications), it must not be a dream that represented only the virtuous and the ideal in life. And so, therefore, as he had written him of Disneyland, great parks and big holiday parades, he must also tell him about the inner-city USA, Edward McKenny, cultural shock, racial and ethnic issues - the acceptance or rejection of one by another, jobs, taxes, unemployment, crime, the NAACP and the KKK, and last but not least: food, rent and car payments.

He went on to read the rest of the letter.

My brother and I had a talk last night about some current events both personal and national in scope. I think he just wanted to know what's going on inside my head. He doesn't like the idea of anybody leaving the country to go anywhere.

He's sort of nationalistic and I really don't know what to make of that. He's almost ten years older than me and I guess at that age there are things he sees and understands which I don't right now.

He said that I'd be selling myself cheap to the U.S. going there with my college education after I graduate and would be depriving our country of its manpower resources. If everybody did that, he explained, there won't be anybody left here to develop the country and help improve the quality of life. There won't be anybody left but the corrupt politicians and the soldiers - the military who are getting worse.

You see, he's a lawyer, passed the state bar exams three years ago - made the top twenty in the country, and I think he's starting to get into politics which my father objects to.

My father is a storekeeper, as you know (I remember when he used to ask you to tend the store with me when he had to go away for a little while), and he knows practically nothing else but doing that for making a living. He now has three stores which help send me and my sister to college although business according to him, and I know it because I still tend the store once in a while when I can, isn't getting better.

So my brother says he knows what the problem is with local business. Competition. Japanese, Korean and Chinese products. The country needs to keep up or catch up with foreign industry. But if the educated and trained people of the country leave, things could only get worse.

But the politicians, he said, can't see that. And my father is too busy to worry about me dreaming about America.

He found the copy of the handwritten reply he sent, next to the bottom page, and went on to read most of it too.

I hope you like the picture. Melissa picked that one out especially for you because I and my parents are in it too.

Yes, it's great to be finally out of school. No more books, no more homework, exams, papers and deadlines. Now I'm getting back the money we spent for my education, working for an engineering firm designing big steel-framed warehouses, plane hangars and structures for big shopping centers here in southern California.

California is like a country by itself. Everything the rest of America has it has, and more, like the mountains, the ocean and the desert, and of course Hollywood. It's a nice place to live. I could easily get used to it here and that's what I'm afraid might happen.

You see, I didn't want to leave Washington for a number of reasons. I went to college there, known many people and things, the kind of people and things in America that matters learning about and stays with you for a long time.

I guess what I'm saying is - the important part of growing up happened to me there.

I had planned on moving back there, to Virginia, this year but because Melissa just got married and is gone from home, I wouldn't want to move out too this same year. It'll be too much for my mother to see us both go almost the same time. Hopefully it wouldn't be as bad for her if I go next year.

I think I understand what your brother is saying. He's talking about what some people call brain-drain. With some country, it is a problem. But there, I'm not sure because from what you've told me and I've heard the same from a lot of people, every year there's more and more surplus of college graduates. In any case, it always boils down to the question of one's future against the country's.

I believe this is what your brother is trying to tell you. And that's very noble-minded of him.

If you ask me, I'm glad he's that way. That's one way to be nationalistic. A good way. I myself wouldn't want to see the country dominated by foreign economies, even by the United States. I'd want to see it of a nation on its own, like Japan. Why not? Maybe not as powerful and strong, but self-sufficient and able to withstand foreign competition, as your brother said.

He remembered the feeling he had, when he wrote that letter, of not wanting to sound discouraging to Emil's desire to come to America. He also remembered the times, before and after that letter, when he avoided mentioning some of the unpleasant facts of life - his and his family's - in America.

When he looked at the copies of some of the other letters he had sent, he saw many opportunities to touch on some of the social problems in American society which he did but not significantly. He never wrote Emil about the blacks to any discernible detail, or about other groups including him and his family and some of the barriers they encounter fitting in to the mainstream.

He hardly ever talked about crime in America, the deterioration of marriage and the family, how and why people are choosing not to get married for a long time. He knew - now that he thought to question himself about it, deliberately or through sheer lack of knowledge and facts why he didn't spend much time and thought talking about those things. He was too busy going to school most of the time, trying to keep up the high marks, and when he had some free time to think of other things, he chose to look at the better side of everything, he wrote of the pleasant aspects of life in America to Emil. Also, when people are younger, somehow they are better able to ignore the sore spots of their environment. They are not as vulnerable, not as affected by them as Nicholas now felt. A few years ago, for instance, it would not have crossed his mind for a moment to spend a minute of his time with a bum for any reason.

He decided to make himself a vodka and tonic in the kitchen where he kept the bottles before making another attempt at writing a reply to Emil's latest letter. While he was mixing the drink, the phone rang.

"May I talk to Ma?" Nancy said over the phone.

"She's not here, Nancy. She went over to visit your grandma."

"Is it alright if I go to a movie tonight?"

"I don't know, Nancy," Nicholas said after some hesitation. "Who are you going with?"

"A friend. Two friends. They're just down two blocks from here. Okay? They're waiting for me. Could you tell Ma, please?"

"Wait a minute. I can't tell you it's okay if I don't know if it's okay or not like the last time I said okay and I got into trouble. This time I want you to ask her. You have your grandma's number?"

"Well, just tell her, okay?"

"No-o, Nancy, it's not okay. You call her up first and get her okay. I'm only second in command, you understand?"

"Nicky, plee-e-ase?"

"Do you have your grandma's phone number?" Nicholas insisted and the other end went quiet. "Nancy! You have the number over there? Here, take it down -"

"Never mind," Nancy said, disappointed. "I have it."

After he hung up, he sat for a time with a blank sheet of paper and a pen in front of him at the desk. Ten, fifteen minutes, collecting his thoughts and feelings with the help of the vodka and tonic. Then he began writing.

Dear Emil,

I'm glad to hear things are moving right along with you there. Job promotion, going on your own, plan to get married. I wish I could say the same for myself here. But don't ask me. After twenty years in America, it seems I'm just now opening my eyes to the whole reality of the American way of life. And I mean whole, not just the part of it most people care to talk about like most of the things I've written you about, but also the part we'd prefer not to notice, if it were possible.

But it isn't.

Sooner or later, some of these unpleasant part of the American Way begins affecting you personally. Catches up with you in many different ways.

I never told you much about the social conditions of many of the population centers of the United States. The major metropolitan areas and the parts in them we call the inner city. The people who live in them, and how they live in them. I don't know how much of this stuff you get there through the media.

I never told you much either about the blacks and the hispanics except for some innocent things I remember mentioning to you about some such classmates I had in high school back in Michigan. Neither have I talked much about the other minorities, my kind included, and about the immigrants from all over the world, myself and my family included, and some of the difficulties they face adjusting to the American way of life (assimilating is the right word for it, I believe).

I went through that stage myself and now personally I feel I'm as American as any immigrant who comes here as a child could ever be. However, where certain values are in question, particularly those that are tied in with one's culture and ethnic heritage, tradition and these sort of things, one just can't tie in with the American Way. It just doesn't tie in. One would have to have been born here, have no other past and know no different in order to truly adapt to the native ways and belong to the land.

I really don't want to dig in to all that at present. I'll save most of it for another time. Right now, as an example of that other part of life in America, I want to tell you about somebody I know - a friend. Yes, I consider him a friend. He's a bum. A real bum, believe it or not. A homeless person, a natural-born American who got tired of everything, gave up on life and now lives in the streets of Washington.

He went on to tell Emil about Edward McKenny up to their last meeting tonight. He wrote first of the man, this one American man who happened to have fallen on some hard times, as much as he understood the man; and he wrote of the bum, as much as he understood the bum in the man, and the life he now lived.

I know you might find that hard to grasp from a firsthand account like this. But such life does exist here in America for real. Not just on television and the movies. The way I see things at the moment, from this man's example, when it comes to what goes deep inside, people aren't Americans or Asians, Europeans or whatever. They're creatures who live not only with their material possessions but with what they hold boldly and dearly in themselves: love, anger, beliefs, some set of values. You take these away and the fellow falls apart. Goes nuts. Dies inside. Turns into a bum or does something as a gesture of dying or saying 'I give up; I don't give a shit anymore.'

More on this next time.

I'm anxious to know more about the business with your friend Greg Carson. And how involved you and Arthur are in that business. I'm not sure if it was a safe thing to do writing what you wrote me about it.

I know the country has become less and less politically stable the last couple of years. It's been in the papers here a lot lately. The rebel movement, the suspension of many civil rights in a number of provinces because of government suspicions of people's support of the rebels; military atrocities kept quiet from the press, some body counts here and there.

And then there was a news report here a few weeks ago about the National Intelligence Service deploying agents in several major cities in the United States.

> I want to know how deep you and your
> brother are into the political situation there.

Nicholas stopped at this point and thought hard. He began to worry that if it's a matter to consider that the government might be on to Emil's correspondence going out, it must be the same for that coming in. It became almost impossible to continue as he didn't know what else he could say and, if any, how he should say it. Out of desperation, he forced himself to write.

> Tell me what's happening. And most important, how should we continue our correspondence? A suggestion at this time: if it's at all possible, I want you to make an overseas call to me at work or at home, collect. I'd rather be the one to make the call, but you would have to give me a number where I could reach you.
>
> Please let me hear from you as soon as possible.

⌂ 3 ⌂

A LUNCHBREAK

Some people in the office didn't mince words in most given situations talking work, personal business, politics, religion or ideology. Even prejudices.

Even those who normally engaged only in light conversations frequently got drawn into a somewhat over-stimulated interaction. This was often because of Norman Tilley and his lack of language manners.

Some of his co-workers thought they had him figured out a long time ago. His vulgarity. His lack of couth. His total disregard, at times, of other people's sensitivities. They said he led a dreadfully boring life at home with a second wife whom he didn't love and who, likewise, didn't care if one day he never showed up. He had a son from his first marriage who wouldn't have anything to do with him except when father fell behind on the child support and the child upon learning of it from mother would call father at work and speak his mind to him.

These, people learned from Norman Tilley himself who placed little value in keeping such personal things private. Thus, everyone understood that to make his day interesting, Norman Tilley either subconsciously or deliberately precipitated his human environment, making himself the focus of everyone's attention, regardless of the nature of such attention. Everyone knew the personal life circumstances he was coming from and nobody was supposed to take offense at anything he said or did. He was a man who just needed some acknowledgment of any kind at all.

People went along with this as calmly as they could, as far as they could. But every now and then, someone would snap and signal Norman Tilley - enough; that's as far as I go along. Cool it.

Norman Tilley ordinarily heeded such signals although sometimes, Lester Jenkins, a mild-mannered professional middle-class black, had to give him a second signal to stop. Sam Goodman, a son of eastern European immigrant Jews but a native-born from Silver Spring, Maryland, who could be as verbally abusive as Norman Tilley, a wasp, told him explicitly to cool it twice. And if he found it necessary to tell him a third time, he'd tell him to 'cool it, asshole'.

That seldom failed to take effect, and a scene never got any uglier than that for a professional engineering consulting firm, although this was not to say it couldn't.

Nicholas tried to avoid Norman Tilley, limit their contact for anything not work-related. Fortunately, his assignments didn't involve working much with Norman who did site utility development plans on a separate project. Nicholas worked closely with Lester Jenkins, even shared an office with him. Together, they headed a team of engineers and drafters on the structural design of a sprawling department store complex being built in Centreville, Virginia.

Nicholas had a clean rapport with Lester Jenkins. He knew how Lester reacted to Norman. And he knew how the black man would like to react further to Norman Tilley but 'I wouldn't stoop to soil myself with such dirt', so he uttered under his breath to Nicholas once.

Another man who took part in this scenario of reluctant office camaraderie was Harold Forker, the division chief, or the boss. Harold Forker, like Norman Tilley, was a wasp and had similar prejudices. The difference between them in this respect was that Norman Tilley mouthed his recklessly while Harold Forker, though he didn't deny it and wouldn't if asked, kept his to himself.

It was like one was the genuine, live example and the other a demonstration or talking model. Where their similarities ended, the difference in the way they displayed such similarities began.

Harold Forker was one of those who only engaged in light conversations. In fact, it seemed he only spoke to the guys for two reasons: one, so as not to appear asocial; two, to break up a scene when it starts to heat up, usually between Norman Tilley and somebody else or everybody else in the division, although Sam Goodman wasn't far behind in this too.

Sam Goodman had a streak of paranoia every three or four weeks, Nicholas had observed during which Sam would try to play the role of Norman Tilley in the office and touch off an ideological, ethnic or racial controversy which brought Harold Forker out of his office.

Lester Jenkins, like Nicholas, always tried to avoid getting sucked into any controversy but wasn't always successful. And once he got sucked into one, usually through Norman Tilley's instigating, he got really involved in it. For him to be 'really involved', from Nicholas' vantage point during or after a scene when Lester Jenkins would fall back at his desk in their office, would be to hear him use the same vocabulary the others did, during and after.

"Why do I listen to that shithead?" he asked himself and Nicholas back in their office one morning after the ten o'clock coffee break. "Why do I even care what he says to me or to anybody? What the fuck do I care whatever comes out of his filthy mouth? It's always the same thing that comes out of his other end."

"Absolutely right," agreed Nicholas without reservation. "He's nothing but a big round butt-hole that's just full of it. And he's got to let some of it out somewhere somehow. Everybody knows that, so don't let any of it get to you."

Norman Tilley had gone down to the cafeteria to get a warm pastry at the beginning of the coffee break and when he came back asked Lester Jenkins in front of everybody what he was doing for lunch.

"Eat," Lester had replied, "why do you ask?"

"They got chicken gumbo down there and watermelon as dessert for today's lunch special," said Norman Tilley naturally. "Thought I'd let you know."

It took Lester Jenkins pretty much the rest of the morning to put that one behind him and do some work, with some coaxing from Nicholas who tried to lighten up everything. Close to noon break, he said to Lester: "Actually, I think we ought to be thankful for the way it is now."

"What?" Lester turned an incredulous face from the set of blueprints on his desk. "You mean with him? That white sonofabitch?"

"Take it easy. Yes," said Nicholas, nodding wisely.
"Look at it this way: do you have any idea how many other
Norman Tilleys are there in this country?"

"I'd say half the entire white population over the age of
three," replied Lester Jenkins, emphasizing the word entire,
"not counting the mute and the blind."

"If you say so. Now, considering that many, aren't you
glad we only got one of them here?"

"I know."

"How would you like to have five of them here, maybe
ten, or twenty -"

"I know what you're saying. Things could be worse.
But why can't it be better? One butt-hole may not be too
bad, but isn't zero butt-hole better?"

"It's getting there. This country's getting there."

"What do you mean?" Lester Jenkins arched his
eyebrows at Nicholas. "What do you know I don't?"

Occasionally, their rapport extended beyond their
concern for their immediate surroundings, turning more into
an exchange of ideological beliefs and theories. These few
minutes before lunch time became one of those occasions.

"I mean," Nicholas answered thoughtfully, "that's the
whole idea behind this national movement for racial
equality. Civil rights. Equal employment opportunity.
Desegregation or integration."

"Seems more like disintegration to me."

"Seriously, the wisdom that's at work behind this
movement and the collection of all the laws, local and
federal, that have been passed since is not just the
elimination of racial prejudice and discrimination and their
practice in society, but the survival of this nation."

"Which part of it -"

"All of it," Nicholas said quickly to spare both of them
more of Lester's cynicism, even only for a moment. "The

whole American nation, its society and culture as we've seen it develop to now. You see, somewhere back of the collective minds that have worked to pass those laws is the thought that if America is allowed to disintegrate racially, we can only expect it to go through a similar process culturally, ethnically and every which way you can imagine to break up the pie.

"After you separate the nation by color, what next? Separate each color by culture: by how people worship, by their customs, by what they eat and drink, by how they cook their food? No. They want to keep America one nation, indivisible, etcetera, not a whole continent made up of little ones like South America or Europe."

"That's very profound, Nicholas. And that sounds really beautiful too. And I agree to the idea. But don't get me wrong, though, if I may say I don't think it's working quite that way."

"Don't you think there's been some significant advancement of the colored people in America since... since the big march? More respect between the races? More equality, since Martin Luther King's death?"

"Yes, yes, of course."

"Then you do acknowledge -"

"Yes, I do. I do."

"Then if you got any smarts in you Lester Jenkins, besides that highly sought engineering smart you got in your head which I wish you'd share with me sometimes especially when I need it, you wouldn't let one single butt-hole shake your feathers."

"Lemme tell you something, Nicholas, ole buddy," said Lester Jenkins, closing the set of the structural working drawings of the shopping center and glancing at his wristwatch as he turned directly toward his officemate, "you're right about the government, and about them laws to keep this country whole. And you're right, as I said, about the significant progress that have been made in racial equality, civil rights, equal opportunity. But one thing we all must learn to admit is the belief we know we all have that integration is never going to work. You can pass all the laws you want to keep this country racially whole, on paper. But that's as far as it goes - on paper.

"Now, I have no problem with this, though, because *I don't believe in racial integration. I don't want racial integration.* I think it's bad for people. I think it is wrong. I think firmly that it is a violation of the laws of nature. Because of it, a lot of people have died, suffered all kinds of losses and pain, felt all kinds of hatred and anger for one another. It has distorted people's perception of themselves and of others, forcing upon them many a number of unrealistic expectations and certain values that are alien and totally unnatural with them."

"You're entitled to your thoughts and beliefs as everyone else is."

"Those are facts, Nicholas. They're not just my beliefs or something I worked up in my head. You've seen how some black people - women especially, try to adapt the physical characteristics of the whites. Could you think of anything more unnatural than a blond or a redhead black? And there's all these other blacks who are constantly trying to iron their hairs. Make them straight as if they don't know that it's going to grow back to what it was, the natural way it is, the way nature or God or biology designed us. If you ask me, I'll tell you that's about as far as integration has got in this country. Sure, this country is whole according to its laws. But socially, economically, it's not. And it will never be because it could never be."

Nicholas was beginning to think of backing off from this. He seldom saw Lester Jenkins get so strung up on any issue.

But he didn't feel right about leaving him that way without any benefit of a doubt.

"You're not looking far ahead enough," he said with some thrust, "and you're not looking back far enough either."

Lester Jenkins held himself in thought for a couple of seconds, then said: "I understand what you're saying. And I'm telling you, Nicholas - friend, this is as far as the thought of those collective minds you talk about is going to carry the different racial, cultural and ethnic groups of this country: a society of tokenism and polite acceptance."

"I don't think that's for you or me or anybody to say now or tomorrow or the next day. Things are still happening, and they will continue to happen. This country hasn't stopped moving. It's continuing to evolve. Like I said, it's getting there, slow but sure."

"Getting where?" Lester Jenkins couldn't be more sarcastic. "Continuing to evolve into what?"

Nicholas looked him straight in the pupils and answered: "Into a society of zero butt-hole."

"And slow but sure. Real slow, like a hundred years from now. Maybe a thousand. In the meantime, it'd be a big step in that direction if somebody could get rid of the one butt-hole we got here." Lester Jenkins got up to put his jacket on in haste and headed out of the office.

"Hey," Nicholas called after him. "Have a good lunch."

Lester Jenkins halted on his third step out and replied: "I will, thanks. You do the same, man."

One thing Nicholas and, he was certain, most other people in the office especially Lester Jenkins noticed about Norman Tilley's brand of prejudice was the man's display of sensitivities, though minute, in varying measures toward different people. In spite of his attention-getting controversial verbal spills, Norman Tilley maintained certain limits to it, a reserve of subtleties, especially with Lester Jenkins. This, however, only made Lester Jenkins feel worse. He told Nicholas once: "I'd feel better if he'd come right out sometimes and call me a nigger."

With Sam Goodman, the Polish rabbi as Norman Tilley joked once, Norman Tilley displayed lesser measures of sensitivity as he did the day he read the highlights of a news article about a white supremacist organization somewhere in the midwest.

The organization firmly believes, says Peter Jorgensen, a spokesman for the local chapter here, that America is no longer a country, a sovereign state as its ruling class insists. It has become a corporation, a giant conglomerate run by the descendants of the old-world powers who - through their softness and incompetence uncharacteristic of the supreme Northern European white race - have allowed their power of government to be usurped by the Jews, the Japanese and the Chinese, the Negros, the Latins and the Arabs.

We cannot and must not tolerate any longer the abuse of the humanitarian privileges we have afforded these inferior peoples, added another leader of the group, a woman who refused to give her name. We must re-assert our sovereignty upon this land by rule of our superior Caucasian instincts and strength, she said, weeding out among us those who are weak and submissive. We must sever the roots of this Jewish economic and political strangle-hold that's choking America through the lobbying halls of Congress, the media airwaves, films, television and the press. We must push back the threat to our economic well-being brought on by these Asiatic entrepreneurs of cheap labor. And we must remind the blacks and the Latins, the same with the others, to what extent they may indulge in those privileges we have allowed them.

"Now, what do you make of that, Sam Goodman?" Norman Tilley asked facetiously in a lunchroom full of people as most of them were just finishing up eating. "These people really mean business. Listen to what else it says here."

Members of the organization speak openly of not paying taxes and defying the IRS. They describe a thriving barter economy where even non-members participate. Moneys change hands without ever going on record. Goods and services are exchanged in measures based on units of the essential human needs: physical, emotional, mental, spiritual.

Our most important goal at present, says Peter Jorgensen, is to survive the conglomerate forces of the Zionist, the oriental and the black cohorts of this hapless corporate American government. And this could only be done by a sustained effort to build strength through our ideology and through arms buildup.

In separate incidents in Wyoming and the Dakotas, combined federal and state troops in the past three weeks have uncovered and seized stockpiles of assault armaments, among them

dozens of hand-held rocket missile-launchers,
boxes of fragmentation grenades, a cache of M-
16s with hundreds upon hundreds of
ammunition rounds. A government spokesman
said the armaments were powerful enough to
hold Cheyenne captive for months.

"So what do you think about that?" Norman Tilley asked
Sam Goodman again, this time putting the paper and his
lunch litter away,

Sam Goodman who sat one table away facing Norman
Tilley didn't respond immediately while he thought some of
those people in the news sounded like they might be
Norman Tilley's immediate relatives. Over at another table
sat Nicholas and Haj Fujiwara, a Japanese-American born in
Kansas shortly after his parents' post-war release from their
internment camp. Concentration camp, he called it
whenever he told pieces of his family life story. Haj
Fujiwara was a civil engineer whose current project was the
interstate highway that would link those from Pittsburgh to
Richmond directly across the Allegheny Mountains. It was
he, instead, who responded to Norman Tilley first.

"I think there's a lot of truth to some of what they're
saying there," he said, "especially about America being a
giant corporation. In the first place, I think that's what this
country has been all along. It was like one of those British
Companies such as the Hudson Bay Company up north, or
the British East India Company of old. Now it's an
independent company."

"Come o-on," Norman Tilley complained. "Don't be
stupid."

"Do you think anybody really cares whether or not
there's a government running this country and if there is,

what kind of government it is, as long as people eat and has a place to live and live healthy and comfortable lives?"

"Yes!"

"Who?"

"Me! People like me!" Norman Tilley barked at Haj Fujiwara.

This was where Sam Goodman jumped in.

"You?" he barked back at Norman Tilley, mockery written all over his face. "Of all people. Hah!"

"That's right, Sam. I care what happens to this country. Maybe you don't. Maybe people like you don't. But I do."

Sam Goodman told Norman Tilley to look at the window to their side for a moment and Norman Tilley did.

"When you see a blue pig fly by that window," Sam Goodman said, "that's when I'll believe you, Norman. I think Haj is right, not that I like the thought of it: people, such as you, couldn't care less what's happening as long as they don't go hungry, as long as they have money in their pockets and are comfortable with their lives."

"Hey, hey, you want to know something, Sam Goodman?" Norman Tilley had an evil smile on. "I don't care what you think I am. What you think about me don't count, and the same goes for Tojo over there. But let me tell you something else, about this country. This country is my country. And the only thing the matter with it is it has given so much to so many that now everybody has become greedy and wants more. That's what those people are talking about in the news and I can't say that I disagree with them altogether. Not when I think about all these interest groups throughout the country and I see their people come to town to lobby for their cause. The corporate lobbies, the various industry lobbies, many of whom aren't even Americans or bankrolled by foreigners; ethnic and various minority lobbies, the equal opportunity and... and these affirmative action groups and all the rest of 'em hand-out groups, you name them."

"That takes on a lot of people," Sam Goodman commented. "You think maybe you left somebody else out, though."

"I probably did but I believe I included enough to drive my point across."

"You talk about this country. This country which you say is your country. Just what country is that? Of what nation? Of what people? Your kind of people?"

"Americans!"

"Which kind? Your kind? White, Anglo-Saxon, Northern European? Christian? What?"

"Let's break it up, okay you guys?" Harold Forker suddenly stepped in, moving nonchalantly between the tables occupied by the two and going to the vending machine for a soda.

"Which people is it in this country that has given so much to so many who?" Sam Goodman continued, heeding Harold Forker only with a quick glance. "Just who are you to say who is the giver and who is the taker in this country?"

A can of Diet Coke came hurtling down the dispensing chute of the vending machine with a loud clang. As Harold Forker picked it up, he spoke again this time with more firmness in his voice.

"I said break it up! This is a lunchroom, not a TV talk show studio. The rest of us here might not care to listen to either of your arguments. We got rights not to have to listen to any of it."

"That's right," Nicholas, sitting with Haj Fujiwara, said. "So the next time you want to read a news item, Norman Tilley, read it to yourself. And read it without moving your lips."

"Just trying to make conversation," Norman Tilley replied, his voice straining.

"That's fine. Nothing wrong with that," said Sam Goodman. "Just don't make a dumb one."

"Cool it, you two!" barked Harold Forker.

Not long after things quieted down, some people began leaving the lunchroom to go back to their offices. Nicholas remained with Haj Fujiwara at their table. They watched Norman Tilley pick up and strut past Sam Goodman with a pesky grin on his face on his way out of the room. In response, Sam Goodman compressed his nose with his fingers in the same manner one would in the proximity of a skunk and inched away as Norman Tilley went by.

Nicholas and Haj Fujiwara, together with the other employees who remained, laughed at the scene. Whenever Nicholas and Haj saw each other in the lunchroom during breaks, they usually ended up sitting at the same table. Nicholas noticed how much more at ease Haj was with him than with anybody else. He could only guess that perhaps this was because they both came from the same region or corner of the world and that Haj Fujiwara counted this for some sort of a common bond, something they shared, though a superficial one.

In any case, this was mostly how Nicholas came to learn some of Haj Fujiwara's personal and family background. His mother was born in Japan and lived there until his father, who was himself born in Japan but brought up in California, went back and found her for his bride to take back to America. There was never any big problem with cultural differences and adjustment between his parents, Haj Fujiwara said, but with him it was a slightly different story.

He was, first, Japanese and later American. Becoming bilingual was as natural as growing up. He had no trouble assimilating through adolescence in Kansas. In the late fifties, they moved to Japan and lived there for four years during which their native culture quite naturally just took over what American part of them there was.

Haj Fujiwara spoke of how, when he first came back, he realized what undisciplined people Americans were, especially the young. Unruly, and how wasteful they were. Senselessly wasteful. Those four years never left him. He never fully recovered the American in him. The Japanese which those four years had instilled in him went so deep he couldn't, wouldn't knowingly adapt to the value systems he saw in high school in Kansas and in college at MIT.

For a number of years, his last in college and a few after when he began working for his state license as a professional engineer, it was a constant struggle trying to reconcile his life at home and the world outside. Especially at work, the way he worked, did his job, and the way 'they' did theirs.

He told Nicholas one lunch time: "I wish I could spare myself some of the insights I gain coming to work from day to day. Do you ever feel that way sometimes?"

"I'm not sure exactly what you're talking about, Haj," Nicholas said then. "Explain."

"Individualism," Haj said emphatically. "There's too much of it around and not enough teamwork or group effort without one single person taking credit for himself alone. I'm not saying individualism is bad. Of course everybody wants to be a star or, at least, a pat on the back once in a while. You can't stop that. That's one of the major ingredients of the freedom we enjoy. But there are times when something else must come before the 'I', 'Me' or 'Myself'. What I couldn't help seeing here and other places I've worked is an attitude people have. It's everywhere. And that is to go home at the end of the day content in the knowledge that they've proven themselves a match to the challenge of the day - that is, if it had been such a day.

"That, they do actually for their self-satisfaction. Fulfillment, I believe it's called here. Their ego, or macho, if you would, more than anything else. They don't accomplish the day primarily to produce anything, or create anything but simply to feed their ego. In Japan, you don't work and go through the day for the sustenance of your ego and the affirmation of the individual. That's not what counts the most there. What counts there is your productivity and the quality of your output. Nothing less than that. The self-satisfaction you derive out of it you do not make a part of the process."

Nicholas felt he understood this nisei then, as he told him later on during another lunch hour, well enough to share his own insights. And more so, he said to Haj Fujiwara, when he recalls his father years ago talking about his own similar experiences.

"The newcomers always try harder," he recounted his father saying. "They have this instinct of survival as if the consequences for them are far worse than for others if they didn't do good work. So they put in their best, and many get into this habit for life."

With that, he learned in the years that followed together with his father and the rest of the family, that throughout most of their lives, immigrants never fully get over that sense of insecurity they get when they first set foot in America. And that instinct of survival remains strong to buffer them against any threat to their security, real or imagined, even after they've become successful, to say the least, in resettling in their new life.

In the truest sense, he shared Haj Fujiwara's insights surely not only because Haj revealed them to him but because he had many of his own: insights gained through two decades of survival in America working constantly upon rising above that sense of insecurity that wouldn't quit. And like Haj, he could only wish he could spare himself from gaining those insights because in the long run, all they really do is encumber him with knowledge he does not need to better equip himself to survive and secure a place in society. But the process of learning is a part of living one does not and cannot thwart.

For this reason, he was thankful for his family with whom he shared the knowledge that came with this learning process through adolescence, especially through his secondary-school years and even partly through college. He was thankful he was not alone when he came to America as many other immigrants did on their own even while they were children.

There were things, though, he perceived which he kept to himself. Things he simply felt comfortable keeping to himself. But a time came when, around his junior-high year in Michigan, all those thoughts and feelings he kept bottled up began crying out for release. That was when the letters between him and Emil poured halfway across the world. He wrote as often as twice a week. Long letters to Emil. As long as ten pages. And short ones. As short as three quarters of a page. Emil did the same, responding promptly to every letter he received.

Nicholas wrote to his boyhood friend then, whom he missed dearly, things that he somehow would not deem appropriate to share with his American friends, or even with his family. But he also wrote often of things he shared with these others for somehow he felt more freedom of expression and more sense of release when he wrote about them, especially for Emil to read.

When he was sixteen, he wrote Emil about a weekend trip he took to Canada with the whole family.

Father took me with him to a house party of a close friend of his, one of the people he went to see in Toronto. The man works for a Canadian government office that helps new immigrants get started with their new life. He invited several of them to the party and I got to meet them.

They were all Europeans. For the first time in my life, I met a Greek, a real one, from Greece. A Polish from Poland, a Hungarian from Hungary. A Portuguese, an Italian, even a Russian. They all came directly from their own country. I was very very surprised to learn that none of them could speak straight English. Only the Italian knew enough words to express some of the things he wanted to say and the other things he did with his hands and face.

One of them, the Polish, is a dentist and he was very disappointed that Canada won't let him work with his profession. He told me he wants to come here to the U.S. instead but he has no papers and didn't know how to go about applying. He got very excited when he learned we came from the United States. You should have seen him as he listened to me talk. He said I speak perfect English and wished that someday he would be able to sound like me too with my 'beautiful American accent', a sound he had only heard on the radio and TV before, but never in person.

I always thought all Caucasian people speak English. I've never met one before who didn't, just as I've never met a black person who speak Spanish or French.

Also, I thought only English-speaking people are allowed to come to North America. I couldn't imagine father and us coming here and not being able to speak the language like those new immigrants in Canada. It must be awfully bad where they came from that they risked facing such a big problem in life here. But, then, maybe it isn't all that bad for the Europeans because they only had the language barrier to overcome. Racially, and culturally for most of them, they're no different.

The year he finished high school was the year they moved to the Washington suburb of Bethesda, Maryland, after six years in Warren, Michigan. On a cold winter night a few days before his father drove the entire family east for a whole day, he sat up late in his room trying to break down a mass of feelings he had about their lives, past and forthcoming, into separate little ones he could identify and understand. As much of this as he was able to do, he put in a letter to Emil.

We're in the middle of packing everything in the house. Father has hired an interstate mover and they're coming to pick up everything three days from now. The next day we'll all be in Bethesda, Maryland near Washington, D.C., the capital of the United States. I can't imagine what it's like over there, or what it will be like for us. I just hope it helps my parents' allergies. Mother, especially. She's been suffering miserably with the weather here in Michigan.

I don't feel all broken up about leaving here. Just some. A little sad, though, when I look back to when we first came. I remember some of the people we got to know first. Some of them we only knew for two or three years and they've moved too.

It's the same thing at school. I had a couple of friends (I told you about them several times). Nice guys. But they were only at school for two years and they're gone. Their families had to move some place else in the country for jobs. One went to Pennsylvania, the other to Texas.

So maybe that's why I can't feel too much for leaving Warren. Maybe this is one thing people must get used to, living in America: not grow such deep roots where they are for they never know how soon it would be before they were gone someplace else.

I hate to admit this, Emil, especially to you, but somehow I wish we'd be going back to our country instead of to Maryland. Right now, this is how I feel. Maybe I'm just being homesick, uncertain of what lies ahead of us where father is taking us. I know he's doing what he believes would be right and good for all of us. He just wants us to be happy, live a good life here in America.

And we do - live a good life here. We do, since we first arrived, compared to some people - many people and families - I've seen who have been here much longer than we have. And I'm not talking about just the immigrants but also the natural-born Americans.

One thing I learned quick is that there are poor people too in America. People with very little education, and people who are practically illiterate. No-read no-write as we used to say when we first started school back home. I couldn't believe it at first. But I've seen them. Both black and white people. Most of them come from the southern United States. They come here to the north to find work. Start over, from nothing, like newly arrived immigrants although they were born here.

I feel sorry for them and at the same time I get a funny feeling like we're taking something away from them. Their jobs, their houses, their food, their country. I've had this feeling since two or three years ago, I just never told you. I wish you could be here now, Emil, or soon. There are so many other things I'd want to tell you. It really bothered me (it still does, although I know it shouldn't) so I talked to one of my teachers in school. One I felt comfortable with. She's my history teacher. She said - get this: 'You're just experiencing a good feeling for other people. A feeling known as compassion.' She said it is a sign of one's true good nature which I could not help coming out of me.

But the reason for the way I feel is not true, she said. I and my family have as much right as anybody to live in America, to take the jobs we're able and willing to do, to eat the food we eat, to live in the house we live in as long as we don't steal or break the law to do so. In fact, she said, we should feel proud that we are doing it on our own and doing it so well since we came to America without the government or anybody having to help us.

I also talked to father about this. He said it may look that way when people come to America to seek a better life. In fact, in some cases it's true, depending on the type of immigrants who come. But in our case, it's not. On the contrary, it's the other way around. We're not taking more than what America is gaining by getting us. They didn't have to train me to become a doctor of veterinary, father said. What your teacher told you is right. We didn't come poor. We're not rich, but we're not poor enough either to need help. And we're healthy, educated and willing to work. We're as much a part as anybody else is of what makes America America.

📖 4 📖

OLD FRIENDS

Nicholas was on his way to the coffee pot down the hall when, halfway there right by Sam Goodman's office, he heard him pick up the phone and then tell Norman Tilley in the adjoining office area: "It's for you."

It was a few minutes before nine in the morning. The calls rotated inside if they weren't picked up outside after three rings. The front desk girl must be running late again, Nicholas thought.

"Which one?" asked Norman Tilley.

"Third button," replied Sam Goodman. "It's a bill collector. And he sounds like a very young one. Like maybe ten years old."

"Just get off my case, huh?" rebuffed Norman Tilley.
Then picking up the phone, whispered irascibly between his
teeth: "Sh-i-i-i-t."

On his way back, Nicholas ran into three people. First
there were Norman Tilley and Sam Goodman who came out
of their office areas and headed down the hall opposite his
direction. Sam Goodman appeared to know where he
wanted to go for he carried his empty coffee mug. But not
Norman Tilley. He had both hands jammed in his hip
pockets and looked deeply troubled. When he realized he
had fallen into a walk beside Sam Goodman, he turned
around to go the opposite way. But this was not before the
two of them managed a quick exchange of their usual.

"When you gotta pay, you gotta pay," said Sam
Goodman in a singsong.

"Get lost. Just get lost, huh?"

"They comin' to get yuh?"

"I'm going for a walk," Norman Tilley said as he turned
around. "If anybody else calls, tell them I went to church to
pray to God to make the whole world disappear just for
today, starting with you, Sam Goodman."

"Good morning, boys," Nicholas said to them as he
passed by.

Then there was Haj Fujiwara who appeared in the
hallway from his side of it where he occupied a whole
section of their division. Haj Fujiwara led a six-person
design team of soil and sanitary engineers in his section. He
carried a fat roll of blueprints in one armpit and at the same
time peered distressfully at a computer printout in his hands.

"You don't look like you believe what you're looking at,"
Nicholas said as they stopped in front of each other.

"You're darn right I don't. I don't believe this at all."
Haj Fujiwara glanced quickly up at Nicholas and continued
his puzzled scrutiny of the printout. "According to these

calculations, the Allegheny Mountain where this highway is cutting south doesn't exist."

"How did it disappear?"

"I think I have an idea." Haj Fujiwara lowered the printout as he did his voice, saying: "It's these lousy jobs most of these guys in the office have been turning out. A lot of drawings I've been getting from many of them are... terrible. Full of errors. It's bad enough they can't draw. But they can't calculate either."

"I've heard that before. From me and you both. But what about the computer?"

"That's where I'm headed right now. I'm going to run the whole job over myself. I don't think it's the machine. I helped design that system myself and we tested it dozens of times. That system works. But only if you feed it good input."

"Take it easy," Nicholas said as he noticed how really distraught Haj Fujiwara looked. "If you gotta do it yourself, you gotta do it yourself. Simple as that. It's safer that way. Some days are made like this, Haj."

"Yes, but I'm really getting fed up with these sloppy jobs. I can't do all the work here. We need some quality staff. Professionals. And I don't care what school they came out of. Ivy league or bush league. That doesn't mean diddly squat to me. But definitely not any more of what we got here. God. It's as if they just got out of college with no serious experience. Most of them have been out at least four years. But it seems they haven't learned much. And what little they've picked up on, they haven't used much or improved upon. It's like the car manufacturing here. They've been at it almost a hundred years. And now people prefer to buy imports even if they have to pay more." Haj Fujiwara paused as he watched Nicholas drink his coffee. "I haven't even had time for that. It's been bang bang bang since I got in at eight."

"Go get some. There's a fresh pot in there."

"I think I will. And what are you up to this morning?"

"I'll be heading out to Centreville in about fifteen minutes. Field inspection. A couple of major connections the boss wants to make sure is done right, according to the drawings. The architect asks to meet us there today."

"Sounds like fun. I wish I were going with you. I wish I were going someplace. Any place else but here today. Maybe I'll go back to Osaka for a while."

"Get serious."

"Who knows," Haj Fujiwara said, tossing his head to one side a bit as if to deliberate on what he said. He had a grandfather, Nicholas knew, in Osaka who lived in the United States for thirty years and went back to Japan for good while still a young middle-age. "Maybe I will. You have a nice field trip. Let's get lunch together sometime this week, Nicholas."

"Sure, I'd like to."

On his way out of the building at the ground floor lobby, a man wearing a big smile with arms wide open blocked Nicholas' way to the exit door. Nicholas recognized Brian Cooper immediately even if the man looked neat in a new sports coat, dress pants to match and a new pair of shoes. All through college and the five or six months Brian Cooper worked at Hunt, Ingram and Kimura, Nicholas never saw him dress up more than for going to a college game or to a weekend movie. But college was nine years ago, and it had been two years since Brian Cooper left the office.

The man had matured, one would hope, from the ultra-liberal, philosophical and free-spirited young college graduate that Nicholas remembered.

They clasped hands and kidded around briefly before deciding to have a breakfast snack at an L Street cafe down the block.

"Riyadh?" Nicholas was saying in a mock agitation when the girl brought their coffee and pastry. "Riyadh? What the hell were you doing in Riyadh?"

"Working. And learning. Learning about other people, other places. You ought to try it sometime in your life. Everybody ought to, especially people just out of college, before you're too old to do it. I should have done it soon after we graduated."

"I have done that," said Nicholas, unimpressed. "I did it before college. And I'm still doing it."

"You've never been anywhere. What are you talking about?"

"I was somewhere before I came to this country -"

"Yes, but you were too young to know the difference. And, besides, I'm talking about Saudi Arabia, the Middle East, North Africa, the Mediterranean. Places that really open up the rest of the world to you."

"So what did you do there? What's there to do in Riyadh after five o'clock?"

Brian Cooper proceeded to tell as much of his fifteen-month working residency in Saudi Arabia as a civil engineer. Nicholas listened interestedly, noticing in particular how he indeed had matured in the two years they didn't see each other, the way he spoke of his experiences of another culture, another world. He talked about them in detail and colorfully at times that his listener pictured Riyadh and Al-Kuwait, Jiddah and the Red Sea vividly like a postcard in his mind.

"I didn't actually see the city being built," he said, speaking of Riyadh, "but I didn't have to for everything is so new it felt like all of the hi-rise structures, the airports, the commercial and residential zones all just sprouted up in the desert like mushrooms. All in one day. Oil money. Black gold."

Nicholas noticed that Brian Cooper looked a little older too not only with the creases on his forehead and around the eyes when he smiled but especially when he started talking serious. That, along with what was coming from him now - ideologies, way of life, world of Islam, global conflicts, high-tech, put to rest the image of that hollow, materialistic urban American Nicholas knew so well. A man he could easily imagine ranting about today's issues not on a campus stand but on the podium of a political party platform had taken over.

But the man, although he spoke forcefully, was not a loud-mouth or a demagogue. He spoke of his experiences and of what he believed in with care and conviction.

"Everything works only according to a given system," he said during his second cup of coffee. "From the lowest life form on earth to the creation of the universe. Everything in the world as we know it belongs to a system of a certain design."

Nicholas, for the most part of this, just sat and listened. He'd seen Brian Cooper pontificate before, at school and occasionally at work. It was something to behold.

"Religion is a system," he went on. "Everytime it crops up anywhere in the world at any time, that system kicks in. Begins the process of establishing an idea of a supreme being, an idea conceived upon the will and the need to trust in someone else. The rest of the process simply involves any number of worship practices and rituals.

"It's the same thing in all the other aspects of human society: our economic, social and political systems. Our way of life. Each one of them is a system or a subsystem working with others to form one whole system."

Nicholas started thinking maybe the man is doped but it was too early in the morning for that unless he really got deep into that while living in the Middle East.

"And speaking of a way of life. Religion. Culture," Brian Cooper continued in earnest with the pious movement of a hand, allowing no room for any interruption. "Islam. The Moslem world. Talk about taking matters to heart and mind. That's where you see it happen. It's a different world, a different culture. Their Christ is Mohammed. They're called Mohammedans and we're called Christians. Two different worlds, and faith, carving two different cultures and way of life on earth and yet both come from the same system of origination - the assumption of a supreme being. Same system, same idea, or input, but different values.

"I mingled with the natives a little to actually soak in some of their way of life, and what I can tell you out of this is that all these turmoil in the Middle East didn't start with the formation of the state of Israel. It's not the conflict over the Suez Canal or the outcome of the so-called six-day war or the 1973 war. These are only scratches on the surface. If it's not one superficial thing, it'll only be another.

"What it is is a biblical conflict of values. While I was there, I was able to see and feel how irreconcilable certain western values are for instance, with the way of life in the land just as I can see how difficult it would be for us Americans if somehow they came over here and forced their way upon us. It just isn't right for one people to force or inflict their way of life upon another through propaganda, commerce, military, intelligence or whatever means there is. The best thing we Americans, for example, can do to make other people see our way is to show them what it's like here, not there, and hope that they like it and think it's good as we do. Whether they adapt it or not is up to them. Not us."

"Yes, were it only that simple. But you know it's not."
Nicholas decided that this was not the same Brian Cooper
he went to school and worked with at all, not the educated
middle-class white Anglo-American who has yet to be
convinced that other countries actually exist outside of
North America, and not just on television. "Otherwise, we
wouldn't need foreign relations. The U.S. has vital interests
in other countries all over the world from a number of
standpoints: economic, defense, political. Some of them see
things the American way. Some don't. Those who do look
to the U.S. for support. The U.S. can't turn it's back on its
allies. There's somebody else out there who is always trying
to make others see things their way."

"I know there are foreign policies that must be made,
foreign relations that must be established between nations
and we all know which one dominates a relationship when
one of them is the United States, this country being the
more powerful one. But let's not intrude in the way of life
of the little fellow. His culture. His religion. If he wants to
eat raw meat and monkey brains, let him. Don't shove a Big
Mac into his face. And respect his religion, his thoughts, his
faith. Don't proselytize him." Brian Cooper paused for a
moment to dwell on the thousand other thoughts of his
experiences in the world of Islam. He made no attempt to
hide this from Nicholas when he continued: "I think I know
what happened in Iran, why it happened there. A few years
from now, all the crises in there and all these anti-American
demonstrations would all be but forgotten when the real
movement to cleanse the Moslem world of all the Western
and Christian intrusions get into high gear. There's going to
be more terrorism, more show of violence to get the
message across that the way to peace between the two
worlds is through mutual respect. That is the biggest word

the West and the Christians have been missing in their foreign relations and preaching: respect."

Nicholas, at this point, had become certain that Brian Cooper wasn't just an enlightened American traveler who had spent a little too much time in one particular country and got an extra dose of its culture and ideology. He suspected that maybe Brian Cooper was turning Arab or Muslim; one or the other or both. He almost laughed at this to himself and at the same time saw what a curiosity this is to see a native-born Anglo-American after a period of firsthand exposure to another way of life finally 'see and feel' the world including America from a different point of view.

He wanted to tell this to Brian Cooper and give the man an idea of how much he had change. But he didn't know how without sounding personally critical or even insulting and ruining their pleasant morning coffee snack, their first in over two years.

This was another one of those occasions, Nicholas realized, when he wished he had someone close enough to tell it to - this whole coffee-and-pastry scene between himself and this newly enlightened American friend of his. The nearest he could think of was Haj Fujiwara with whom he had shared some personal insights of life in America. But the thought of Emil was instantly there, a live presence in his mind almost like an instinct, before anyone else; the idea of telling his boyhood friend back in the old country another one of his interesting personal experiences in America, writing it down in a letter and always as if he and his family had, only a month ago, or even a few days ago, landed in the new world.

If I didn't hear it from the man himself, I
wouldn't have believed any of it. But he did say

all those things he said to me. And I know he meant every word of them.

He's been back three months from the world of Islam and for the last three weeks has been working for a small consulting firm in Rockville, Maryland, a suburb of Washington. He said he plans to go abroad again within a year and wants to know what our part of the world out there in the Far East is like.

We have all kinds, I told him, our country being like a small United States but not so... anglicized, having been colonized simultaneously at one time by the Americans, the Spanish, the Portuguese and the Japanese. It's a true example of a polyglot society, I said. A nation of mixed Asian and European races and cultures. The population is ninety percent Eurasian. I also pointed out that the Moslems form a sizeable part of society, together with the Buddhists, the Taoists, the Shintoists, along with the Christian majority similar to the Philippines..

He said he definitely must go there soon. If he did, I would like you to meet him so you would see for yourself what an educated native-born American is like when he suddenly comes in contact with the rest of the world personally and gets an actual taste of other ways: an Allah-and-Christ-worshipping society, a rice-eating culture, or a multi-lingual, multi-dialect nation of various skin pigmentation too. All these in the truest sense of the word. A culturally integrated nation.

Nicholas broke off his mental letter-writing to Emil, a cerebral activity which he seemed to fall into more and more often of late, when Brian Cooper said:

"I'm glad the world, the universe is such that there's two sides to everything. And I'm glad too, I must add, that the world, I mean the time we live in now, is a two-party system."

"I gather you're talking about the political system in the United States."

"That's part of it, but I'm referring more specifically to the two world powers, their separate ideologies. It's interesting how they must keep up the balance of power, their propaganda, the influence of their doctrines. Could you imagine what the world would be like if there was only one world power?"

"Which one? Russia?"

"Either one. Think of it."

"That's not hard to picture," Nicholas said, glancing at his wristwatch. He shouldn't be late much longer for Centreville. "Just think of the Soviet Union as the only country on earth. Think of all of us, the whole human race, as all in there, ruled by the supreme government in a police state with all its civil impositions: controlled population movement, controlled foreign travel and emigration, total government control of the economy."

"What made you pick the Soviet Union?" asked Brian.

"We know what it would be like with the United States as the uncontested world power."

"No, we don't," Brian Cooper said quickly. "I don't think so. Here in the United States, we have a general idea. But outside, who knows?"

"It won't be much different than now. For one thing, there won't be just one government in the world. America is not going to rule the whole planet. There won't be any global police state. Each country will have its own sovereign government. And the United States will continue to do its job of preserving human freedom and justice. Isn't that what this country is founded upon?"

"Freedom and justice? Those are big words."

"Well, isn't it?"

"Supposedly."

"What do you mean supposedly?" Nicholas asked irascibly.

"Depends on whose freedom you're talking about. And justice for whom?"

"For you and me," Nicholas blurted out in his mounting impatience. "For the little man and the big man alike out there, everywhere. What happened to you over in those Arabian deserts? Got your brain cooked a little too much?"

"Maybe," said Brian Cooper, laughing. "Maybe it did need some cooking we never had at school. My point is: monopoly is never a good proposition. Kills competition as you know. I don't care how good and magnanimous an entity is especially a political establishment, a ruling party. A government. When it goes bad in any way, who's to counter it? There's nothing to stand in its way. The world will be hurled back to the age of colonialism and all sorts of open-handed exploitation. You're probably more in a position to tell me what it's like, coming from a former colony of the United States. I'm sure somewhere in that period of the country - what, seventy, eighty years? - there were many accounts of cultural suppression, injustice and all sorts of brutality that aren't in history books. I mean American history books."

From now on, Emil, I must learn to take this man more seriously. I truly believe his experiences abroad have opened his mind considerably.

That was very perceptive of him, about our colonial past, assuming he's no certified expert on our country's history. He was right about the injustices our ancestors suffered during all those times - one hundred fifty years altogether. One culture forcing its way onto another, one way of life trying to obliterate another.

And he was right about many of the brutalities against the native citizens. You'll find them in our history books written by our historians. I never read any account of it, not a single one in any of the American history textbooks taught in schools here.

Did anybody ever talk to you, when you were very small, about an old man in our hometown everybody called Nuno? He was called this because he was supposedly the oldest person in town. I can't remember if I ever told you about him myself. He was about ninety years old when I was eight or nine and I remember people used to listen to him tell stories about life during the colonial years, about the revolution in 1920 and his part in it.

His stories were told over and over again by those who heard it. I myself heard several of them from the old man himself not long before he died.

Nuno was a very patriotic man. He devoted most of his adult life to aiding the revolutionaries. He showed a great deal of pride and satisfaction for having taken part in the expulsion of all the foreign powers. But it hurt him so much, he said, everytime he remembers the atrocities those foreigners meted out to our countrymen. He talked about men, women and children being treated like animals - in their own land. He talked about the punishments and tortures our forefathers went through for suspicion of involvement in any movement or propaganda to free the country from the colonizers. Mass executions by firing squad or hanging and crucifixion. Many were decapitated. Women were raped and kept for pleasure. Those who weren't shot or hanged or beheaded and for some reason were spared were condemned to a lifetime of slavery in the sugar and rubber plantations, or the mine sites living like animals. A lot of these are in our history books as I'm sure you know.

When Brian Cooper began to sound as though he was turning Moslem, I joked that he got his brain cooked in those Arabian deserts, and when he started talking as if he was turning communist too, I thought he had it cooked well done. But no, he wasn't advocating communism and its doctrine or world domination. In fact, this was what he spoke against: domination, hegemony, monopoly, colonialism by anyone, even by the United States.

What he was saying of the two superpowers now is that one could be as bad as the other. And that's why, as he said, it's a good thing that the world is such that there are two sides to everything, that it's a two-party system.

One is an evil, if so it is, necessary for the existence of the other.

One thing I keep wondering about, especially for living here in Washington, is what if the two superpowers, let alone the rest of the world, didn't have to spend all those hundreds of billions of dollars on defense budget? Would we have people living on the moon now? Or one of the planets? Working to seed the place with the elements necessary to create a life-supporting environment?

Would illiteracy, poverty and hunger be finally wiped out on the face of the earth?

I put these forth to Brian and he said: no, not in our time. What all that surplus money is going to do is depress the world economy instead. Currency systems would collapse and so new world conflicts would arise. In fact, he said, they would almost have to be created. Most developed countries have economies that thrive more on human conflicts and adversities. Take the humongus insurance industry for instance in this country. And the lawyers. They'd all be out of work if they didn't have any human conflict - domestic, national and international - to build a case on. These types of livelihood, among a few others, generate what you may call a paper economy. They don't produce anything tangible or consumable which meets people's basic human needs. All they produce are mountains of papers to be filed in cabinets or stored in computers. It is an artificial economy, Brian said to me, which feeds on human fears, hostilities and weaknesses. There's big bucks in it, allowing many to live high up on the hogs with an artificially high standard of living.

Meaning, people, perhaps a whole segment of society, the economic elite, living on vast sums of money they got for nothing more than a crisp lip service without so much as producing a bowl of rice or a glass of milk to help the world food supply.

God, I hate the way he put it to me, Emil, and I hate it more that I find myself agreeing with him. But I do.

I'm glad I'm not an insurance man, or a lawyer.

☐ 5 ☐

A THANKSGIVING

He was starting to worry about being late when he got on his way to the Centreville jobsite. But once he reached Route 50 West after crossing the Potomac to Virginia on the Roosevelt Bridge, he remembered a short phone call he got earlier from Gary Clemens, an associate of Zimmerman Partners and Associates, Architects, one of the best known commercial architects in town and a top client of Hunt, Ingram and Kimura. The associate architect had called to say his boss, the office principal in charge of the Centreville shopping plaza project, couldn't make it and is sending him out instead.

With Gary Clemens out there, he didn't have to worry about anything. They worked well with each other. Always had, even in the face of certain differences in their profession as architect and engineer. He relaxed and enjoyed the drive, giving himself time to reflect mostly upon some of the things that came out of Brian Cooper.

He wondered how accurate is the theory, even that of Brian Cooper but especially that forwarded by critics of the United States and particularly its enemies that America thrives best on human conflicts. Within its borders: vast social and economic divisions in its society. And outside its borders: wars, real wars both open and covert, and sustained ideological incursions of foreign cultures. If this were so, wouldn't it hold true too in its spiritual life, and for that matter, in religion in general? The conflict between good and evil must continue to exist. The church loses its role if it does not have the necessary evil that it must play against.

Just like the media, he thought, remembering some of the TV network coverage he'd seen where newscasters were openly hoping in their facial expressions and tone of voice, in spite of what they say, that more disasters would strike, more destruction would occur, more deaths, more killings, more human conflicts and sufferings, so they would have a story to sell, have more opportunity to prove their competence at doing their work, up their rating and keep their jobs.

As he rode along Route 50, one of the most clogged roads in Northern Virginia during rush hours but now empty, a lot of questions induced primarily by Brian Cooper's polemics crowded his mind.

Is the U.S. no better than the U.S.S.R.? But no worse? What are the criteria? In this age of expert propaganda and total, unrelenting indoctrination, how is one on either world to know what those criteria are?

Is it the quality of life? The culture and social order? Is it the form of government which defines and enforces these?

Propaganda and indoctrination notwithstanding, which is really preferable: freedom and decadence or totalitarianism and equality? Privatism or socialism?

America. Where is it?

Is there really such a place? Do people find it once they get there or does it remain a dream in their heads, an ideal that's there only to be pursued through a lifetime of indebtedness?

With the current national debt, every child born in the U.S. is already in debt by over seventeen thousand dollars. Somebody has to be living way beyond his means, enjoying a standard of living he couldn't afford, for his newborn to owe so much in its first light of day.

Where do the goods that make for such a standard of living come from? Who did without them so that those others may enjoy a better life?

How and when are those goods paid for, if ever?

What about people like Edward McKenny? Is there an America for them? Was there ever? What is it, then? A middle-class family and house in the suburbs that a peasant in China and Brazil or even Emil in the old country could only dream of?

Is that what America is? Is that what people think it is? Or is it a bench in a public park? A grate on a cold night?

... *you have an America to go to! I don't! I'm already here!*

America, where are you? What are you?

It was a cool morning of November, the Tuesday before Thanksgiving, sunny and clear with but small puffs of cottony clouds over Centreville. He felt glad to be out when he got there.

The jobsite was some two hundred acres of idle earth that had recently tripled in value after it was zoned commercial. Some sixteen miles of highway driving on the Beltway and Route 66 separated it from the huge Tysons Corner development, a distance its developers felt wide enough for the new shopping center to survive competition and do good business out of the local economy and those of other area communities such as Chantilly, this side of Fairfax City, and Manassas.

All they needed were more people. More people to move farther out west of the Capital Beltway and Tysons Corner which was starting to get saturated, bring their Washington high-tech paychecks and spend them there on mortgage payments and consumer goods.

What it was to be, as planned and designed by Zimmerman Partners and Associates, was already in evidence at the present stage of the project as Nicholas saw when he drove in from Lee Highway not long after he got off Route 66. A main roadway funneled the traffic from the outside in between two sections at first - the three-story central mall with two levels of subterranean additional parking under it, and the specialty section where one can shop for what can not be found in the department stores in the central mall.

The roadway then looped around the central mall separating at the first turn the other section of the shopping center which was the automotive service center, and emptied back out to Lee Highway. The sections were interconnected by enclosed overhead walks over the roadway, making it a less hazardous place for customers as they go around spending their dollars.

"Should this project bomb," Nicholas told Gary Clemens some weeks ago, "it wouldn't be because of the architectural design."

That pleased Gary Clemens who respected architecture itself although he hated the profession, revealing to Nicholas at that time that he did the design of the central mall himself and that the idea of the overhead walkways was his too.

At the construction office, Nicholas was directed by the contractor's clerk-of-work to the location in the mall where Gary Clemens may be found. He had a man escort Nicholas for the quickest and safest way of going about the site amid the piles of construction litters and hazardous obstacles.

The man was a construction worker who had come in to the office with his foreman to help deliver some office equipment. The foreman was only too happy to volunteer the services of his man who in turn was more than happy to escort the engineer in locating the architect.

The construction worker, a forty-year old journeyman mason, would do much more than see to the safety of the man who was the reason for his being there at the site on full-time employment now for almost a whole year. He could hardly remember how long it had been since he had worked year-round before this job.

It was at least a year and a half ago when Harvey Dugan, doing short-term work at another jobsite, came to know Nicholas. Harvey Dugan was the only worker who happened to be around when Nicholas showed up at the site one day and introduced himself. He offered to find his foreman but Nicholas insisted there's no need for he only had a couple of questions which in fact, he said then, may be better answered by a journeyman worker than a foreman.

Their meeting turned out to be more than a blue-and-white collar work session at the jobsite. From it, Nicholas learned that Harvey Dugan was a transient worker from Martinsburg, West Virginia, married and had two young boys, eight and eleven years old. There was nothing to do in Martinsburg, he said, so he comes to the Washington area periodically to look for anything in his line of work even only part-time, short-term, temporary. Anything at all to bring home some money to support his family.

In the process of knowing him, Nicholas perceived a man, an American blue-collar worker who did his best to earn a living no matter how meager and yet continued to exist at the edge of uncertainty in a society of an economic power second to none on earth.

Before they parted then, Nicholas had composed a handwritten letter of recommendation Harvey Dugan was to carry to a man, an official in a general-contractor and developer company in Fairfax, Virginia, who he said would know to get Harvey Dugan a full-time, long-term, year-round work at one of their projects once he presented the letter to the man. Inside of one month after that day, Harvey Dugan had found a place to live in Centreville shortly after getting the job and earned enough money to move his family with him soon after.

In his fluid southern accent, he told Nicholas the next time they met not much later: "Nobody had ever done what you'd done for me and my family, I swear. I thank you kindly, sir. And if ever there's anything, anything at all..."

As they walked past construction machineries, piles of building materials, mounds of earth, men and women in hardhats everywhere, Harvey Dugan tried to cope with mixed feelings at seeing his friend again. He walked proudly beside Nicholas and was happy to be doing what he could do for him but at the same time was feeling embarrassed in himself that he couldn't do more than be his guide. If only there was something else he could do for the man, anything at all before they get to where he's taking him and not see him again for a long time, maybe never.

"How's work with you here so far?" Nicholas asked as they picked their way through a gravel bed.

"Oh, it's fine," replied the mason, big grin on his face, "ever'thing's fine. Real happy about it."

"And your family? How are they?"

"They're doin' great. Thank you for askin'. The boys are back to school regular now. The wife's taken up part-time work at the neighborhood foodstore and she'd never been happier since the day we got married."

Suddenly, a thought occurred in Harvey Dugan which excited him so much he almost grabbed Nicholas by the arm yet at the same time he questioned if it wouldn't be so bold of him to let Nicholas know what it is. He knew if he didn't risk it, the thought of the possibility that it might have been alright after all to invite him over the house for the Thanksgiving dinner would be hanging over his head for the rest of his life. What more proper time to really express his gratitude to the good man than this holiday of thanks giving?

He was certain Nicholas would politely decline the invitation as, surely, he had already made plans for the holiday way ahead. But, still, it would give him a great satisfaction at having tested the possibility regardless of the outcome.

"Mr. Gabriel," he stammered.

"What is it, Harvey?" asked Nicholas, noticing the man's difficulty.

"This week is really going to be a good one for me, and my family, being the Thanksgiving week. We haven't had a good Thanksgiving together in a long time so I'm taking Friday off too. Spend some extra time with the boys. I'm wonderin' if it's at all possible for you to come to my home for a Thanksgiving dinner with me and my family."

It took a few moments for Nicholas to make any kind of response. He realized something like this takes either a yes or a no for an answer. Nothing in between.

"I realize it's such a short notice," Harvey Dugan spoke again with much care in his voice, "so I understand if you can't. I'm just sayin'... if it's at all possible, even for a short while. My wife's asked me a few times about you, sayin' 'what a good man that Mr. Gabriel must be to help when he never even saw you before. A total stranger.' She would really like to meet you. But again, if it's not possible, maybe another time... "

"No, Harvey," Nicholas said suddenly. "I can make it this time. In fact, this is as good a time as any. I don't have any definite plan for the holiday. Not yet." At this point, he had decided that as he had, indeed, no firm idea what Gail planned for the holiday, he would take matters into his own hands and accept Harvey Dugan's invitation and bring Gail along too. "Except for a couple of things," he added.

"Mr. Gabriel, I am so happy to hear you could come. Anything at all I can do, just say whatever it is."

"Howabout dropping the Mr.? I have a first name too just like everybody else. It's Nicholas."

"Alright... N-Nicholas. You betcha."

"And can I bring a friend?"

"Nicholas, you can bring all the friends you have. There'll be plenty to eat and drink all day long. I can't wait to get home and tell my wife. She'd be so happy to hear about this."

Gary Clemens had a light build and was six feet two inches tall. From a distance, he looked a lot taller especially when he's looking up. Up at a hole through the floor above or the guts of the building hanging above the unfinished ceiling. He gave that elongated effect of a subject in a perspective composition with a single vanishing point somewhere in the sky.

This was how Nicholas observed him as he approached the architect at the second floor of the mall building. Gary Clemens, dressed so casually in a loose-fitting pair of cuffed pants and a wrinkled shirt with rolled-up long sleeves, reminded him of Gary Cooper in the Howard Rourke character of Ayn Rand's 'The Fountainhead'.

Nicholas liked this man both as a person and as a fellow professional. He never had any quarrel with him over anything on the projects they've worked together. Differences of opinion - technical, budgetary, what not, were easily resolved between the two of them either on the drawing board or at the site and rarely needed to tax the attention of their respective office principals.

He honestly wished the man would some day soon become a recognized architect, succeed in setting up his own practice and break the hold upon him of - in his words - the barren minds that constantly surrounded him. He tried going on his own a few years ago, banking on a couple of respectable commissions that came along after winning the competition for the design of a large Army officer housing and office complex in North Carolina.

His practice lasted two years. Then, as is common in such an unstable line of work - again in his own words, he job-hopped for the next two years between firms in Maryland, the District and Virginia, sometimes even as far as Pennsylvania, until he ended up at Zimmerman and Associates where he had been for the last four years.

Gary Clemens liked architecture. People can see it in his work especially when no one - his office boss or any of those barren-minded people he had known in his career or even the project client itself, tells him how to do it, how to

88 JAIME ESPIRITU

draw the lines. But he hated the profession as he had so disdainfully told Nicholas a few times.

"There are people in it who shouldn't be," he said. "And there are many who should not even have been admitted to any school of architecture. People who simply have no business being in it and would have been better off being a teacher, a lawyer, or a government paper shuffler."

When Gary Clemens spoke of quitting the profession himself and going into something else, farming he said, sales or even driving a truck, Nicholas thought what a tragedy it would be, what a great loss in a world that suffers with so much mediocrity as it does, if he did. The architect was at the prime of his life, only in his late thirties, so full of creative energy he was so willing and quite able to bring out into the practice of his profession.

One of the reasons that brought them out to the jobsite this day was a structural connection, a point three stories above the main entrance of the mall where a tremendous amount of the roof load was concentrated and transferred to a five-foot deep long-span girder beam which together with the decorative tall columns that supported it framed the entrance to the building. Hunt, Ingram and Kimura had expressed concern about the stability of the structure for lack of additional reinforcements which the architects had refused to allow for aesthetic reasons. But the engineers insisted, showing how serious their concern was by offering to do the additional work at their own expense, in keeping with their good relation with a valued client architect.

Zimmerman and Associates gave in, agreeing to make architectural design changes - to a degree - that would work in the additional structural members the engineers, including Nicholas, felt should rest everyone's safety concerns.

"I want you to know that I personally appreciate what you guys are doing," Gary Clemens said to Nicholas as they hovered over a blueprint on top of a workbench, "pushing us to do this."

"I'm glad you feel that way," replied Nicholas.

"I won't argue with the threat of disaster especially when I have something to do with it. A lot to do with it. I, too, am the one who originally hatched the idea of this monumental main entrance design."

Nicholas wanted to tell him how he admired the originality of the design, how daring and innovative. But he didn't know how without sounding patronizing about it. In their business, engineers are never in any position to make personal observations on the creativity of a client. But just this once, if he had had to, he would have stuck his neck out and told Gary Clemens that anything good and praiseworthy is never without risks and never easy to do. That for anyone to be worth a damn to anybody, he must have that daring of originality, change and innovation. Otherwise, why not just build from the blueprint of the first store architecture ever designed and built, or that of the first automobile, the first skyscraper, the first airplane?

He thought about Haj Fujiwara back in the office and his persistent demands for good quality work. Then at this same moment, he looked closely at Gary Clemens. In these two men, Nicholas saw that most of the better human attributes that have created and advanced human civilization to this day lives on. It continues to suffer in the ever-growing banality of contemporary values, but it endures, it lives on.

He sees it in Gary Clemens' face. A glow of creativity, now absent in many other mortals, but in him, inextinguishable, waiting patiently to burst into flame. He hears it in the voice of Haj Fujiwara and the force of discipline behind it, true and precise, calling for the realization of the ideal. Of perfection, perhaps.

Suddenly, without meaning to bring it on to himself, he felt a load of sadness, a sense of emptiness deep down at the thought of Haj Fujiwara going back to Osaka and Gary Clemens becoming a salesman.

After work, he made sure he remembered to tell Gail about what's up for Thanksgiving, hoping she didn't already have something that couldn't be surmounted by an invitation to dinner with a blue-collar construction worker and his family. He went directly to her apartment and found her in the bedroom about to get in to a pair of jeans from her work clothes.

They kissed and hugged, then he held her around the waist to support her while she struggled with the jeans.

"How's work for Uncle Sam today?" he asked.

"Fine. Nothing spectacular. And how was your day?"

"Interesting, I might say. Went out to the Centreville jobsite. Met with the architect. Got invited to a Thanksgiving dinner by a - friend."

Nancy came out of the other bedroom and poked her head in briefly. She exchanged hi's with Nicholas and went to get a can of soda in the kitchen to bring back in her room in front of the TV. "I stopped by your place on my way here," Gail said. "I put a chocolate mousse in your freezer. I picked up a couple at the store on my way home from work. They were on sale."

"I'm glad we're neighbors."

"Something to drink?" she asked as she led the way to the kitchen.

"Some icewater would do, please."

"You want to eat with us tonight? Chicken a-la something tonight, call it whatever you want when it's done."

"Sounds good to me," he replied, laughing lightly and kissed her on the back of her neck. Then he proceeded to tell her some of the day's story. "Now, did I ever tell you about Brian Cooper, a guy I went to college with who was so immature he spent a lot of time marching in demonstrations, joining student activist groups without fully understanding what he's advocating and running his mouth for?"

She turned around to him with his glass of icewater in one hand, a frozen pack of chicken in the other and a frown on her face. "No," she said, "I don't believe you ever did. But how do you know that? That he didn't understand the side he was taking? And even if he didn't, he apparently believed in it enough to show his support for it, do his part. And that's what counts - having a belief in something as opposed to not having any at all."

"How could one believe in something he doesn't understand? You want to know how I know? Because I just saw him today. He came to visit me in the office and we went out for breakfast. He's recently been back from a contract work in the Middle East. Saudi Arabia. And he's singing a different tune. Ten years ago I remember him in front of a student group delivering his personal doctrine on the impeccability of the American Way and all the systems that make it work and work better than any other way; how the rest of the world must see things 'our way' if they want to live a more meaningful life on earth.

"Now he tells me, after mingling with the natives and learning of another way of life, another set of beliefs, he tells me 'it just isn't right for one people to force its way of life upon another through whatever means.'"

"Well, the man has matured. Maybe that's one thing you and I and the rest of the American people and the rest of the world ought to recognize and be thankful for. A man is entitled to his belief, and he's also entitled to change it."

She turned back to the chicken on the counter without the slightest idea of anything she had to do with Brian Cooper.

"Anyway, what I really need to talk to you about right away," he said after downing most of the icewater and placing himself next to her at the counter while she was getting the chicken ready to thaw in the microwave, "is to find out how much I'm ruining that great Thanksgiving Day plan you've made - two weeks ago or a month ago? by accepting that dinner invitation from this friend of mine at the jobsite today and asking if I could bring a friend along, namely - you."

"Who is he?"

"Name is Harvey Dugan. He's a construction worker and he and his family think a whole world of me for my helping him get his job at the project. I just couldn't say no in the face of such grateful enthusiasm he showed and especially after he quoted his wife saying what a good man I must be and all that. It would really mean a lot to them. Give them a chance to say thank you and make it a really good Thanksgiving Day for the poor folks. So -" Nicholas was momentarily muted when Gail moved quickly to lay an index finger full of cooking ingredients on his lips.

With an admiring look in her eyes, she said to him: "Yes, I would be very happy to go. And, no, you're not ruining any plan I've made ahead of time because I haven't made any except the likelihood of going to mother and being with most of the family there later during the day. I'll drop Nancy over there then tomorrow night."

Harvey Dugan's house, which he rented for three hundred a month, was a one-story wooden house with a forty-five-degree pitched roof of asphalt shingles and a ridge that extended straight in one line from above the front porch to above the kitchen and the back porch. Underneath was the open space that formed the combined living and dining areas. Past this, separated by a floor-to-ceiling drywall partition which Harvey Dugan built himself were the two bedrooms and the bathroom. And beyond, the kitchen and a small pantry and storage cabinet where he kept his tools in his trade as a mason or, occasionally, as a carpenter, a plumber, a roofer.

In this bare and humble American home, Nicholas found a rural American family when an eight-year old boy opened the front door to let him and Gail in to the living room. The boy, the youngest of two, led them properly into the room before his parents who came in a hurry from the company of their other guests who had come in earlier.

The women were introduced first. When Nicholas took his turn to shake hands with Bernice Dugan, he knew from the humble and thankful look in her eyes that he had done the right thing by being part of this one particular day in their lives. It was at this very moment when he recalled an event in his life very similar to this except in it, he was part of the family instead of the guests. It was one of several events he remembered as a child back in the old country and in Michigan where they were newly arrived immigrants in the United States when his parents had invited guests, American guests, into their house.

From those events, he never imagined what it would be like to play the opposite role. Now he saw himself in the young boy at the front door, his father in Harvey Dugan happy to see him come, and his mother in Bernice Dugan anxious to show their hospitality.

Dinner which was being prepared by Bernice Dugan and her mother was an hour away, a time which presented the opportunity for all the guests to get comfortable with one another. The other guests consisted of another couple, Robert and Barbara Grant, from Shepherdstown, West

Virginia, a small town near Martinsburg, also in West Virginia where Waylon Dugan, the only other guest and a younger brother of Harvey Dugan, also lived.

Waylon Dugan, who brought in the entire picture of a rural cowboy bar scene in his faded jeans, cowboy boots and shirt, explained in his authentic southern accent that they all rode down together including Mrs. Alma Bigel, Bernice Dugan's mother, in his '76 Chevy four-door 8-cylinder sedan earlier in the day and that they'll all be going back Sunday afternoon. One reason for this, he said, was for Robert Grant who is a close personal friend and also currently unemployed, to perhaps have an opportunity to meet some people in the Washington area from whom he might get some work leads and perhaps also a direct job recommendation.

By the time he was offered a second can of beer, Nicholas had a pretty clear idea of where everyone fit in the scene. But he didn't view anything at all with any misgiving. On the contrary, he intended to go along with the role he found himself in at an appropriate moment later, by offering to do what he possibly could to help find Robert Grant work in the area. It was looking at Barbara Grant, a timid woman of at least thirty-four years of age who looked terribly pale and impoverished, wearing a threadbare shirt about two sizes too big and which probably belonged to her husband that made Nicholas quickly decide to help.

While Gail talked to Barbara Grant, Nicholas turned directly to Robert Grant intent to be as straightforward as he could be to the jobless man but without bruising his dignity.

"You plan to move down this way too if you could get work here, Robert?" he asked.

"Yes, I sure do," replied Robert Grant. Nicholas guessed that he must be in his late forties with the band of gray around the edges of his hairline and the creases that showed around the eyes when he smiled. "Got to go where the job is at this point. I'd hate to do it - leave the good old hometown finally, but it can't be good being there anymore if I can't get a job."

Nicholas noticed Barbara Grant throwing a quick glance at her husband.

"How long... have you been out of work, Robert?" asked Nicholas with just the right measure of hesitation in it.

"Been sometime now. What? Seven, eight months?" Robert Grant turned to his friend Waylon Dugan.

"Yeah," confirmed Waylon, bobbing his head at his good buddy, "that's 'bout right."

"Waylon got me a temporary job where he works. Lasted a couple of months."

"What kind of work do you do, Robert?"

"I was a truck driver for a while. Just local, delivering auto parts around the tri-state area of West Virginia, Maryland and Pennsylvania. I wouldn't go too far. Takes you away from home too much. The man I was working for sold his business and got out of it. I'd done other kinds of work. Mostly maintenance type or guard job."

"Any particular skill? Something you're specially good at, or something you trained for?"

"Yeah. Paintin'. House paintin'. I'd done a lot of that. I used to do it full time some years back but work kinda just dried up around the area where we live. But now, I'd come down here if I could find a full time paintin' job. It doesn't have to be permanent as long as there's enough work to keep goin' most of the year."

Nicholas felt relieved when Harvey Dugan came around to offer more beer. He abstained for now and excused himself instead to go to the bathroom. As he got up, he heard Barbara Grant telling Gail: "We have two children. A ten-year old boy and a fourteen-year old girl. We thought it might not be too polite to bring 'em along for the entire weekend so we left them with my mother. I'm looking for work too. Anything, just anything to help keep us all going and keep the family together."

Once inside the bathroom, he took a minute to just stand in front of the mirror to allow himself to react naturally to everything he learned before he asked himself: what now?

His first thought concerning the Grants was that of several contractors and sub-contractors he had dealt with who used both union and non-union labor from structural steel workers to painters. It wouldn't take him more than a phone call to any of them to put Robert Grant to work. They're always looking for a few good workers, some even for cheap labor they could field in some of their short-term projects which they always have plenty of lined up. Hopefully, Robert Grant's ability and experience would put him above that and get him a better-paying long-term work assignments so he could - Nicholas thought with an irrepressible urge - afford to buy the poor wife some new clothes immediately.

He spent a couple of extra minutes in the bathroom thinking beyond the Dugans and the Grants.

Whose doing is it that these people from West Virginia, family-oriented, simple and uncomplicated folks but honest and willing to work, exist the way they do, living in a clapboard house like this, while those people in places like Foxhall Road in Washington, McLean in Northern Virginia or Potomac, Maryland enjoy a lifetime of affluence generation after generation. What separates Robert Grant and Harvey Dugan from all those wealthy people, and even from ordinary white-collar wage-earners like him?

Whoever said America is a classless society? And what's really at work in it, and in control? Is it a democracy, or a plutocracy, dressed up as a democracy?

In the living room, Gail learned further that Barbara Grant had finished high school, even gone to a vocational school for a year and worked for three years in an office before she started having the children,

"I could still type," she told Gail. "I'd have to brush up a little, though. My spelling is good."

"Where do you work, Gail?" Waylon Dugan asked.

"I work for the Department of the Army in Alexandria," replied Gail, and before she had to correct anybody as she often had to do in this kind of situation, added: "I'm not a soldier. I'm a civilian employee."

"And what do you do there?"

"I'm a personnel specialist with the Army Civilian Personnel Office. We process and keep track of civilian workers' records as they come and go, and anything that happens in between."

"How did you get a job there?"

"Yeah," seconded Robert Grant, leaning closer to Gail across the coffee table. "How does anybody get a job in the government? And especially in Washington."

"You do the same things you got to do to get a government job anywhere in the country."

Barbara Grant, sitting next to her husband, just sat there and only listened to the others for she and Gail had already gone over the same set of questions and answers. In fact, Gail, upon learning of her work experience and abilities, had encouraged her to try applying in the government and even offered to help her through the red tapes.

"First, you find out what kind of job openings there are, and where, and which ones they are presently accepting applications for. When you see an opening you think might fit you - and you can apply for more than one job at the same time - you ask for a copy of what we   call 'job announcement' which describes the job, the duties and responsibilities, the location, salary and what's required of the applicant to qualify and be hired. Then you fill out an application form, it's a standard form they'll give you along with the announcement, if you ask for it, the same one everybody has to fill out -"

Gail had just about wrapped up a mini-seminar on how to break into the U.S. government service and launch a career in it when Nicholas rejoined them. A minute later, Bernice Dugan, twirling a kitchen wet-cloth in her hands, her husband beside her, stood before them and respectfully announced dinner's ready. She then moved forward and literally took Gail's hand to lead her up to the table. Harvey Dugan took care of the rest by motioning everybody to rise, starting with Nicholas.

It was a buffet dinner with a twenty-pound bird as the centerpiece which Bernice Dugan had started preparing the day before by shopping at discount prices at the foodstore where she worked part-time, and working in the kitchen all day today with her mother.

Nicholas couldn't help being aware of the satisfaction and happiness that radiated from Harvey Dugan at the sight of his family and friends celebrating a real Thanksgiving meal like they'd never had before in his own home. But more than this, Nicholas found it difficult to ignore the fact that everything everybody did was directed toward him and Gail as a gesture of thanksgiving and respect.

It was a wholesome meal which everybody enjoyed and for which the hosts were repeatedly complimented. Later, as Nicholas and Gail prepared to leave after Gail explained that they would like to save part of the day to spend with her mother in Chevy Chase, Bernice Dugan cupped both hands over her mouth as though in a terrible bind.

"Honey," she gasped at her husband, "we almost forgot."

"What?" asked Harvey Dugan.

"The... you know what. They're in the bedroom."

"Golly, you're right. Please, don't go just yet for just one more minute," he pleaded to their guests.

"Jimmy!" Bernice Dugan called aloud to the bedroom where the two boys had been all day, watching the games on TV. "Please bring out those things laying on the bed now."

The same boy who opened the door when they arrived came out carrying gift-wrapped presents that filled both his arms under them: a big one for Nicholas and a small one for Gail. Seeing this, the most Nicholas could do was clasp Gail's hand to steady himself as they stood motionless near the front door.

"Now, this is just a little somethin' we just couldn't pass up doin', Nicholas," Harvey Dugan explained apologetically as he prodded Jimmy to step forward. "I hope you folks don't mind."

"Please -" Nicholas looked helplessly back and forth at the man and the woman in front of him, throwing a quick glance at Gail too. "I hardly think we deserve all this honor."

"It's not much," said Bernice Dugan. "I know it's a little early for Christmas, but like Harvey said, we just couldn't pass up the opportunity to do this now. After all, Thanksgiving is supposed to be the start of the Christmas season. Now, Jimmy," she said to the boy, "give the presents to Nicholas now. Come on. Don't be shy now."

The boy stepped up to Nicholas and offered the gifts.

"Now, what do you say?" his mother asked.

"Happy Thanksgiving and Merry Christmas," said the eight-year old.

"Thank you very much, Jimmy, and I wish you and your family the same," said Nicholas, choking, as he reached down for the presents.

◻ 6 ◻

THE REBELS

News of the old country made the lead item in the world event section of the Post every now and then. Eight years ago, the president - as the opposition had suspected and feared - not ready to relinquish power after two six-year terms finally made his intention to stay in office known by skirting the constitutionally mandated election of the executive office.

This he did (but which he denied) by staging a military coup led by several hand-picked Generals who sacked the People's Hall, imprisoned all the Members - the people's duly elected representatives, shooting to death a few of the strong of the opposition among them right in their Hall Offices including some of their staff members who were at work. Those who were absent from the capital were rounded up in their local provincial offices Others escaped and went into hiding. Those who were abroad at the time, especially the known members of the opposition, remained abroad. Within four years, six of them had been killed: three in the United States (Los Angeles and Washington, D.C.), two in Manila and one in Hong Kong.

The military takeover of the civilian government was a sweep. Within weeks, the business of government was back in order with the president restored both as head of state and as active military commander of the armed forces. His supporters in the People's Hall, now abolished, who were temporarily jailed along with the rest were summoned back to draft a new constitution in their capacity as an interim supreme council of state.

These events resulted in the rebel movement, which until then had been widely disorganized, gaining strength and solidifying both in the rural provincial areas and the cities. Incidences of open encounters with government troops mounted, and so did the casualties on both sides. In the years that followed, there were many accounts of government assaults and their brutalities not only against the rebels but the citizenry who supported the rebels. But the movement, joined by the disenfranchised political opposition, only gathered more strength, became more widespread and even established foreign operations bases for arms procurement.

The government maintained, as it had all along, its non-aligned foreign relations policy. Its embassies remained in Tokyo, Beijing, Washington, D.C., Moscow, London, Paris, Bonn. The same could be said of the rebel movement in the sense that it did not succumb to any offer of aid either from the orthodox communists or the West.

The conflict was purely internal, and remained within the scope of the ideology of nationalism. But the government voiced its protest against certain foreign countries that it claimed allowed and even encouraged rebel activities such as raising money, arms deals and shipping into the rebel-controlled areas of the country. It in turn intensified its intelligence network it had operating in those foreign countries.

The result was the killing of those opposition figures in the United States, Hong Kong and Manila, not to mention a number of other liquidation again in the U.S. and other parts of the world which had yet to be officially substantiated as the work of the government intelligence.

Although subject to certain restrictions such as access to the inner core of government and travel in some ideologically sensitive regions of the country, the media - local and foreign - had been allowed pretty much on their own. But during the first week of December, a month after the last U.S. presidential election where the incumbent was soundly beaten, the government suddenly clamped down on the media, nationalizing all the major metropolitan dailies, the TV and radio broadcasting networks and several of the most influential weekly magazines in the country.

All foreign news correspondents were expelled on short notice except for three - a Japanese, a French and an American - who were allowed to stay as unofficial observers. They became the only link between the nation and the rest of the world. And such a weak link for they were allowed to send out only five hundred words each coverage they were permitted. And those words passed through the sieve of the Media Bureau of the Ministry of Foreign Affairs which then turned them over to the president himself for the final go-ahead or no go-ahead.

It took a few days for these events to reach abroad for it took as long for many expelled foreigners to be transported out of the country. It was another week before the first of those five-hundred word coverage appeared as a lead item in the world event section of the Post.

Nicholas read it during lunch at work. From it, he learned that the rebel movement had recently made significant progress in de-stabilizing the government which in turn had quickly stepped up its counter-operations nationwide in its resolve to bring down the rebellion for good. In one short paragraph, it included a government statement blaming foreign intervention for the increased aggression of the rebel forces.

In the meantime, according to official reports, it is limiting foreign travel of its citizens to official government business and 'regulating media operations in the interest of national security and the country's reserve to be free from foreign interference during this critical time.'

Anybody could have read into that very easily, especially somebody who had the interest to keep up on the happenings there. From anybody's point of view abroad, especially in Washington, the country was ruled by a military regime under a dictatorship which can deny all human rights at any time, and therefore suspend freedom of speech, press and assembly at the dictator's will. The new constitution which supposedly provided for civilian participation in the means of government had been scorned by ideologists at home and abroad as an instrument of injustice and (human) oppression.

As soon as he got home, Nicholas turned on the television in the hope of catching anything else on the news. Nothing, outside of what had already been reported by the foreign correspondents expelled from the country: Fierce battles between the rebels and government troops as close as within twenty kilometers of the capital, more arms shipments intercepted by the navy, headed ashore towards rebel-controlled areas from the sea lanes coming from Guam in the southeast and Hong Kong in the northwest; nationalization of several major corporations, local and foreign-owned, and of the media as had been previously reported over and over.

It had been more than two months since Emil's last letter when Nicholas received the next one, three days ago. News of the suspension of the press and, therefore, most of the freedom of speech in the country, prompted him to take out the letter from the drawer and go over it again.

Emil had written short letters before. Two pages, one and a half pages, widely spaced and handwritten. But this one had to be the shortest as far as he could recall. One page consisting of several short paragraphs.

He was almost certain there were things Emil was trying to tell him in it which Emil couldn't put down explicitly in writing.

You won't be hearing much about us from now on. We don't know how long this news blackout will be. Much as I want to myself, I can't - right now - tell you much of what's happening... other than the fact that the rebels have gained control of several of the major industrial regions of the country. The government has placed those regions under a state of military emergency. Meaning - a state of civil war.

My family is doing fine, considering. Arthur, however, as we expected had been investigated by the government. He was actually taken out of the house one night and interrogated for two days by the NIS and the military intelligence.

I was questioned too, but only for a few hours. They asked me about Greg Carson, and

any knowledge I might have on the rebel-academia connection. Also, the rebel-USA connection.
Greg is now held in a top-security state prison, almost incommunicado.
And how's your family? Your father, in particular. How is he ? Have you spoken to him lately? Please tell him *we* wish him well, and take care.
We will be in touch, shortly, or as soon as possible.

For a while, he sat at the desk in the office-bedroom just looking at the one-page letter after he read it, moving his eyes gradually up and down the paragraphs trying to reason out where Emil might have deliberately skipped saying something. Something as little as a word or two, or perhaps even a whole line, that Emil expected he might pick up on.

He went to the kitchen and made himself a gin and tonic, placing the letter on the counter close enough so he could still glance at it and read it. Then as he moved to the living room, drink in one hand, letter in the other, he concentrated on the last two paragraphs.

And there it was, something peculiar. Not at first. It was just odd. Emil asking about his father in particular. And when he thought about it a second time, it became peculiar. And especially so when he noticed the personal pronoun *we*. Not once but twice. Why couldn't he have said *I*?

What did *we* mean? Him, Emil, and who? His family? Or some other people?

The rebels? The rebellion? But what has his father in California got to do with all that? What's the connection? The connection!

He looked at the letter again. Hard. And he read the word twice.

...the rebel-academia connection.

...the rebel-USA connection.

He almost spilled the gin and tonic which he was about to sip when the phone rang. It was in its fourth ring by the time he got to it and when he put the receiver to his ear... nothing. Just a click followed by the dial-tone.

Back at the couch, he picked up the drink and took two big gulps, intent upon resuming his analysis of the letter. What else is Emil trying to communicate to him in it? And what about the one before this? The one where he wrote about Greg Carson's capture. And the university professor.

He wrote openly about the rebel movement in that one and he reasoned that it was safe from the government intelligence because it was going out with a secure courier via Hong Kong. So he didn't have to hide anything there. But now, could the government have picked up on the courier route? A possibility. One which Emil was not taking a chance on and which should explain the brevity and content of his letter.

But, what's with his father? Could it be that he was in on it too? And... had been?

The rebel-USA connection. The words rang in his mind and this time he didn't even look at the letter.

He tried to recall as much as he could of anything at all he had heard his father speak about politics, national issues in the old country and particularly the rebel movement. Nothing that he or anyone in the family could have tied in any serious way with the ruling party or the opposition. Or the rebellion. Everyone knew which side he was on. The opposition. But ever since they immigrated to the United States, all that was just talk. He was too busy trying to get settled in America, trying to support and raise a family and find a good place to do it.

That certainly must have been enough to keep him tied up and to sever any political connection he might have had in the old country. Unless of course there was another side of him in this which he didn't share with the family.

Nicholas then tried to remember the people his father had associated with personally and professionally, from Michigan in their early years in the U.S. to Washington and California: native-born Americans and people with roots from the old country like themselves. He suddenly realized that he really had no basis for deciding whether or not his father participated in the political movement in the old country and if he did, how actively? What did he do? And how did he do it?

Again, as he immersed his thoughts on all these suspicions, he was interrupted by the ringing telephone. This time, he got to it just as it started ringing the third time and said a quick hello. But, again, he got no response. The caller, however, didn't hang up. Not right away. Nicholas listened closely and waited for about five seconds. He knew somebody was at the other end. He could almost hear the person breathing, waiting.

Waiting for what? For him to say anything. Anything at all to establish an identity of his voice, he guessed. This, he began to feel more sure of as he remembered this morning when he was getting ready to leave for work at seven o'clock. This exact same thing happened. Twice within five or seven minutes, the phone rang and - nothing.

Three or four times, though, he couldn't be sure now, he said hello in the first call. He even asked who it was in the second call.

The line went dead and the dial-tone came on. Nicholas replaced the phone, now starting to feel a little spooked.

He actually even went to the bedroom window of the third floor condo overlooking the street and looked out at the telephone booth at the corner across. He didn't see anybody in it or leaving it.

He went back to the living room and finished the gin and tonic, making firm in himself the decision to call his father in California as soon as he could work out a way he might directly or indirectly get the man to talk to him, if he had anything at all to say, about the rebel-USA connection.

***

The day Nicholas received Emil's shortest letter, there was another one Emil had written, about ten times longer, which was on its way through the courier route although it hadn't actually begun its long journey to the United States from the pickup point at the University of the South East. To be exact, in the classroom of History and Political Science professor Joseph Hugo Livingston during his 7:30 PM lecture class.

Standing on the seven-inch high platform in front of the class of twenty-five juniors, a mix of economics, commerce and law majors, he cut a very respectable and formidable figure. Physically formidable. The professor stood about five-foot eleven, just a little above average height of the country's male population. At fifty-nine, he looked ten years younger. This was because of his excellent physical condition which showed with his smooth skin, bagless eyes, dark with very few gray hair and the muscles which especially under his Hong Kong custom-tailored suit were very prominent on his shoulders and limbs.

Formidable. But students respected more than feared him. And this was the reason, he knew well to his great satisfaction, why they behaved so well and did so well in his class as he knew they would even right now as he eyed them, everyone of them, taking the weekly quiz.

The students shifted position in their seats once in a while, made thoughtful gestures with their head and hands without taking their eyes off of their papers. Professor Livingston caught every movement even only through his peripheral vision although he understood. The ten questions he had on the quiz weren't true or false or multiple-choice questions. Most of them required logic and judgment answers which must use some words - between fifty to a hundred and fifty.

He glanced at the wall clock at the opposite end of the room every five minutes almost right on the dot. And once in a while, his eyes would drop on the student right below it, then travel to the chair behind the professor's desk on the platform. On the chair was his briefcase. On top of this was a zippered leather case, about twelve by sixteen inches, bulging to over an inch thick with the materials it contained. Among them was Emil's letter addressed to Nicholas in Alexandria, Virginia, USA.

In less than two hours, the professor expected the leather case to be safely on its way to Hong Kong on the 9:45 flight from the international airport after the last of the students, the one underneath the wall clock - the pickup man, had left the classroom with it.

Professor Livingston, also known in the rebel movement as Commander Utak, leader of the movement's national capital region, now looked out the window of his seventh-floor classroom in the Business and Finance building of the University of the South East, one of the most highly respected institutions of higher learning in the entire Western Pacific.

Cotamaru, the capital city sparkled like a jewel at night. Being at the northernmost tip of the island country, it provided a panoramic view of the major waters of this part of the world. In a hundred and eighty degree turn going west to east, one could get a glimpse of the China Sea, the Philippine Sea and the Pacific Ocean.

He loves this country, the professor thought, looking over the tree-lined avenues below, the parks and the buildings illuminated by the colorful city lights. And he fully intended to see in his lifetime and that of his children, that freedom and respect to the citizenship of the people is restored. Not to any particular racial, cultural or ideological group or class but to every citizen of this multi-cultural polyglot nation.

He could not accept the idea that everything his father and grandfather and their generations did to reclaim the country piece by piece through the past one hundred years from all those foreign powers - first the Spanish and the Portuguese, then the Japanese and the Americans - they did so that a power-hungry military regime run by a crude egocentric dictator would one day rule the country. When Guillermo Tobias Sakai, the president, ordered the suspension of the press two weeks ago, he was so infuriated he considered the possibility of organizing a commando squad from one of his region's battalions to assassinate the bastard.

Professor Livingston understood clearly the reason for the news blackout. The current U.S. administration had practically been groveling to the dictator to tip the balance of the country's non-aligned foreign policy even a little to the West's side. This of course had cost the Americans some dollars in the form of special economic and defense aids.

The dictator had had the Americans pretty much at the end of a lure for the past four years, biting consistently. But in a matter of six weeks, a new U.S. administration would be coming into power and with a president-elect who was no pushover and was said to be aching to come out swinging, so to speak, at the communists, all those fanatics and terrorists in the Middle East, and all the dictators and suppressors of human rights all over the world. On top of this, the regime hadn't been getting good marks with the world press for the past several years.

The professor was quite certain it hadn't been a difficult decision for the government to shut down the press. Now, he realized if their fight for freedom must continue, the lines of communication between the freedom fighters throughout the country must remain open; and not only in the country but abroad. They must continue to have contact outside the country. The arms deals must continue, the shipments already negotiated and scheduled for the planned delivery dates must proceed.

The courier routes must not be cut off; the flow of information between activities at home and abroad can not be interrupted.

The leather case must make the 9:45 to Hong Kong.

Those close to the high command and who were part of the rebel intelligence activities knew very well the importance of the courier routes. They also realized, and they believed more than Commander Utak did, how precarious they were especially now that the government had employed the hated National Intelligence Service which according to some rebel agents had fielded a number of moles to burrow deep into the rebel movement. This they had done not only in the rebel strongholds in the country but also abroad. Specifically in Paris which had, supposedly, the third largest number of expatriates, Madrid the second, and Los Angeles, New York ,Washington, D.C. combined, the largest.

One rebel undercover had suggested to the commander that the Hong Kong route be discontinued immediately, stating that he had strong indications that the NIS had already picked up on the courier trail and that they were just waiting for an opportunity to spring a big bust. Another agent, only recently recruited into the rebel intelligence and who had close personal contacts in Los Angeles where most of the arms procurement activities were conducted, and Washington, D.C. area supported the discontinuance of the courier route.

In the previous pickup, he hardly wrote anything in a one-page letter to a personal friend in Alexandria, Virginia.

Commander Utak had agreed to pull the route but only after tonight's pickup from his classroom. The dispatches that went with it were all very crucial to strengthening their positions in the regions they already controlled and there was no time to find a new way to send them out of the country.

It was a mistake.

The pickup man did complete his run from the classroom to the transfer point at the airport which was in the office of a cargo officer of the Pan Pacific Airlines. But that was as far as the leather case got.

The NIS had a man waiting to receive the package instead of the cargo officer who was diverted to a nearby area just long enough - eight, ten minutes - to miss the arrival of the courier. The leather case then quickly got on its way, through the government stakeout at the airport, to the high offices of the civilian and military intelligence while the NIS man now with an identical leather case containing the same amount of material but made up of old newspapers, and posing as the courier, waited until the cargo officer returned, and made the face transfer.

That gave the government intelligence time to determine, depending on the content of the leather case, their next move. It could take the rest of the night and early morning the following day, counting the few hours flight to Hong Kong and the time for whoever received the package there to discover that the courier route had been blown. And it would take still more time for them at that end to inform this end of it of what happened.

The basement second level of the Executive Annex, which housed the high command communication and control center of the of the National Intelligence Service, was a virtual fortress. But when Major General Leopold Moore Kato, army commander of Defense Intelligence Command, stepped out of the elevator, the vault doors and other iron barriers that stood on his way along the corridors to the nerve center parted or swung wide like paper before he and his entourage - an army Major to his right, a pair of armed presidential honor guards front and rear - got within ten feet of them.

And he was mad. Newly mad.

Coming out of the Executive Palace two blocks away not fifteen minutes ago where he had a brief audience with his supreme commander, the president, his aide-de-camp, the army Major, had informed him that he had just received a report from the NIS about the identity of Commander Utak and a major breakthrough in penetrating the rebel intelligence. What made the General mad was that he wasn't told immediately by those incompetent idiots, those civilian careerists in the NIS. Idiots!

It took them a whole day, twenty-four whole hours to get to him something as vital to the survival of the government as the identity of an arch enemy like Commander Utak and possibly his quick capture.

The last doorway they went through opened into a combined office, conference and communication area. To the right was a low-partitioned section which accommodated at least a dozen personnel busy either at their computers or live audio-visual monitors receiving data from the government intelligence networks locally and abroad. To the left was a bank of communication exchange stations about thirty feet long, tended by a dozen men and women each busy either listening in their earphones or talking into the tiny microphones hanging before their mouths.

Up front was a glass-enclosed area wherein an egg-shaped conference table with a red telephone at each end may be seen. None of the staff paid any attention at all when the six military men burst in to the area. Two well-dressed and robust men each wearing a redoubtable welcoming grin on their faces stood on their way to greet them.

"Good evening, General," one of them said. He was almost a foot taller than everybody else in sight including the General himself who stood at six two. "Good to see you again, sir."

"Look, I didn't come here to banter with you or anybody," the General bellowed, undaunted. "I've come to talk to only one man, and right now! Now, where is he?"

"Yes, sir, General," said the other man whose narrow-eyed polite manner was so perfect it looked like a put-on to everyone. "He's been expecting you. We've all been expecting you, sir. If you would please follow us to the conference table."

They all marched toward the conference area. The aide-de-camp posted one pair of the guards at the entrance to the glass enclosure, the other pair behind the chairs for him and the General. The two civilians placed themselves behind the two chairs at the opposite side of the table.

The General didn't sit down and so neither did the Major. Instead, he took a sheet of paper he asked of the Major which he looked over now for the third time and with a look on his face as if he were having a difficult bowel movement. About two seconds before he started screaming for the man he came to see, two men walked in and stood opposite them at the table. They reminded one of the American brothers John F. and Robert F. Kennedy: light-gray suits, darker tie, lock of hair bobbing down their foreheads and youthful smiles on their faces. Except that they're not Americans, nor were they Irish. And they weren't Caucasians. Not a hundred percent. More like between forty to forty-five percent, the balance a mix of the Asian racial stock - Malay, Chinese, Japanese, just like the rest of the men in the room and the rest of the country.

The one who stood opposite the General opened his arms in joyous greeting, saying with a wide smile on his natural-tanned face: "I'm glad you could make it this soon, General. Please." He motioned the military men to their chairs.

But the General didn't take heed right away. He wagged the paper he was holding at the man he came to see - the Director of the National Intelligence Service, an old acquaintance and one of his keenest competitors in government service under the present regime, though just about only half his age.

"Thomas Sebastian Reed, why wasn't I told about this immediately?" he half-shouted, flagging the paper with the back of his other hand. "Why? You better have a very good reason for holding it back for as long as you have!"

"Why don't we all sit down first and relax," the NIS Director suggested calmly.

Everyone waited for the General to sit down first before doing the same.

"Well?" said the General once seated, his face tensing and then relaxing a bit as he exhaled audibly. "So who is this Commander Utak? Where is he hiding?"

"Take it easy, General," said the Director. "First, the reason we couldn't get word to you right away was because we didn't know what to tell you. We didn't know what to tell anybody until we've gone through the package we intercepted and done some authenticating, as much as we are able to, of the content. We could be looking at a lot of false leads here. These rebels could be playing us into their hands. They've done it before, as you're well aware of, and it had cost us dearly. Especially this Commander Utak."

"Who is he?" asked the General, glaring at the man across the table. "I want to know right now. This man has cost me hundreds of soldiers. Thousands over the years!"

The Director tried to keep up his calm appearance while, underneath, he scrambled for every possible way he could fence with the General without turning his bag of (intelligence) goodies inside out to the military. The military is too gruff, too inarticulate, too maverick. They would shoot-em-up and settle for chopping the surface growth, leaving off the weed underneath to sprout again later.

He made no preparation for giving the soldierman the run-around. When the palace notified them that the General was coming, there wasn't any time at all to format a briefing. Now he must practically handfeed him as frugally as he could, hoping he gets a bite every piece he serves, and every bite calms the bully's wrath down before he had to turn every damn bit of NIS intelligence over to these military neanderthals.

"General," he said firmly, "we have this man. As good as in the bag. But we don't want to bring him in yet. Not for twelve to twenty-four hours, at most, from now."

"According to this transmission," the general said forcefully, exhibiting the paper in his hand, "you have intercepted information regarding the core activities of the rebel movement enough to disable it. Enough to crush the whole damn rebellion. This requires immediate military action. I want a complete copy of the materials containing these informations."

"You will have them, of course -"

"Now!"

The Director stalled for a moment, sizing up his position and quickly realizing the DIC commander was not going to sit there and tolerate a run-around of any sort from anybody. So, he turned to the man sitting next to him, the First Deputy Director of NIS, and the two of them conferred for about three seconds with their eyes. The Deputy then nodded and dutifully but not without dread pushed a three-ring folder on the shiny Philippine mahogany tabletop over to the Director who took it firmly in both hands.

"General, I can't emphasize enough the importance to all of us of how carefully and effectively we must use these informations."

"Major." The General, for the moment ignoring the Director, motioned for his aide-de-camp to take the folder from the civilian without waiting for it to be offered. The Major rose to reach for it as the Director picked it up to hand over to him. Then the General commanded the Major: "Go over it as quickly as you can right now. If you see anything you think I must know immediately, interrupt." Turning to the Director, he added: "Thomas Reed, I have been in command of the nation's Defense Intelligence for a number of years now and prior to that have been handling top secret informations that would give you and the entire NIS goose bumps, long before you got out of high school. I don't need to be reminded of how important things are and how they may be used to our best advantage. Now, tell me, why can't you bring him in now?"

"As I said, he's as good as in the bag. We have him tagged with a half a dozen field agents - him alone. His house is under surveillance twenty-four hours a day. And at the university, we have over a dozen agents working two shifts."

"University? What university?"

"The University of the South East, sir."

"Why the university? Don't tell me it's infested with rebels -"

"Yes, sir, General," said the Director quickly. "Reports have been coming in from the stakeout for the past eight hours. There are scores of students in there who are active rebel soldiers, perhaps hundreds, we don't know exactly how many."

"My god," the General mumbled, shocked. "My own alma mater." He snapped a fierce look at the NIS Director and asked: "What about this Commander Utak?"

"I know who he is, General," said the Major, not moving anything except his eyes which he lifted from the folder to the space above the table between them all. "He's a faculty member. A professor of History and Political Science. One of the best, I could personally say the best teacher I've ever known in all my school years. Professor Joseph Hugo Livingston."

A cold silence prevailed while the General regarded his aide-de-camp incredulously. Then turning back to the civilians across the table, he barked: "I want him brought in now! This very hour. Major, get me the president on the phone."

The NIS Director and his deputy literally shot up to their feet and the bodyguards standing behind them shuffled back in alarm to give room to the chairs as they were pushed back "Wait, General! Please. Before you do that -" the Director had now openly acknowledged with this imploration his vulnerability in the power struggle with his military rival. He knew how well Major General Kato and the president got along. "Give us twelve hours at least."

"Mr. Reed, every minute you let him go free, he could be packing up to go underground. Word could have gotten back to him by now from the other end of his courier route that they've been intercepted and, therefore, his cover blown. If this were so, he's probably aware by now that he's under surveillance and he might be just waiting for a chance to break out. And how many men did you say you have on him? A half a dozen? What chance does each one of them stand against a group of students - rebel soldiers, who might seem to have innocently wandered on his path and then seize him quietly and kill him?"

"A few more hours, General. Six, eight hours." The NIS Director now considered how he had underestimated this one soldier. The General was exactly right, about everything he said, although the Director knew it himself all along. He knew he'd risk allowing Commander Utak to slip through his fingers by not arresting him immediately. How real a risk it was he only vaguely imagined, until just now, quickly after the General reinforced it to him so straightforwardly. But still, he must continue the field operation presently in progress. They must get to the root of the rebel movement, let Commander Utak lead them from one to the other of his kind - peer, subordinate or superior - and weed them all out of society, round them all up and defeat them. This he told the General as intelligently and convincingly as he could.

"At the same time," he added, "we've been working the international phone lines to our agents abroad. America, Europe and Asia. There are people named in that courier package located in Los Angeles, New York, Washington, D.C. and Paris that we must tag immediately."

"Major?" The General turned to his aide-de-camp.

"Sir. I see the point in what the Director has chosen to do. These materials are dynamite. Catching Commander Utak at this time would amount to catching one rebel. According to some of these documents, he had already done what we must now prevent from continuing to happen. Three big arms shipments are scheduled within the next two weeks. No mention of where they're coming from, abroad, and none where they're unloading in the country. There are, however, points of contact named in Madrid, Paris, Washington, D.C, Los Angeles and Manila."

There were short, urgent knocks on the opening sides of the glass enclosure behind the civilians. It was the head operator of communications who was admitted with a subtle nod by the Director. She was in and out quickly after handing the Director a sheet of paper and whispering something to his ear.

The Director read the paper as fast as he could, anxious for the information it contained and for not wanting to put the General on hold for too long. Thus, just as the General was starting to protest the interruption, the Director raised his head from the paper, saying:

"We just completed a worldwide alert. The last station just confirmed their orders. All our people abroad are updated except Manila. We're not too concerned with that. We've got the rebel connections there well covered. We're more concerned with Washington, D.C. and Los Angeles.

We've issued a double alert to all personnel there: in Washington on orders to tag some people there whose names appear in those materials you're looking at right now, Major; in Los Angeles on orders to, likewise, tag as many as ten people. Two of them to be put under control immediately and squeezed dry of every information we can get out of them. Both to be... terminated after that.

"Station chiefs have orders to report here on any progress of the operations within an hour, but no later than eight hours no matter what."

The NIS Director then yielded the space, the entire surface of the conference table, all the air in the room and all the time the military men needed to respond, voice out their reactions. But there was only a prolonged pause that followed during which the NIS Director saw a soldier's aggression on the face of Major General Kato diminished by a ponderous look in his eyes; reason calming the anger within.

Exhaling from a vigorous breath, the General finally said: "Eight hours, if you caught no more than a firefly in the dark by then. At that time, I want Commander Utak in ball and chains under maximum security. I'm going to put out an order to shut down the university at noon tomorrow, with everybody in it; place it under military control. No one is to go past the military cordon going in or coming out. I'm going to need full cooperation from your field agents out there, as well as from you for the current operations data."

"You have them, sir. Whenever you're ready. We can have a briefing right here tonight if you like."

"Very well," the General said, checking the time on his watch. It was a quarter past seven. "Let's set it at no later than twenty one hundred hours. That'll give us time to grab a bite. I haven't eaten anything all day except coffee and cookies at the palace this evening."

"Not to worry, sir," said the NIS Director. "We'll have anything you like brought in."

"Wonderful. Major -"

"Sir."

"Get busy on the phone right now." The General proceeded to name the DIC staff officers and the combat force commanders he wanted in the briefing. He added that if the latter wanted to bring along their on-duty field combat officers who will be deployed tomorrow and would be doing the actual shooting if necessary, so much the better.

While the General gave orders to his aide-de-camp, the Director of NIS did so too to his deputy, the man known to the rebel intelligence as Bobby Kay. At one point, he turned to the General to ask what he would like to eat. The General responded with total indifference, even saying that he didn't mind junk food if it came to that.

When he had finished conveying his essential dispositions on the planned military action to the Major, the General took over the folder from the Major who immediately went to the telephone at his end of the table to begin gathering the participants for tomorrow's siege. The General peered anxiously at the rebel documents in his hands. He didn't leaf through the folder. He simply looked at the page the Major had it turned to.

The document did not contain any such materials as troop movements or tactical maneuvers. It was easily recognizable as a personal letter from a rebel to one who appeared to be a valued friend living in the United States. Alexandria, Virginia. The General decided it might provide a good lead in gaining an insight into the heart and mind of a rebel and, possibly, the rebel movement.

Dear Nicky,

This, more than any other letter I've sent you, is one I pray to God would fall safely only in your hands. Some of the things I must tell you here concern other things beyond the matter of our friendship. One of them is my direct personal connection with the rebel movement, another your father's in Los Angeles and, therefore, yours as well by blood relations (this would probably come as a surprise to you as I know your father never told any of you in the family anything about it. In one of our recent contacts with him, he suggested that I be the one to let you know finally, at this time, saying that it might be easier that way for all concerned and also for security reasons).

I indicated some of these in my previous letter to you. I didn't want to speak openly about anything then because word got around that the government had discovered our courier route. It was a crucial decision to make between the leaderships here in the national capital region whether or not to stop the route immediately. It was decided that one final delivery be made before it is discontinued.

Professor Livingston is confident it will get through the airport one more time. We had to share in his confidence for this last courier run is vital to the movement and we have no other route for it to go out of the country immediately although I personally - as now one of the rebel intelligence officers - couldn't emphasize enough the risk we face.

Your father expects you to get in touch with him as soon as you read this, assuming you would. If not, however, he would get in touch with you instead, ten days but no later than fifteen from now at the latest.

Yes, as you might have guessed, I have decided to be recruited, and as I mentioned, I am now a rebel agent, appointed by the intelligence committee at the full recommendation of the capital regional commander, Professor Livingston, or Commander Utak.

There are a few things I must tell you, actually, more than a few things, why I've decided to join the freedom movement. First, there are the examples of the many brave and sacrificing men, and women, who have put the peace and security of their homes and families as a pawn for freedom. And many more are doing it as I began doing it only recently.

Others who have been working for much longer to free our country from the present dictatorship deserve even more praise and admiration which I, a citizen who now know the value of freedom, feel may best be demonstrated by joining their ranks. Among these gallant freedom fighters, I count your father who, I learned just a few weeks ago, has made many very important contributions to the cause in the years he has supported the movement (I will let him tell you of these himself).

Second, there are the realities themselves I see in our daily lives here: the brutality of the military, the debasement of the human spirit. the destruction of high ideals - the very same ones that motivate creativity and elevate man above the level of animals. Third, there is Professor Livingston with whom I had a heart-and-mind talk before and after I joined. He said that freedom is enough cause for anyone to risk life. But for him, the movement means more than the pursuit of freedom. It is a struggle to recover the country from the tyrants, the thieves who stole it from those who fought and died for it, namely his grandfather, one of the many brave heroes of the 1920 Revolution, and his father, killed in the Second World War defending the country from a returned former colonizer - the Japanese.

He said it angers him more to see our own countrymen oppressing our people than to see it done by foreigners, conquering enemies who naturally think it is their right to exploit the country. Professor Livingston is fiercely nationalistic, and understandably so. He questions why, in spite of our abundant manpower and natural resources, high literacy and a fairly well-ordered society - no race riot, very low crime rate, we've hardly progressed since the last world war, economically first of all, and politically. He believes this is due to the colonial mentality that the succession of governments up to and especially the present one inherently practices. Once in power, it simply emulates the ways of the colonizers which are borne of pure greed and ruthless exploitation.

The colonizers have not really left us. Not completely. They are still with us, he said. In us. And so we must continue the struggle to defeat them in those who are in power, those who are in control of the country's fortunes, where and when they oppress and disgrace us. The colonizers have brought both good and evil to our land, our culture, he said, and I do not mean to overlook the many ways we have benefited from them. The Americans, for instance - he does not hate them. He's convinced the American way, the constitutional foundation of their society with its guarantees of human rights and freedom, is the only sure way in this age to bring about economic progress and stability, although it may not be so when it comes to meaningful human existence and preserving the sanctity of the family. The Spanish and the French and the Germans - he does not fault them for the persistence and dominance of their cultures over those of other peoples such as ourselves. It is to our advantage, he told me, that we learn and even adapt some of these cultures.

And the Japanese - what better culture there is on earth to learn from in its simplicity and discipline, in its charm and concept of beauty. If they tend to have the attitude of racial supremacists, again you can't fault them for it because they have shown themselves equal to or better in many ways than other races, Asians or Europeans, particularly the Germans and the English who have the same idea about themselves.

What the professor wants, and he has a horde of advocates in this among the educated and the intellectuals from all parts of the country, is for our people to weed out the evil that the foreign powers have seeded our land with and retain the good they've shown us, mold it into our culture, our way of life, and raise a strong nation out of it, one that will gain the respect of the biggest and the smallest nation on earth, one that will make every citizen proud to be of this land and culture, as the Japanese are of theirs.

The General stopped reading for a moment and his eyes started to wander in space. It was difficult not to be affected, one way or the other, by what he had just read. His pedigree was as average as anybody else's could be not only in his generation but in the entire present population: one-fifth native Malayo-Chinese, one-fifth Japanese, one-fourth Portuguese-Spanish, one-fourth Caucasian-American (of no specific European roots) and one-tenth Polynesian. A good blend in the making of a Eurasian: light complexion with a natural golden tan, a bone structure that is a model of the human species, and a physiognomy that mirrors the affinity of all of humankind.

A beauty. But in it all, too, came ugliness and pain as he had seen and experienced himself. There were the stories from his elders of the inhumane suppression of the native peoples by the invading world powers who in turn fought and killed each other for the spoils. Those who were defeated became part of the spoils themselves. Out of those spoils came his great-grandmother, born of half-European (Spanish) and half native East Asian (Malay-Japanese) blood. She grew up to become a slave-mistress to one of the administrators of the Japanese ruler who governed the portion of the country then colonized by Japan. This woman, he was told, bore thirteen children. It was his father who told him their family came from the thirteenth child, a girl, who became his father's mother.

The General never saw her, his paternal grandmother, in person. Only in picture. One picture which his father showed him, when she was twenty. She had just then given birth to her second child, a boy, the General's father. Not long after that, his father narrated, she being of great beauty was abducted by the Americans across the Japanese-American colonial border and was never heard of again.

Her children, left behind, grew up in many different homes, until one day when the youngest was fourteen years old, a man showed up carrying the picture of their lost mother. The man claimed to be their father and later helped them migrate to the American part of the country to look for their mother. They never found her, for not long after, the Revolution that eventually forced all the colonizers - the Spanish, the Japanese and the Americans - out of the country began.

Major General Kato tried hard within him to ward off any sympathy for the rebels that the letter triggered. Much as he identified with the personal background of Commander Utak, a man of his generation, perhaps the same age, and understood his cause, he insisted in his mind that he was an enemy and that it was his duty to his country, as a soldier, to his government and to his supreme commander the president to crush the rebellion. Whatever changes were needed for the good of the country, the people, the economy, foreign relations and all that, will be done afterwards.

The NIS Director had stepped out for a minute and when he came back caught the General in a sort of a trance.

"Excuse me, General. General?" He was going to snap a finger at him just before the General came out of it.

"Yes. What is it?"

"General, I've just finished consulting with the palace Chief of Staff and he suggested we notify the Ministry of Higher Education regarding the university."

"Don't worry about that. I'll be talking to the president shortly tonight and they'll handle that sort of thing from there: the city government and its police, the media, the foreign students. Routine."

The General then turned back to the letter of the rebel intelligence officer to his friend in Alexandria, Virginia.

I have put my personal life on hold at this time. I still work the same job, live at home, see my girlfriend, go to the daily routines on the surface. But I believe this won't be for much longer. I have been visited by NIS agents again and I'm almost sure they know about my part in the rebel movement so that the next time they come, they'll take me away.

I had no idea at all before everything started happening how the course of my life would change, and how much more it would differ from yours. I still hope, when things settle down here eventually and if we survived, God willing, to go to America, experience life there and know for myself the origin of part of our heritage.

However, after listening to Professor Livingston, I realize how I and my family and everyone I care about here are as much a part of what he's fighting for. But more than that, I do care about our country. And, yes, I believe we can make it as good a place to live and die for as America or Japan or any other country whose citizens ever cared to live and die for. We can be more proud of ourselves to the rest of the world than we've ever been.

Time is running out fast the way things look from the events that are taking place, and are about to take place soon. This goes for my personal situation as well. I can not remain on the surface much longer. A week at most. Maybe just a few days from now.

After I deliver this letter to the courier, I am going to see the professor and suggest that I go underground. I am going to suggest the same for himself if possible immediately.

I don't know when you might hear from me again. We are working on a new communication line to our foreign supports via satellite. We expect it to be in operation within two weeks. I will be in touch with your father in Los Angeles one way or another, and if everything works out alright, I will call.

Until then, hope for the best for all of us here, that we may succeed in our struggle for freedom and gain honor and a better way of life for our people.

As ever,

Emil.

The General stared for a few seconds at the name and wondered who the man is: How old? What manner of a man is he? His lineage in this polyglot society, the other languages he speaks - Japanese? Mandarin? Spanish? French? How much and what kind of education? Surely he must be college-educated, to be able to write and express his thoughts and feelings so well, to be so articulate with words. And he must live in the city to be able to do his work for the rebellion. He also wondered who Nicholas Gabriel is.

"Director," the General spoke suddenly, giving the men across the table a start especially the NIS Director who had been keeping busy analyzing some of the newly arrived field intelligence reports on Commander Utak's movements, the people he went in contact with in the places he visited within the past few hours. "What do you have on this Emilio Sabater?"

"Oh, that fellow. Interesting young man. We've only recently tagged him. A week. ten days. He's the one that led us to Commander Utak. Our agents simply followed him to the university, and another time to the professor's house."

"What made you tag him?"

"We've brought in a rebel undercover who was about to go underground. His defense lawyer is the brother of this Emilio Sabater. Nobody has admitted anything yet but we're pretty sure our captive rebel, Greg Carson, had asked Professor Livingston to obtain the services of Arthur Sabater, the defense lawyer, through his friend and former university classmate Emilio Sabater. This connection between the two - their friendship, we know. We did some research on it. We also know now that Emilio Sabater was recruited by the professor only last month, replacing Greg Carson in his post as an intelligence officer responsible for securing communication routes between rebel bases throughout the capital area. We will arrest him at work tomorrow afternoon. We've got plenty enough out of him to bring him in."

Major General Kato regarded the NIS Director through narrowed eyes as if the two of them were a mile apart.

Mentally, he was more than a mile away. More like ten thousand miles away as he imagined another friend of Emilio Sabater, the one in Alexandria, Virginia, reading the letter.

"Do me a favor, will you, Director Reed?"

"What is it, General?"

"I want you to let this letter through. You keep the original, I trust, including the envelope?"

"Yes, we have them." The NIS Director ruminated for a moment, then said: "I guess there won't be any harm in doing that. In fact, I think it's actually a good idea."

***

Professor Livingston didn't get the phone message until after he came out of his 5:00 o'clock class. He found it on his desk, placed there by the secretary of the Office of the Faculty where he was planning to do some paperwork while waiting out the half hour prior to his next class.

The message which was taken at 1:15 PM was brief. It said: 'Pls. return call immediately. C2CRXA.'

Upon seeing that string of characters which the innocent secretary had written down so significantly in uppercase, he realized no other phone message could have looked so ominous to him. C2CR was the acronym by which the deputy commander, his second in command (C2), of the rebel capital region (CR) was known in the movement. XA was one of the message codes out of several pages they used. It meant critical alert. To the surface intelligence agents, it could mean a geographic re-assignment or an instruction to submerge. Go underground.

He made the calls to C2 quickly, taking the precaution not to use his desk phone but the public phone at the far end of the corridor from the faculty office instead. He had a half a dozen numbers he could reach C2 but under the circumstances they knew which number to call to reach one another. The suspicion he feared most was true. The last courier dispatch was intercepted. The package did arrive at the rebel base in Hong Kong at one o'clock in the morning but it wasn't opened until six when it was found to contain nothing but several old issues of The Daily Tribune, one of the dailies the government had recently shut down.

And then it took Hong Kong several hours to get the alert call through. They tried to reach both C1CR and C2CR all day long. They finally contacted C2CR at one o'clock in the afternoon who then spread the alert throughout the command region immediately. C2 was one of the persons who knew as well as C1 the contents of the dispatch.

Commander Utak ran the scenario quickly in his head. The government have had at least sixteen hours learning about the most current rebel activities not just in the capital region but nationwide, as they would know from the dispatch package. They would also identify and locate him as well as C2 and several other important people in the freedom movement within the capital area and the adjoining provinces under another regional command.

As efficient as he knew the government tried to be in cornering any of its oppositions, let alone the rebels, Commander Utak shivered at the thought while he was still on the phone with C2 that he could very well have been under close surveillance by the NIS since the night before. They could have arrested him even before he went to bed last night but they didn't. And they haven't, yet. Why?

He knew why, when he thought of where he went, what he did today during the day. The trip he made to a southern province for a meeting with several other rebel leaders.

And then a late-lunch gathering with a number of his field agents at a Japanese restaurant a few blocks from the university, for their daily intelligence update.

There was no time to lose. Not a single moment. He became acutely aware of his situation. He knew suddenly that he had become a quarry, had been for some time, and now he must take evasive actions. He must escape, but could he, still? Is there time? Is there a way?

Think!

Think fast, while C2 is on the line. NIS agents, even government soldiers could suddenly appear from behind and shackle him away like an animal right this very minute. He glanced over his shoulder and saw no one. There was only the faint view of someone at the end of the corridor some thirty meters away carrying a gym bag and looking up at a bulletin board.

First, everyone in the freedom movement he got in touch with personally today must be warned and told to submerge, if he or she hadn't already been arrested. He gave the code names of everyone he could think of as quickly as he could to C2 and instructed him to enlist as much help as he could get to do this immediately. Second, everyone whose identity was compromised because of the courier bust like the professor himself must be told to do the same. This goes for C2 as well. C2 said at this point of their frantic telephone conversation that he had already done so - gone into hiding. And this after he discovered two NIS agents who must have been tagging along all day long, and shook them off his tail. He said he couldn't possibly go home first to pack up before he went underground so that all he had with him was literally the clothes he had on and a small amount of money which fortunately he estimated should be enough to allow him to reach the nearest rebel-controlled area and join the armed rebel forces.

They decided to make the area everyone's escape destination where they would all later re-group and re-organize. Everyone is to proceed there within twenty four hours.

Finally, after he hung up, Commander Utak came to deal with his own situation at hand. C2 had offered to send some help, a rescue team to get him out of reach of the NIS, but he declined, saying that he had enough men close at hand, within a minute's notice, at the university. While saying this, he was fingering a row of three tiny buttons on a beeper he had in his coat pocket and at the same time scanning the view, through the glass window, of the lawn and the parking lot where he could see his seven-year old Toyota Cressida. Getting to it from where he stood, he suddenly felt, would be a long hazardous journey.

He didn't doubt that the whole campus was by now ringed, jutted and secured with government agents. And he was right. At a slight turn of the head, there they were: two NIS agents, the hated enemy, scum of the land, one positioned at the exit driveway of the parking lot near one side of the faculty building, the other at the open end of the pavement where a car could be driven across the green directly to the road.

The three buttons on one side of the beeper each had a corresponding colored signal light on the top end of the communicating device which had a range of over ten kilometers and sent coded signals to at least two dozen other beepers carried in secret by the rebel-soldier students attending the university. Each beeper carrier was actually a rebel undercover with a following of at least a dozen recruits. This constituted a team which for the past year or two had contributed greatly to the freedom movement materially as well as ideologically. Their allegiance to the cause was unquestioned, and so was their personal loyalty and admiration to their leader, Professor Livingston.

There were several color-coded signals only Professor Livingston may use. One of them was an alert signal - a blue and a red repeated at least three times - which meant standby alert until code canceled. Another was a green and a red which meant active alert - bear arms, take defensive action if necessary to vacate present location and rendezvous at pre-designated meeting place. This the professor rarely used except on one occasion when a crack platoon of the Civil Guards conducted a raid drill with the school ROTC on campus and he thought government intelligence had finally caught on to them.

Another signal was a pair of red repeated at least five times. A red alert which told everybody - team leaders and recruits - to submerge.

For a nineteen or twenty-year old student, it was like being told one day to leave the life that he had known, leave society, friends and family, and begin living in a different world altogether. Bear arms up in the hills, come out at night on a mission perhaps to kill, or be killed.

Professor Livingston had hoped he'd never have to use it. But now, the urgency to send those red signals overwhelmed him. Without a moment's hesitation, he did.

Then he looked out the window again before starting back to the faculty room. Now he saw three men staked out on the parking lot. As he hurried down the corridor, the man with the gym bag at the other end behind him was joined by two other men and they all began moving toward him.

He was only a few meters from the door when a handsome young man appeared from the intersecting corridor hurrying toward the faculty room.

"Emil!" called the professor in a controlled voice.

"Professor -" Emil Sabater looked at the professor and saw the three men beyond who were now on an open pursuit.

"Hold it!" one of them ordered. "Don't move!"

"Run, sir!" Emil yelled. "This way!"

They raced down the corridor where Emil came from which led to the adjoining main library building of the school. There were people coming in and out of doors at each side of the corridor. They headed for the one with the exit sign above but before they got there, four young men coming the opposite way also in a hurry called after them.

"Professor," one of them said, catching his breath while trying to be polite, "anything we can do for you right now, sir?"

"You got my signal. That's my standing order. You all know what to do. Where to meet. We're being pursued right now. Three men behind us."

"We'll take care of them, sir. Go! Go! We'll catch up later!"

Emil led their way through the exit door and out to a small loading dock driveway where they got in to a Toyota Corolla.

"I got the alert from C2 at two o'clock. We've been trying to reach you all afternoon, sir." Emil maneuvered the Corolla out of the loading dock onto the street as if he did so everyday at this hour, careful not to appear in any hurry to get out of the area. "I had to escape as soon as I heard from C2. I discovered two government agents staked out at our house. I hardly had time to get a few things together before I left. And I had the car parked two blocks away from the house." Emil suddenly turned to Professor Livingston and asked: "Where to, sir?"

The professor pondered for a moment before replying: "You can't go home anymore. For a time, anyway. And neither can I. Let's go to the designated red alert rendezvous point. Let's head for the hills."

📖 7 📖

FULL CONTACT SPARRING

From a back stance (Foogoolse), Brian Cooper began the motion to deliver a high hand-knife to the side of Nicholas Gabriel's head. But halfway through the motion, he broke the momentum of his forearm and the open hand slicing in the air, angled the upper half of his body to the outside of the left leg upon which he pivoted and delivered a right roundhouse kick (Dolyuh Chagee) instead to Nicholas' left rib-cage.

"Sonofabitch!" Nicholas growled, quickly recovering into a steady sparring stance from the blow which really pissed him off more than hurt him. It couldn't, for the impact was easily absorbed by the protective cushions they wore on their torso, head and extremities, particularly their weapons which were their feet (Tae) and hands (Kwon), as

140

prescribed by the International Martial Arts Conference for the American League of Amateur Tae Kwon Do.

"There's plenty more where that came from," Brian taunted as they shuffled irregularly from a left to a right fighting stance, trying to confuse one another as from where one might launch an attack.

"Shutup and fight like a man," Nicholas quipped, then threw a quick succession of side punches from the horseback stance (Kimase). Brian beautifully deflected each punch with an in-to-out block but in the next moment realized it was all a ploy. The instant Nicholas saw his opponent confidently immersed in one line of defense, he switched his attack to a combination side kick (Yup Chagee), back kick (Dui Chagee) and jump roundhouse accompanied by a chilling yell. This last caught Brian on one side of the face and sent him tumbling down the canvas in a heap, face first, some eight feet away.

"Get up, old woman, and come back here," Nicholas chided, standing firm in a forward stance (Jungoolse) and beckoning at Brian with a fist, "I got something else for you."

Brian snapped back to his feet looking vengeful and charged his opponent in a fierce yelling rush, a technique much like that predator animals use naturally to panic their prey. He leaped in the air, turning gradually to one side to get a good angle of kick as he descended. But his target was quicker in moving out of harm's way. He landed flat, nary a shake, on his bare feet like a cat on four, and they were again facing each other, shuffling with quick, snappy movement, switching stances, looking to launch an attack at the least expected moment.

Then the bell above the closed door rang three times. Their time in the sparring room was up. It went so fast. Fifteen minutes. And each felt he could go another fifteen.

But there were others waiting to begin their fifteen minutes in the room, one of only three in this facility of the Northern Virginia Martial Arts School in Arlington.

They faced away from each other to fix their martial arts uniforms (Doboks) and the belt around it as was the customary courtesy before they turned around to bow to each other and shake hands. This was the end of their sparring session which also indicated to the school's Master Instructor (Sah Bum Nim) who could see them through the glass windows that they heard the bell. Everybody made sure the Sah Bum Nim never had to ring the bell a fourth time before ceasing any activity in any of the workout areas - the sparring rooms or the class gyms. A hundred sit-ups or fifty push-ups or both were the routine penalty. Discipline in every respect topped all the requirements for being allowed to stay, once accepted, in the school, and of course for advancing in rank which was signified by the color of the belt one wore.

Nicholas wore a blue belt as the outcome of his previous schooling in Tae Kwon Do at another Virginia school six years ago, and the additional hours he'd had here since he signed up for a six-month course three months ago. Brian was a couple of ranks higher. A two-stripe red belt. He had had two years of previous training in this same school, then quit when he traveled, and re-enrolled only a month and a half ago. They were glad to know they were in the same school when they ran into each other one day.

They had gone to the 6:00 o'clock class this Friday with some twenty-five other students, a mix of blue and yellow belts, a few reds. Friday classes were usually big compared to the other days of the week. People needed to unwind after a whole work-week, let out all their aggressions in a disciplined and productive way, they thought. Brian liked coming to the Friday class for the same reason but particularly because it had a female instructor whose high side kick simply amazed him completely. That on top of the fact that he was attracted to her. In one of his attempts to become personally acquainted with her, he had once suggested a ten-minute light-contact free sparring with her after class. She declined, saying that she did not tutor individually outside of her sixty-minute scheduled classes.

While they dried up in the locker room after the shower, they agreed on the Pawnshop at Bailey's Crossroads a few miles on Columbia Pike from the school for a bite to eat.

Nicholas had sensed even while they were just warming up, doing stretches an hour and a half ago before the class, a certain state of restlessness in Brian. Brian worked vigorously on the stretches and throughout the sixty-minute workout class, executing the forms (Poomse's) they were asked to do, fiercely but with finesse and all the physical power he had in his body. Nicholas didn't particularly feel inclined to do the fifteen-minute full-contact with him after the class but they had already reserved the room and he did feel he needed to do it as it had been a while since he had done it with anybody.

"You scared the hell out of me there for a minute," Nicholas confessed over a tall glass of Gatorade at the restaurant. They drank it at the advise of the school consulting physician to make up for the potassium loss during the workout. "Like you really wanted to spill somebody's brains out."

"You weren't exactly just waving your tailfeathers there either," replied Brian. "I can't remember the last time anybody kicked my face to the floor before tonight. You're good."

"I got some work to do. You're better. I know. So, tell me - what's eatin' you?"

Brian gazed at Nicholas like a stalker, pulling away from the table as he did. Something's bugging him alright and he thought how sharp Nicholas was that he knew.

"Nothing, really," he said, moving his head slightly sideways in the manner Nicholas remembered characteristically in their college classroom days when Brian wrestled with an academic problem or a personal one, usually either a girl or money problem. "Nothing," he repeated.

"C'mon, you can tell me. I don't mind. Not that I give a shit, though. I got my own problems."

"Well, screw you, Charlie Brown."

They laughed and gulped their Gatorades down.

Brian took another half a minute shuffling his rear end in his seat as if a real bug literally gnawed at it before he let out: "I don't know, Nicholas. I feel so... so unsettled right now. Do you ever get a feeling like that sometimes? Like, uh -"

"Yeah, like what?"

"Well, like... like you'd done what you had to do. Pretty much what's expected of you. And now, where do you go from here? You know what I'm talking about? No, you don't know what I'm talking about. You're just an innocent naturalized American who's still going through your cultural shock."

"Why, screw you too, Charlie Brown, twice."

They cracked up again. Then Nicholas said: "I know exactly what you're talking about. I'm not sure if I care to hear about it, but I don't mind. So you feel unsettled and you ask where do you go from here -"

"Yes!"

Nicholas stared at Brian Cooper, young white educated middle-class American, for about ten seconds, expecting to hear something else from the man, but Brian remained as he was - a face like a clean sheet of paper waiting for an answer to a mystery question.

"This is really sad," Nicholas said, shaking his head, disappointed. "No, it's not just sad. It's stupid!"

"What's stupid?"

"To hear a young professional American man say something like that. Especially someone like you who have traveled just recently, lived abroad, had some exposure - firsthand personal exposure to another culture: its way of life, its food, its religion, ideology, its smell, its extremes, its rot, and I imagine most other things that make you see the difference between you and other people which should cause you to either appreciate your own condition in life or hate it. Either case, learn from it. Do something about it. Anything. I mean don't waste the experience, because if you did, then you're wasting your life too!"

Brian appeared partly shaken but he kept his eyes locked thoughtfully on Nicholas. Slowly, he realized he was reacting to what he just heard and though it made him feel insulted and even angry, it was good that he was reacting.

When he first got back from abroad four months ago, he felt anxious for the return to the lifestyle he had put on hold temporarily. He felt so hungry for the ordinary walk of life in America: the trip to the foodstore, a casual evening at a bar, American girls - or women, the weekend games on TV. But now, now that he had been back to the routine between the job and the two-bedroom apartment in Rosslyn, it seemed as if he had never gone away.

The things he had felt missing in his life he again felt, or remembered. And a certain awareness of a lack of challenge came back. In short, now he was thinking, he was falling into a rut, if it hadn't already happened. But why? Hell if he knew.

What's happening? Is this some kind of a rite of passage? If it is, usually one moves from one stage of life to another. But it doesn't feel like he's moving anywhere from where he was at all.

"What do you mean 'don't waste it'?" he suddenly heard himself asking Nicholas, puzzled. "I'm gainfully employed. I'm a contributor to society, not a burden to it. I'm a productive citizen."

Nicholas thought of Edward McKenny, the homeless man. There was a similarity that suddenly struck him between that man, that American man and this one he was sitting with not on a cold bench in a park but a dinner table in a cozy restaurant. Although they filled opposite roles in society - one a contributor to it as he just declared, the other a burden, one was just as unsettled as the other, as lacking in direction, as lost, as helpless.

"Being gainfully employed - having a job, you're saying, and paying taxes I hardly think makes for a meaningful life." Nicholas tried not to sound more critical than helping. Their orders had arrived and he was separating the two halves of a thick roast beef sandwich on his plate to start eating.

Brian had only eyed the deluxe cheeseburger in front of him when it came and turned back to Nicholas to continue to listen.

"What you've done - traveling and living abroad, learning about another world, is admirable. It's good experience. A very good source of learning. But learn from it, man, is what I'm saying. Don't let the experience go to waste. Otherwise, you might as well had just watched it on TV or read it in a book and forget about it the next day. That's why I think you can't tell where you're going. You're not picking up on things as you go along. You're not alone in that, though. A lot of people especially the younger generation are the same way. Why do you think a lot of people get into drugs and all kinds of trouble? Because most of them don't know what they want to do with their lives."

"Not me, boy. I've seen what drugs can do to you. And don't lump me with the rest of society. I can't relate to that. I got my own life to deal with first."

Nicholas didn't think Brian did drugs, ever, or smoked pot. The most Brian had done of marijuana was in college, as a matter of fact, with him and some other people usually after their final exams. But neither of them did it regularly. Brian was as straight as any native-born, middle-class college-educated American man could get. The only drawback he had, Nicholas thought, was that the man never knew what it's like to worry about where the next meal was coming from, to be sick of hunger, to be oppressed, to be without freedom. Just the usual lack of appreciation for all the good things in life in America people take for granted.

This one American man, Nicholas now thought, is suffering from a boredom borne out of the lack of the basic motivations to improve upon himself, the lack of the desire to relate to others in a meaningful way.

"Tell me," Nicholas said cheerfully as if they were just starting a brand new conversation. He had just finished the first half of the roast beef sandwich and washed down the part of it in his mouth with the beer. "Have you ever thought of getting married? Settling down? Taking on some new responsibilities?"

"Why, sure," Brian replied thoughtfully, giving Nicholas a long look. "Who hasn't, at our age? I'm thirty-three. Certainly I'd like to get married too one day."

"Maybe that's why you feel so unsettled. Maybe we need to get you settled down, find you a nice woman and get a life."

That sounded almost like a joke to both of them. Nicholas only wanted to see how Brian would take it. He didn't think that was the best solution to the man's sense of aimlessness in life.

"You're probably right," said Brian, and Nicholas worried. "But - I don't know, though. The kind of women I see today, I find it hard to think of marriage. I've gone out with many of them and, boy, I can't figure them out." He took a bite of his burger shaking his head. "If they're not out there doing their aerobics, obsessed with themselves, they're visiting their shrink trying to get their heads straightened out. And the straight-headed ones, they want the whole fucking world. They want your job, your salary and more. And they want to make it with you only when they want to make it, not when *you* want to make it. They're so damn self-centered and domineering you can't figure out how to relate to them anymore. And talk about homemaking. Forget it. Some of these women I've gone out with, the only thing they know how to do in the kitchen is open a can of tuna."

Once again, the two of them cracked up. They chewed their food and drank their beer, enjoying each other's company.

Then Nicholas resumed their conversation. "I don't quite agree with you, though, on today's women. I'd have to make exceptions with some of them. You said you don't like being lumped together with the whole of society, and that's what you're doing with the womenfolk."

"Alright, alright, then maybe there's a few good apples out there. But where the hell do you find them?"

"They're out there, in their work places, their apartments or condos, pushing carts in the grocery stores, loading up their charge cards at shopping malls. You run into them in a lot of places. But before you start looking, it would be a good idea if you decided first what you want. Make up your mind what you plan to do with your life."

Brian Cooper just sat quietly for a while, chewing on the cheeseburger, masticating slowly, looking at Nicholas as if dumbfounded, but thinking.

Thinking: I don't need to listen to that. I know that.

Now talking to himself, mentally: But like the man said, what do you plan to do with your life, man? So you're feeling in a rut right now. Some kind of a rite of passage. You got to get past this. Do something. Find some new challenges. The Agency? Maybe something else this time. Yes. Something to get started with.

He made a gesture to Nicholas with his glass of beer as if to propose a toast, saying: "Hey, we got to do this more often."

"What, kick each other's brains out?"

"That too."

⌑ 8 ⌑

THROUGH FREEDOM
AND JUSTICE FOR ALL

The first thing he did as soon as he walked into the apartment was pick up the phone and call Los Angeles. For the past four days since he re-read Emil's short letter and started getting those mysterious phone calls, he'd been working in his head how he would open up to his father the question of the man's involvement with the rebel movement in the old country.

He had mixed feelings about its possibilities. At one instance, it excited him to think that his father didn't just settle for a secure and comfortable life in America and forget about the old country; that maybe aside from that stable family-man image he had projected of himself to his family, there was another man in him. A political man, an ideologist, a soldier, a patriot.

150

Nicholas felt proud and was intrigued at the thought of this. But in the next instance, he worried that his father and all of them in the family could be in danger. Government agents from the old country had been known to liquidate not just the well-known opposition leaders but their supporters as well, including members of their families as a measure of further intimidation.

If it were anything like that, he was certain, though, that his father would have let them know or done something to protect them. No. He simply wouldn't do anything so carelessly to endanger any of them.

Maybe he was just reading too much out of Emil's one-page letter. He quickly recalled what was in it that brought all these on and kept holding the telephone to his ear. The answering machine picked up and he left a message to say simply that he called and will do so again later.

They were either out having brunch at their favorite restaurant in Santa Monica only a few miles south of the house in Brentwood Park, or visiting his sister and her family in Westwood Village. He went into the kitchen to make a cup of coffee and then came back to the living room to look at the Sunday paper to pass some time before calling again.

There was nothing but a filler item in the world news section about the old country, not much more than a hundred words, which reported government advances in rebel territory in a number of fierce encounters with rebel troops; three major university campuses shut down after (government) intelligence uncovered hub of support activities for the rebellion; many students arrested; rebel arms procurement sources and shipment routes from abroad, as far as Eastern Europe, South America and southern California, uncovered in a courier dispatch intercepted by government agents.

Southern California, he read a second and third time, his eyes glancing at the telephone in between times. He decided to continue waiting a few more minutes and skimmed through the rest of the newspaper section.

He turned next to the sports section. The 'Skins weren't doing too well this year. They were out of the playoffs.

Nothing else caught his attention in the paper especially now that he began to be preoccupied with the thought of his family. The kind of life they've lived in America, as well as his own personal life, what he had made of it and what it had meant being here thus far. Most often, whenever he thought of his father, he thought of the whole family. And this was because, he knew, it was his father for the most part who made the decisions and the many personal sacrifices that determined the course of their personal lives, from the old country to where they were now.

So much of his father's thoughts and beliefs affected their lives even now, and perhaps not just their lives but the many they left behind in the old country, depending on how encompassing those thoughts and beliefs were. Presently, the nearest one in his mind was his sister. Melissa.

If anything in the world gave him any sense of satisfaction simply by knowing it, it was nothing else but the life he knew his sister lived. Married for more than eight years now, she couldn't have been happier with the people in her life: two healthy and adorable children, a five-year old boy and a seven-year old girl, a hardworking husband - born in America of immigrant parents from the old country, who loved his family and treasured every single day of his life with them.

He remembered how they all worried when his sister got engaged to the America-born man that their marriage might not last long, mostly because of their differences in values and upbringing. But they were wrong. The man turned out to have held on strongly to the values his parents drilled in to him from the old country.

Growing up in America, he didn't succumb to the pull of decadence outside the home and survived all peer pressures at school and in society in general.

Nicholas couldn't have been happier for his sister, his only sibling whom he cared about deeply. It would hurt so much had he seen her go through that cycle of dating, marriage and divorce. Once, or perhaps more, God forbid. Not in my family, he had thought many times.

He remembered some of the women he had gone out with since college, many of whom had now gone through the cycle at least once, if not in the process. Then, later on and until recently, those big-city divorcees, mostly career women, he met socially and got involved with, including Gail Phillips.

Next, he thought of Harvey Dugan, friends and family. It seems the poor thrive better in human relationships especially with the ones fraught with material difficulties. They tend to care more for each other, value their relationships more although they have little more than themselves, their caring, to share with one another.

People are like countries: the poorer they are, the longer they remain poor, the stronger they feel about their values. The richer they are, the sooner they change and become less of themselves.

Once he had pulled himself and his family out of their impoverished life in West Virginia, assuming his continued good fortune in making a living in the capital area, Harvey Dugan and his wife and children, as they all grow older, would be faced with some changes in their relationships to one another, changes they must cope with and learn to live with in one another. The price they must pay for the new values they acquire, the opportunities and the new possibilities of life they've opened for themselves.

And the same would be true of their friends Robert and Barbara Grant who didn't waste any time at all in following up on the job-leads from Nicholas and Gail. Early in the week following Thanksgiving, the couple got in touch with them immediately. Nicholas arranged for a job interview for Robert Grant with a drywall subcontractor, one of the busiest he knew in the business around the area. Robert Grant went and got a job offer before the end of the week.

Gail took Barbara Grant to their personnel, the Army civilian personnel office, where the two of them, with the help of a placement counselor, spent two hours rummaging through several folders of job announcements looking mostly for entry-level openings. That same day, Barbara filled out an SF-171, in longhand, finished and turned it in to a personnel specialist who after going over it made several copies, made several phone calls and asked Gail to accompany Barbara to a room in another floor of the huge government building for a preliminary interview for one of the jobs they'd picked out that matched Barbara's qualifications. Three other interviews were arranged for her through the rest of the week and by the time she got out of the building when her husband picked her up, she was assured of a job inside of two weeks. She held one of Gail's hands in both hers before they parted and put a few drops of tears on it as she bowed her head and tried unsuccessfully to stop herself from crying.

Nicholas called Los Angeles again several times. It was early evening when his sister finally picked up the phone. They talked for a few minutes before he asked for their father. Mother got on the line instead to tell him father was out in Long Beach with a group of expatriates at a reception for a newly-arrived former Foreign Minister from the old country who was now the leader of the opposition in exile.

He could always tell when she was being open since he was a kid so that when she's not, he knew even better. He was going to insist that she level with him, but this time, he had some thinking to do before he pried into her thoughts. All their lives, he never thought they kept secrets in the family. But now, just as he was about to tell her what he wanted to ask father, he had to ask himself: if father is involved with the politics back in the old country, did he share this with mother? How openly, if he did? And if they were both in on it, they had probably decided to keep their children out of it for very good reasons.

He decided he wanted to talk directly to father and asked mother to tell him to please return his call as soon as possible.

America. Land of expatriates. Land of immigrants. A refuge to the freedomless. A sojourn to the victims of human oppression.

The thought flashed in Nicholas' mind as he sat in the lunchroom with Haj Fujiwara during the Monday noon break. But after listening to what Haj had just said to him, he had additional thoughts about America.

America is also a place to learn personally about other people from all parts of the world. And it is also a place where one may come not only to share in its freedom and opportunity but to find one's self, to know one's self.

"I am going back to Japan," Haj had stated factually, causing Nicholas to practically stare at him while searching for any sign to doubt it. Nicholas found none.

"When did you come to this decision? Not that I take you seriously, yet."

"Two nights ago. I had a talk with my parents."

"What did they say?"

"My mother is very happy about it. She was born and raised there. In the city of Kobe, near Osaka where my paternal grandfather still lives. She believes this is the right thing to do with my life - to live the rest of it in the homeland. She said she would like to be able to do the same thing but that her place in life is with my father, wherever that might be."

They sat quietly for a few moments not even looking at each other. Just weighing the magnitude of Haj's decision as if it were some form of a buoyant object floating and turning slowly between them, there for their careful scrutiny.

Haj broke silence first. "I talked to my parents separately," he said, only glancing at Nicholas quickly and gazing at the invisible floating object. "I never saw her face light up with such life when I told her. Yet, at the same time, it made me feel sad."

"Why? I don't understand -"

"One thing led to another very quickly. And I started thinking about our entire lives here in America and imagining that part of hers she lived in Japan before my father went there and brought her here when she was seventeen. Her feeling happy to know of my desire to go back to Osaka betrayed her own and even stronger desire to go back. But more than that, it dawned on me how unhappy she might have been with life here in the United States all these years even with my father's devotion to her."

"You don't know that for certain."

"No, I didn't. In fact, I refused to even think that for the past thirty or thirty-five of her forty-four years here in America, she had been unhappy. She never talked about how she feels about life here until I saw that happy look on her face two nights ago and she started telling me a few things I never expected to hear from her."

"America is a good land," Haj's mother had told her son in her fluid Japanese accent, "especially for one who has not known any other, who has not belonged to any other."

"And for you, mother?" her son, her only child had asked then. "Has America been a good place for you too? Have you been happy being here?"

Haj's heart sank when he looked in his mother's eyes which did not conceal a shade of sadness that went deeper than she would admit even to herself. And his eyes nearly watered when she raised her hands to hold his face in them gently, as gently as she used to when he was little and she would smile fondly at him and say in a sing-song: "Pretty, pretty little Japanese boy. Pretty, pretty little American boy." She spoke to him in Japanese then as she still spoke more Japanese than English even when she'd been in America for fifteen years.

"I am happy being with you and your father," she said with just a trace of that old kind smile that could not prevail upon the shadow in her eyes. "I am fine, my son. What is more important is your happiness. You are young and must live a full life. You must marry soon and give us pretty, pretty -" this time, the same old smile of fondness came fully, "- little Japanese-American baby grandchildren. But first and more important is your happiness," she said again and the shadows returned to her eyes. "So I ask you, more than you should ask me, my son Hajime, have you been happy being in America?"

He took her hands in his and looked down at them - the same hands that brought him into the world, cared for him and raised him in America - as if to meditate and draw the answer from them.

"Yes, mother," he said, looking up shortly at her and then down again. "I have been happy."

"Speak to me the truth, Hajime. The truth, my son."

"I have been as happy as anyone born in America to a good family can be. You have given me a good life, and so has father, in this good land as you said. I might say there are other things one discovers and learns about in life which may only be found in other places, and perhaps not in America." His mother's face lit up at this instance. "Those things I found in Japan, our land of origin, your homeland, mother, during the years we lived in Osaka. True, I am an American, by birth. But I am also Japanese. Pureblood Japanese. I am part of you, and even that part of you which I know longs for Japan, for home, is in me too."

It made her happy, gave her a great sense of reassurance, he knew, to hear him say that. But that was only part of the truth she asked him to speak to her. Much as he ached to share with her many of his personal experiences in life in America as early as his pre-teens back in Kansas and on up, especially those that now brought him to the decision to move to Japan, he simply couldn't.

Through the years, he had spoken to his father, on occasions, of some of his difficulties at school and in their home neighborhood. But talking about them, he knew even then, would not alleviate anything and on the contrary only add a burden to his father's own difficulties in life, in his bigger job of trying to survive to keep his family together. Likewise, he did not see the point in his mother feeling the hurt he felt by telling her of his hardships then, for instance the catcalls directed at him at school and most everywhere else - Jap, gook, yellowbelly.

He did not see the point of it then and he did not see the point of telling her now, that he had been a very lonely man in America, that the values he learned at home all his life, the very same ones he saw in Japan, he could not fully reconcile with mainstream America, with those he saw at work in people's work habits and attitudes, at institutions of learning in people's efforts to learn and develop themselves intellectually, and at people's homes and other places where personal human relationships are involved, in the way people treat one another. He simply could not tell her now that he had no idea that he was never at peace with himself until he experienced the peace of mind, the sense of belongingness, the feeling of being truly at home he found living in Japan with their own kind.

He hoped that the day his father himself decided to bring back his bride to her native land to live with her there would not be far away from the day their son returned.

"And what did your father say when you talked to him?" Nicholas asked, clearing up his litter on the lunch table.

"He said that I won't fit in that society even though I'm a hundred percent Japanese by blood and speak the language fluently. I would be considered an American, at best. An outsider, in any case."

"He's probably right. And I might add that you wouldn't last more than a couple of years this time, before you're back in the States."

Haj smiled confidently. "This decision has been cooking a long time. And I don't mean weeks or months. I mean years, like ten, fifteen."

Nicholas realized now that he must take Haj seriously. At the same time, he became acutely aware of the implications of the man's decision upon himself and his own life in America.

Here was a fellow American, natural-born and therefore more of an American than he - an immigrant, a transplant - could ever be, and he's leaving America for his ancestral land. Whatever reason brought him to this decision could only be as strong as his convictions in life and the principles he adhered to without question. Nicholas flinched at the thought of this. What reason could he himself possibly have to decide to go back and live in the old country? What principles? What convictions?

A sudden urge to learn what was realistically at the core of Haj's decision nagged at him.

"What finally made up your mind after all these years?" he asked solemnly. He had no idea how Haj needed him to ask that question exactly the way he did.

At last, Haj had the opportunity to voice out some of those things which for better than half of his life in America up to now he did not see fit to trouble his parents with. And now, he did not care if he appeared to lay bare in what may seem an unusual way to Nicholas, his deep feelings as he spoke.

"I finally convinced myself," he said reverently, "that I am not accepted in the American society as it is now. That I don't fit in it and therefore don't belong in it. I must therefore go to where I belong."

Nicholas looked shocked. He was shocked.

"You don't know what you're saying, Haj!" he burst out but in a controlled voice. "And I always thought you're of a higher intellectual level than that."

"Watch it there a little," warned Haj with a feigned threat in his tone of voice.

"Damn it Haj, you realize what you just said? If you don't belong here, then I don't belong here either, and so with my family, and your family, and ninety-nine point nine percent of the whole fucking American population."

When it became apparent that Haj did not intend to say another word until Nicholas had calmed himself down, Nicholas got a hold of himself and asked softly: "Would you mind telling me why you feel the way you do, enough to say what you just said to me?"

It was clear who had more self-control and was better disciplined with himself when Haj spoke again. "Not at all," he uttered gently. "I have two words, each with a very important meaning, to respond to your question: the first is value, and the second is peace. I'll be brief about this. I have not been at peace with myself ever since freshman college, I would say, two years after I came back from Osaka. Things have never been the same since. And I know why: because I can't connect to the value system everywhere - scholastically, socially, with the one I grew up with which I won't give up. Or can't. Don't get me wrong, though. This is not a matter of a failure in the process of assimilation."

"I understand, I understand," said Nicholas, waving Haj down. "And I agree, you should not have to give up the value system you grew up with especially if it is better and more beneficial than the one you see around you. But you got to hold your ground. Don't run away. Stand up for it."

"What do you think I've been doing all my life? But I don't see living another thirty-four years of my life here the same way I have: no friends, true friends, no meaningful relationship, no roots. To tell you frankly, I never felt at home anywhere we've lived. Kansas, California, here. It's been a very lonely life." Haj whispered the last sentence and Nicholas would have choked if he had tried to talk after hearing it and seeing the empty look on Haj's face.

"Listen, Haj," he managed to say after waiting a few seconds, "America is a big country. The genes of just about every nationality on earth has found their way into this country and the question of how good or bad a nation grew out of it is open to anybody's interpretation, depending on who one is: what racial background, what culture, economic class, so on and so forth. But I'll tell you something: I don't care how big it is, how good or how bad it is. You shouldn't let that matter to you personally unless you're running for public office. And even then, you only appear that way in your speeches, when you're platforming, like any politician. What should concern you more is how much control you have over your own life here in America. Do you control it? Or are you allowing somebody else, something else, to control it?"

"I know I have control over my own life. Not total control, though, but some. Enough that I could live with. If I knew I didn't have enough, then I'd have to work on getting more: make more money, get a more powerful job, have more control or influence over other people's lives, make changes so I could be more in control of my own life. There is a big difference between having control, having power over other people, and being accepted by them. Fear is not respect."

"You're too civilized, Haj. You talk of respect. Acceptance. You know how somebody gains respect and acceptance? Nine out of ten times it's not out of sheer reverence, love and fondness or any form of personal admiration. People respect the law, when they choose to, that is, not because they want to - there are certain laws some people openly resent - but because they're afraid they'd be punished if they didn't.

"It's the same thing with human beings. People respect somebody not because they like the guy but because they're afraid of him. Because he has control and power over them. Power to make their lives miserable enough to make them quit their jobs, change their ways, make them move out of the neighborhood, or move out of the country."

"I'm not a politician," Haj muttered. "I'm not a bureaucrat. I don't want power over other people. I'm an engineer. I want to use my knowledge and skill the best way I could. I'm also a human being who needs acceptance and respect, not for the pain and hardship I could inflict on people but for what I am and who I am. A Japanese-American. A person of this complexion and appearance and who ordinarily eats rice seven days a week."

"You're not only too civilized," Nicholas observed coolly. "You're also too idealistic. I won't try to make you change 'cause then you wouldn't be you. But I wish you would recognize how important it is in this country to get what you want by being in control. Especially if you want respect, even if you have to gain it through fear. I understand what you mean when you said it's been a very lonely life. I've felt the same way, many many times, throughout my life here in America. And it's because it's not easy to hold on to our values, our ideals, without being gradually dragged down to the level of mediocrity we see all around us."

Hearing somebody talk like that, Haj thought, was like finally having thorns pulled out of his chest. Little spikes that had been driven into his body and soul long ago, being withdrawn. Not all of them, though. Only some. But, still, it was a relief.

He did not question the relevance of Nicholas' feelings to his own. He did not doubt Nicholas' own experience of that lonely life in America, especially considering his foreign origin. But his decision to leave America for Japan was settled. He had talked to both his mother and father. It was final.

Nothing could change it now, even as Nicholas continued to speak to him, in an attempt perhaps to make him give a second thought, or justify his own - Nicholas' own existence and life situation in America.

"You want to know how I feel right now, Haj? I feel like trash. And you know what I see when I look at them?" Nicholas indicated their co-workers - fellow engineers, accountants, management experts and other professionals - on one whole side of the lunchroom by pointing with his chin. "I see a bigger pile of trash."

"What the... don't be ridiculous, Nicholas."

"You see, what you're saying is you're good, and no one here, including me, and in the whole of America is good enough so you're leaving the country."

"C'mon, Nicholas -"

"You know that's true," Nicholas continued. "Everybody knows that's true. You're good, professionally and in a lot of other ways. And that's the more reason why you shouldn't run away. I know you're not happy with the people you work with." Nicholas lowered his voice halfway through that sentence. "I don't blame you. Most of them are credentialed half-literates. But that's the way it is nowadays no matter where you go in America. You're lucky you don't work in the government, like my father does. I hear things from him about work. Something's got to be done about this. Somebody's got to do something. And you know who the people are who can do something about this decline in American competence, literacy, productivity, character? It's people like you, Haj. It's you and your kind.

"Unfortunately, though, you are so vastly outnumbered. And your count is even continuing to decline. I doubt if there's ten percent of the entire population you could consider the prime-mover of the country now. It's probably more like five percent, meaning that pretty soon the condition of life in this country, the determination of the quality and way of life in America will be in the hands of a few, a very few, if this hasn't already been happening."

Nicholas' assertiveness suddenly stalled as the memory of a day in his life in the old country came to mind. This was the day he sat in his grandfather's lap, when he was seven which somehow seemed to have found a permanent niche in his memory. Shortly before the 1920 Revolution, grandfather, then a young teen-ager had been employed in the residence of a Japanese General for a variety of duties - gardening, driving, courier errands, among others. He also lived a dangerous life for he spied for the revolutionaries. In this position, he learned many things that in many ways helped liberate his country from all the colonizers. He also learned some of the ways the Japanese think. Grandfather was having a conversation with his son, Nicholas' father, that day while he rocked the grandson in his lap. He recounted one of the many occasions the General spoke to him ardently about some serious matters, during which the General said to him:

"Your country is a very important country, if not the most important, in Asia. We, the Japanese, the pre-destined leader of all East Asia, must lead you out of bondage, cleanse you and your land of the Western decadence just as we must do with the rest: China, the Philippines, Malaya, Indonesia, and others."

Of America, grandfather recounted to his son, unaware that his grandson was absorbing what he was saying and would recall them years later when he would be living in America, the Japanese General said:

"It is big, and it is rich. Very rich. What a tragedy it has been for its original nation. Its native peoples. If only we, the Japanese, had been the one who had occupied that land instead of those European mongrels, with their African slaves, who now spend and waste its resources the way they do with their inefficient, wasteful, ignorant and often destructive ways. Ah, I couldn't begin to imagine what a better world this could have been for everyone."

When Nicholas re-focused on the man sitting across the table from him, he felt for a moment that Haj was a different person. Haj was first an Asian, then a Japanese. The thought that he was American didn't enter Nicholas' mind at all. He then recoiled at the magnitude of the impact upon him, and the whole American nation, of Haj's decision to abandon his land of birth.

What possible anguish and pain could life in America truly have inflicted upon him to come to this? What loneliness? Social isolation? Cultural inhibition? Racial discrimination and prejudice? Is it a question of what America, the true face of America is, or is it a question of what a man is?

The complexity of such questions was so engulfing that Nicholas succumbed to gazing languidly at the invisible floating object between them. While in this state of arrest, he heard Haj's voice.

"Tell me, Nicholas," Haj said in a gentle and inquiring tone of voice, "honestly, how do you truly feel about yourself being here, in America? Do you really consider yourself an American?"

There was a long pause between them, its silence isolating them from the rest of the people in the lunchroom, from the rest of the world. Nicholas felt a kind of loneliness in this silence, one that prevented him from responding to the question.

"Do you feel like an American?" Haj added.

Nicholas, earlier, had thought of asking Haj this very same question but thought better for you did not ask one born and raised in America if he is an American, hyphenated or not. Faced with the question himself, he had to take a few moments to consider his answer.

"I swore allegiance to this sovereign state, and to what it stands for," he said as if to weigh every word of it. "I am a citizen of the United States of America." Their eyes locked and drilled deep into their consciousness, exchanging thoughts that neither one would dare put into words. "I am an American, as you are."

They both knew in those thoughts they communicated to each other that that was not an answer to the question. But with it, they were both willing to pass it up for one and to skip the question.

Haj drew away from the table, indicating that he was bringing his lunch break to an end shortly. But part of that motion was out of a realization that he was not right about being able to satisfactorily discuss with Nicholas either what he, throughout his life in America, could not with his parents, especially his mother.

It just wouldn't be right to tell Nicholas his long-held belief that the mixing of all the human races in a country to form a nation is not good and would never work to the benefit of the most, let alone the whole; that it's not right to force people in the creation of a mongrelized society which would inevitably result in endless racial and cultural conflicts. These he simply could not tell Nicholas no matter how much they might explain to him the loneliness he felt, they both felt, in their lives in America, for Nicholas' country of origin itself, its multi-racial polyglot nation was founded through that process. In fact, Nicholas himself represented the result of this.

But he will go and live in Japan, the origin of his blood, and where he will be home. There, he will find many among his kind, beginning with his grandfather in Osaka, to whom he could voice his beliefs.

There, he will speak of his lifetime experiences in America where he lived among the rich and the poor in a mix of dominant cultures and others less assertive. He will speak of the personal knowledge of the world and its peoples one learns only by living in such a large country of mixed nationalities; and by this knowledge he will let everyone know that the entire world to this day since the birth of human civilization actually remains to be a battlefield of contention in every way between the Asians and the Europeans. The entire western hemisphere, Africa and everything else besides are just battlegrounds for each side to probe one's strengths and weaknesses. The superpowers are going to continue to escalate their rivalry for supremacy in arms and ideology, but this will last only for a few decades, if they last that long, before the rot and decadence in their society and governments ate them up from the inside out. By that time, the whole of Europe and the whole of Asia would have polarized completely and they would have become the two major and final world powers. An Armageddon, when they finally come to that, will then determine the fate of the human species.

**

Around one-thirty, just before it happened, the office just getting settled back to work from lunch, Nicholas sat at his desk in the office he shared with Lester Jenkins, alone. Most of the things he just learned from Haj Fujiwara during their noon break, particularly those that hit home, still fresh in his ears. He wanted to talk to somebody else about them, and did so by writing a letter to Emil, in his head.

I was totally surprised when he said it and that he would say it. I was stunned at how directly he said it as if it had been in him for years. 'I am not accepted in the American society as it is now,' he said. His exact words. 'I don't fit in it, don't belong in it. I must therefore go to where I belong.'

I have a feeling he's holding off on some things. I have an idea of what they might be and I can even guess why he doesn't want to - or couldn't tell them to me.

I believe him when he told me it's not a question of assimilation. He's a native-born American. He's more American than I am, in spite of the fact that he's pureblood Asian and I'm only half, and half Caucasian. But there are other sides to the question of assimilation, not just the matter of being born and raised here or not, picking English as a primary language and adapting to the lifestyle.

There's also the matter of how strong one's cultural background plays in his personal life, at home and beyond. How long or how short a leash it has him on. And then of course there's the matter of race.

I can see how America can become one big lonely place for someone born and raised in it to discover later certain limitations he has to face because of his race. It's not the same for Haj as it is for the blacks. The blacks grow up recognizing fully those limitations since the first day they begin to shed their innocence. With Haj, as it is with me in some ways I have felt in the past, this recognition comes rather late into adulthood and it comes rather abruptly. It's somewhat similar to cultural shock. Racial shock.

Now, this I don't see Haj talking to me about openly. I don't see him getting into any specific personal experience of racial prejudice which I'm sure he's encountered many times and probably accounts for most of what he said to me today.

I agree, racism is still very much a part of the problems America faces today. There was this Filipino I used to work with on a project not long ago. Not a bad-looking guy. Very intelligent, highly educated as most of them are as we both know (there was a time when nearly a third of the faculty of all the colleges and universities in the capital were Filipinos). Once in a while, he lapsed into a morbid mood, really felt depressed and his language would deteriorate. I guess this helped him let out some of the untidy things in his life he had bottled up inside him.

One of those occasions, he was telling me how torn up he felt, intellectually, emotionally, socially - inside out, he said, between two cultures; like being caught in between two big rocks closing in on him. He even tried to be funny about it: like Samson, he said, with no hair. Totally bald.

And his language then went down the gutter level:

'I'm so fuckin' lonely in this damn country of over two hundred million people sometimes I can't think straight,' he mumbled to me in anguish. 'I feel so damn useless, living my life for nothing. Wasting it away. I now believe cultural assimilation is wrong. People should stick to their own. Stay where they belong.'

Nicholas remembered the fellow well. One of the few professional people he had known and worked with in America who'd be hard to forget. The Filipino man held a master's degree in Architecture and in Civil Engineering, from Harvard. He was all at once bright and naive, serious and jocular, harsh and soft. And he was the first person to ever cause Nicholas to seriously look back to where he came from, to view the old country and see how it looked from America, on that one occasion the man was in a depressed mood. He also looked deeply into himself, and his life in America.

Now, it was Haj.

He continued with the imaginary letter to Emil, feeling glad that Lester was not in the office and no one else had come in to distract him from this.

I tried to disagree with both of them. When I look back, I see our island country almost as I see America. People from every nation on earth could come together and live as one people, form their own sovereign state and government, their own country which they'd be willing to defend and die for.

America is fifty times bigger. That is the only difference I see, which makes racial and cultural assimilation a slower process. Our native country had to go through the same difficult process throughout its entire history.

It was difficult alright. Agonizing, brutal and painful, lonely and a lot of other ways we can never imagine exactly for everyone who was ever born to live and die there during the process. But the country has survived. It became united. It grew strong, drove out its foreign rulers and achieved freedom and independence.

I wish there was a way I could share this view with Haj, with every immigrant, and with every immigrant's son and daughter who ever set foot in America and felt the way Haj does now. The thing in question here is not really what America is or what a person is as I asked myself during lunch with him. Rather, it is the existence of America itself, the concept it is founded upon. A concept based on the preservation of human dignity through freedom and justice for all.

Does America exist? *That America*? Is such a country possible? My answer is, yes. It exists. It may not yet be such a country for all its people and those who yet seek to be a part of it. But it exists and continues its struggle to achieve the basis of its conception for all its inhabitants.

It will take some more time than it already has. That process. And there will be many more Haj's. Many more hurts, loneliness, brutalities to the mind and heart, racial hatred, disillusionment, broken dreams. But America will persist. It will survive. Human dignity will, for all.

He stopped his mental letter-writing to stretch his neck, which made him turn to look out the window on 18th Street seven stories below. Tiny snowflakes were floating down from the sky. It was a very thin snowfall but still mid-December usually was early for the area even for such a light one. It was pretty, though, and evoked a sense of tranquility. Nicholas thought of Emil and his longtime dream to come to America. He wondered how Emil would see America. How he would fit in. What life awaited him. Would it be a dream come true, or a dream turned into disillusionment? It would depend, he surmised, upon how much a part of that process he becomes when and if he eventually set foot in America, and the kind of person it makes out of him.

He was about to turn to the work that awaited him on his desk - a set of blueprints and construction specs for one of the projects he was working on, when the whole thing began to happen.

First, he saw Norman Tilley appear in the drafting pool area through the glass partition that separated him from there. Norman turned to look past him, at Lester's desk and seeing that Lester wasn't there began to move on apparently to look for him. He only made two steps then stopped, raised an index finger in a hook, palm up, and with it beckoned at somebody at the other end of the area. Nicholas couldn't see who it was. He thought it looked like Norman was trying to call the attention of a little kid or a stray puppy dog.

Then Lester came to view, moving in measured steps toward Norman.

"Can you move it there a little faster, Lester?" Norman said in a loud voice. Nicholas tensed when he saw the look in the black engineer's face as he moved closer to Norman. He knew something was about to happen, and for certain when Norman added: "I want some answers from you about this job," holding up some small sheets of drawing in one hand. "And I want them quick, *boy!*"

The next thing everybody saw, Nicholas from his office and all the workers in the drafting pool area from their drafting boards, was pandemonium. Lester snatched the papers from Norman's hand, tore them up and threw them in Norman's face.

"Why, you fucking black sonofabitch!" Norman snarled. "You savage bastard -"

That he didn't finish as Lester swiftly connected some right-hand knuckles to his mouth. It was a straight blow, so powerful that it immediately split his upper lip and splattered blood throughout the lower half of his face. It also sent him crashing backward on a young drafter who didn't have enough time or room to avoid him. The two of them fell on the drafting board and demolished it.

Lester's rage didn't let up. He was tossing swivel chairs and drawing racks and book shelves out of his way to get to Norman again. He was going to kill him. Tear him up and get the most satisfaction out of it. This was the only way, the sweetest way to let go of one's racial hatred that's been tearing him up inside: let it tear up on whoever, whatever's causing it; let it break down his human dignity too, and spill his blood and destroy him physically. Kill the goddamn white sonofabitch!

Everything flushed out of his mind except for one thing left in it: a signal, a switch that triggered a primeval instinct. The instinct to prevail, to subdue. To kill. God, above all, didn't exist. And neither did ethics, morality, law and justice, compassion and understanding. There's only one thing he knew and felt: hatred, deep gnawing hatred that he had lost control of.

He was going to finally get himself his first white man who would, by the time the whole bloody scene was over, probably be his last. The cops would come and then... no. Maybe he'd get a couple other white sons of bitches in the office too.

He lunged at Norman with the fierceness of a long-starving predator, but Norman was quicker this time.

Norman leaped out of the young drafter's ruined pile of furniture, grabbed hold of a loose-four-foot long steel drafting straight-edge and started swinging with it in blind rage as if it were a medieval chopping sword.

The entire work force of the office within sight of the area had gathered around at a safe distance. Several male workers ventured to move in to break up the fight but hesitated. Someone called the police instead. Another called the security guard downstairs.

With reflexes enhanced by sheer animal instinct to kill, Lester moved much faster than Norman could swing at him with the wobbly straight-edge which thus became more of a burden than a weapon. Norman let go of it to run away behind another drafting board from the on-rushing Lester, looking frantically for another weapon, a knife, a pair of scissors, anything to defend himself with against the fury of the black man.

Some of the spectators moved along with them in a circle, maintaining the same safe distance. Nicholas was one of them. Everything was happening so quickly that he couldn't resolve clearly any thought of intervening. Though Lester was bigger than him by a couple of inches in height and some thirty pounds in weight, he knew he could safely place himself between the black man and the white man and level the black man's attacks with some routine technique. But he wasn't sure if Lester, in raging fury, would recognize him at all and even if the black man did, if he would stop or continue attacking. At this moment, Nicholas wondered, feeling rather odd about it, whether Lester, in all their working days together, saw him as a white man or not. While he was going through these, the fight went on.

The black man swept the drafting board and everything else on it and under it out of his way, went for the white man's throat with one hand in a lightning charge and delivered a succession of heavy blows with the other hand on the white man's face, head, kidneys and anywhere he could hit him. The white man got away, screaming for help. The black man caught up with him, spun him around and broke his jaw and some more teeth with a hurtling steel fist. The white man crumbled to the floor half-dead but the black man had no sane thought of stopping as long as he suspected there was one breath left in the white man. At this point, just as the black man was about to deliver what might be a coup de grace, somebody - a white man, stepped out of the circle of onlookers to intervene. Behind him stood another white man, Harold Forker, the division boss who looked totally petrified but still had the presence of mind to urge, literally push the man in front of him. The man was as big as Lester, looked a little heavier and moved more like a wrestler than a boxer: slow and threatening.

When Lester turned around and saw him, the man held out a hand in a gesture for calm, but Lester instead decided that he was going to clobber and mutilate his second white man all in one day, maybe even a third, and then they could all get him and lynch him. Hang him, shoot him, do whatever they want to do with him.

Nicholas remained nearby. He was almost there, any moment now, into stepping in and knocking some sense into Lester with a lock-joint hold perhaps and a quick chop over the carotid. At this instance, he looked past the combatants to the faces across the ruins of the office area and caught a glimpse of Haj Fujiwara.

The Japanese-American simply stood there without registering shock or any kind of reaction to what was taking place. He just looked with a passive expression on his face as the black man rushed the second white man who hardly managed to counter with a slow punch that went past the side of Lester's head. He was just there as if seeing something normal, expected, all a part of daily life in America.

Lester proceeded to demolish the second white man mercilessly with all the power of racial hatred that burned inside him, behind a series of kicks and punches to the face, the rib cage, the liver, after he floored him with one vicious punch to the mouth.

Nicholas finally decided to move in.

America will persist, he thought as he leaped in the air to everyone's amazement and landed in front of Lester in time to thwart another blow the black man was packing for the blood-drained face of the half-conscious white man. Nicholas caught the murderous fist, swung it over his head quickly and locked it in a reverse-joint hold, at the same time pinning the elbow down low with his other hand so that Lester's shoulder and face, side down, pressed hard against the floor, his entire body paralyzed by the pain being inflicted on his twisted wrist.

America will survive. Human dignity will... for all.

"Kill me! Kill me now... " Lester squeezed the words out of his throat while his Adam's apple scraped on the floor. His eyes were shut tight as he endured the pain which Nicholas meant to calm down his anger. He struggled some against Nicholas' expert grip on him but the additional controlled dose of pain Nicholas responded with quickly discouraged him from trying any further. "Kill me, white man, or I'll kill you if you don't!"

"Lester, it's me," Nicholas said softly, bending closer on one knee to Lester's ear. "It's me. I'm going to let go slowly, okay? Okay? Now, open your eyes. It's me - Nicholas."

Lester opened his eyes while keeping the contorted expression on his face. Seeing Nicholas restored some of his sanity and returned him from the wild animal loose on a killing rampage a moment ago. "Everybody please back off and clear out, right now!" Nicholas called out to the people around them. "Somebody get an ambulance." He saw how badly hurt the two white men were as they now lay unconscious and bleeding. There were wide patches of blood through the path of battle, on the floor, the walls and the furniture. He worried about Norman. He hoped Lester didn't kill him. But from the deathlike appearance of his mangled face, it didn't look like there was any life left in him.

Everybody did as Nicholas said, stepping back slowly, scuffling, still in shock.

"Everything's going to be alright, Lester," Nicholas whispered to Lester's ear. "I saw and heard everything that happened. It wasn't your fault. You were provoked. I'll testify for you. I'll be your witness. Now, let's just ease on out to our office. Just don't do anything more. They all got the message. You can bet on that."

The two security guards showed up first just as Nicholas was leading Lester into their office. They stayed close outside after they heard what happened. Then the police finally came only slightly ahead of the paramedics who worked right away on the injured, checked their vitals and carried them out on stretchers.

Norman was alive. But from the report the office received later in the afternoon, it was said that he would most likely spend the rest of his life in a wheelchair either as a quadriplegic or - with God's mercy - a paraplegic. His central nervous system was irreversibly damaged.

There will be many more hurts, brutalities, hatreds. It will take some more time. That process. But America will persist. America will survive.

Human dignity will, through freedom and justice...for all.

◫ 9 ◫

MAN WITH VODKA
ON A MANHOLE COVER

The police listened first to Lester Jenkins' side of the story and took notes at the same time. Then a few minutes into it, one of the officers stepped out of Lester's office and took statements from witnesses. Three people who claimed to have seen everything that happened from beginning to end offered to speak. One of them was the young drafter whose office area was demolished, another was Sam Goodman who had enthusiastically monitored the racial confrontation word for word, blow by blow, and the third one was Nicholas who simply told the police exactly what he heard as they were being said and what he saw as they were happening.

Lester spoke normally. He was back in full control of himself, all the gut-wrenching anger and hatred in him drained, satisfied.

"I snapped," he said to the officer questioning him, a young robust black D.C. policeman. "I couldn't take it anymore. It had to happen sooner or later. I'm glad it did today. As for the consequences -"

"That," the officer interrupted firmly, "we will determine later on, for everyone involved, sir."

"I wouldn't know how else to put it if you were to ask me a dozen more times, officer," Sam Goodman said to the other policeman questioning people outside near the drafting pool area which was gradually being restored by the workers in it. "The man has been a regular, genuine pain in the neck not only to Lester but -"

"Just the incident today, as much as you witnessed, please," the policeman asked patiently.

"Only one way to describe it: Lester finally snapped," replied Sam Goodman peremptorily, holding out the palm of a hand, as if that was the only thing there was to say, naturally, about what happened.

"Lester was provoked, not for the first time, I must add," testified Nicholas directly, unemotionally. "As to whether it was done intentionally or out of carelessness you'd have to ask the man who did it."

"Understand, sir," said the officer. "Thank you, sir."

After the police had gone, the entire office turned a stony silence. At quitting time between four-thirty and five, people picked up quietly and left with their curt and barely audible 'good nights' to one another. On his way out, Nicholas looked up at the corkboard on a wall of the reception and found a phone message for him tacked on it.

All it said was 'Lafayette Park.' The message was from Edward McKenny.

A serene late-autumn night was falling when he walked to the edge of the park after finding a parking space at one of the minor streets nearby. The snow flurry which first came in the early afternoon had been off and on. At a few minutes to five now it's on again, lending a touch of the holiday season in the air together with the Christmas lights which had proliferated at the surrounding streets including Pennsylvania Avenue and the big house across it behind the high iron fence and the uniformed guards that surrounded it day and night.

It took him a few minutes walking from one end of the park to the other to locate Edward McKenny who happened to see and recognize him first. Sitting on a manhole cover wrapped in a blanket and shielded from the busy H Street by a hedge, Edward McKenny watched his visitor wander about for a while, bend to look at the face of one bum stretched on a bench and another huddled against a trash can under a tree.

It cheered him to see Nicholas again after several months. And it wasn't just a matter of feeling glad about it. It also gave him a sense of triumph, of power, that he could actually reach out in the upper world out there beyond the streets and the parks to someone and bring him out here for a visit.

He felt comfortable sitting on the manhole cover which was just warm enough for this kind of weather. It must be some kind of a steam mainline running just under it, he had guessed, or maybe a hot water one. He sat hugging his legs with one arm so that his chin rested on his knees. His other hand held a three-quarter full bottle of vodka.

He delighted at watching Nicholas carrying a half-full plastic grocery bag look around for him. He couldn't help guessing what the sucker had in it. He hoped he had some cigarettes in that bag. He hadn't had a decent drag the past couple of days.

"Hey, you miserable -" Nicholas opened up upon reaching the bum he was looking for and bending down to recognize him.

"Hello again, old friend," Edward interrupted, a smile revealing a set of yellow but even, unbroken teeth. A remnant of his middle-class life in the upper world somewhere in time past.

"Didn't you see me looking around for you?" Nicholas scolded.

"Yes. How d'yuh like the scenery out here today? Isn't it pretty? All those lights -"

"Never mind that! Why didn't you call me? Get up or raise a hand so I'd see you instead of letting me walk around here like a fool!"

"And all those people rushing about to get home, go shopping. Getting ready for the biggest Christmas holiday of their lives. Every year it's like that."

"What the hell do you care about all that? None of that exists for you. You're dead, that's what you told me the last I saw you, remember? Dead! So how are you, anyway? How've you been?"

Nicholas couldn't decide whether he should stay stooping down over the homeless man or sit down and join him on the ground. Edward McKenny resolved this for him.

"Sorry I only have one manhole cover," he apologized, "But - here, you can sit on this." He reached for a hefty bundle wrapped in what looked like a half-size bedspread with the four corners tied together with a string and heaved it over to Nicholas.

"Thanks for being so hospitable," Nicholas said, placing the bulk under him and sitting on it like it was a bean bag. "What do you bums keep in this thing?"

"I don't know about others, but that contains my all-season wardrobe. So, tell me - have you gotten anywhere much in the world since I last saw you? Money? Power? Women? Recognition, and all the rest of those things everybody else is after in this town?"

"Don't poke fun at me because of what I am or whatever kind of life I live. Do I make fun of you because of what you are?"

"What makes you think I'm making fun of you?"

"The way you sound and look at me from under that blanket." Nicholas snuggled his rear end deeper into the bum-sack under him until it was holding him comfortably in place. "You don't have to make a mockery out of all those things just because you've given up all your cares about them and liberated yourself from them."

"Sorry if I sounded so insulting. All I really wanted to ask you was - how are you? And did you have a good day?"

"Now, that sounds much better. I'm fine, thank you. My day?" Nicholas considered it for a moment, eyeing the tiny feathers of snow floating in the air and settling down on his winter coat, on Edward McKenny's blanket and on the ground to vanish quickly as they touched. "It was, I would say, not a very ordinary day, let alone the fact that it's coming to a close with me squatting in a park ground in the cold in the company of a homeless man."

"You don't look too cheerful about it. You don't look too cheerful, period. I'll let you tell me about it, my friend. But first, let's have a drink."

"I don't have any drink."

"I do." Edward shuffled under the blanket. Then his hands came out from under it, one holding out a yellow three-and-a-half ounce disposable plastic cup to Nicholas and the other the bottle of vodka.

"Since when did you take up drinking?" Nicholas asked, holding the cup as Edward poured about an ounce into it.

"Oh, a few weeks ago. Beer makes me go a lot and it's just too troublesome since I don't have my own private toilet. I picked up a bottle of this stuff outside the back wall of a bar one night and it's not quite empty yet so I tried it and I found out it works good with me especially on a cold season like this. Keeps you warm at least in the head and the stomach but it doesn't make you pee as much as beer does. Now I know why those Russians living in those icepacks in Russia invented the stuff."

"I've never done this before," Nicholas said, sniffing the vodka. "Drink solid booze with no mixer." He looked up to watch Edward pour himself one in another cup.

"C'mon," Edward urged assuringly, "it'll do you good. You'll loosen up so you can tell me all your life's troubles."

They said 'cheers' and held out the cups to each other before bringing it to their mouths. Edward did a bottoms-up while Nicholas drank only half of his and gave a couple of vigorous coughs. Edward chuckled happily and urged him to finish it, which he did following it up with a long aa-a-ah.

Edward poured them another round which they sipped slowly this time while they talked.

"Here, I brought you some stuff I thought... maybe you could use." Nicholas handed the plastic grocery bag over to the street man, making sure neither of them were looking at each other like it was nothing.

"Oh, yeah?" Edward muttered, somewhat embarrassed and looking away someplace else across to the other side of

Lafayette Park, as far as Pennsylvania Avenue and the residence of the President of the United States of America.

"Yeah," Nicholas repeated, sniffing at his cup of vodka. "There's something in there to put on when it gets real cold. And there's some cigarettes in there to,"

"Oh, yeah?" Now Edward turned to the bag and dug in to it. He found a brand new pair of gloves, a knit headwear, four packs of cigarettes with some books of matches, two cans of soda and two sandwiches in plastic containers.

On his way out of the office, Nicholas had decided to make a quick stop at the vending machines in the lunchroom for the cigarettes and the foodstuff. The dry goods he picked up at a small men's shop nextdoor. He didn't know why he did it or how it occurred to him to do it. All he knew was that when he read the phone message on the corkboard, he was going to see the bum and somehow back of his mind, it followed that since he was, he might as well make it worth his while and of course the bum's as well. After all, it wasn't like he did this on a regular basis.

Edward tore at one of the cigarette packs greedily, forgetting everything else for a moment: the booze, the food, the company, the cold, the pride. After the first puff, he withdrew in satisfaction back under the blanket and after the second, he resumed his don't-give-a-shit posture: aloof, stand-offish, self contained.

"So what kind of a day was it today?" he asked in a philosophical tone of voice: a wiser man invoking the responses of a less experienced traveler in the path of life. "Things didn't go your way as you planned? As you wanted? What makes it not a very ordinary day for you, young man?"

"Don't talk down to me, please. I really had a rough day and I'm still trying to put myself back together. Up here,"

Nicholas pointed to his head and touching his chest with a fist, added: "And here."

"He-e-y, c'mon, now. You shouldn't let a woman get to you that bad. She couldn't be worth gettin' your head all tied up in a knot like -"

"It's nothing to do with a woman, Edward. It's something to do with -" Nicholas unexpectedly found himself groping for words to describe his experiences of the day since the lunch break with Haj Fujiwara and the thoughts and feelings he now had bottled up in him about those experiences. He hadn't had the sufficient calm of mind to resume his mental letter-writing to Emil since the last time at his desk.

Suddenly, he realized what a good opportunity this was to uncork himself and let things out as much as he felt like doing it. So what if it amounted to no more than telling things to one of the statues in the park talking to a bum? But he knew it wasn't like that talking to Edward McKenny. Not exactly, or he wouldn't be spending one minute of the day out here with him. This bum had seen both sides of life as real as anybody could see it. As a matter of fact, he had an advantage over most people because he had freed himself of all the cares and materialism which ordinarily enslave an average person through most of his life. He can mock them, laugh at them, scorn all those pursuits in life many get ulcers and cancers and die for.

Nicholas, thus, found the words to uncork himself, not caring much how Edward responded, what the homeless man thought and said and how he said it. The important thing was, he had somebody to talk to and talk to as freely as he felt in any form or manner of speech.

"It's something to do with personal beliefs," he continued uninhibitedly. "Things like what I think of this country. It's people. Like you, or all those folks rushing home to get their Christmas shopping done as you said. And people like me too, and even people like those who live in that big house."

"And what brought all of those on today?"

"Thank you. I thought you'd never ask. A fight. And I mean a real fight. Have you ever seen a black man go after white men in a rage to kill? Have you ever seen racial hatred unleashed?"

"Sure I've seen black men fight white men. Happens all the time. Joe Louis and Muhammad Ali beat up on a few of them -"

"I don't mean that kind of fight. Stop being facetious. I'm talking about the fight we had in the office this afternoon between this black guy I work with and a white guy who always gives him a hard time." Nicholas emptied his cup and held the vodka good this time without coughing. He's really getting uncorked now. "Gimme some more of that stuff," he said to Edward, holding out the cup between them. "I'm beginning to like it."

Edward, now clearly enjoying himself with present company poured better than half the cup. Nicholas took a quick sip and grimaced.

"Tell me something," he said, peering into the unwashed and unshaved face of the street man, "you're a white man. Tell me how you feel about the black people. Do you see them, and really see them, as fellow Americans?"

"Is this some kind of a trick question?"

"I'm serious, Edward. And you'd be helping me gather myself together if you could just give me some honest answers. Alright?"

"Hm-m, I'll try."

"Alright. Now, I want you to look inside of you and see what you really have in there. And while you're doing that, forget everything temporarily. Forget that there's rich and that there's poor people in the world. Then tell me how you feel and what you think about the blacks."

Edward McKenny turned his eyes down to the grass at his feet and reflected but only for a short time.

"Of course they're Americans too," he said, stating a fact. "If they're not, then I'm not either. And what does that make me and the rest of us?"

"As a white American then, tell me how you personally feel about them. Don't be afraid to tell me anything. I don't give a shit. I just want to know. If you're prejudiced against them, say so. If you're afraid to shake hands with them because you think their blackness would rub off on you, say so. If you don't want to breath the air they breath, you can tell me. I don't give a shit. You can be any way you want to be. It doesn't make any difference to me. I just want to know."

Edward pulled back a couple of inches from their huddle and regarded Nicholas suspiciously through narrowed eyes.

"You're not asking me for what I personally feel," he said in a clever tone of voice. "You're asking me for what all white people feel about the black people. I can't tell you that 'cause I don't know. I can't tell you what those rednecks down south for instance have inside of them just as I can't tell you what these bigots we have here in Washington and all the way up north to Bangor, Maine have cooking in their heads. I can only tell you what I got. You'd have to ask Joe Schmoe over there for what he's got. It may or may not be the same. I say, yes, I'm prejudiced against the blacks. Why? Obviously because of the color of their skin. If we're the same color then there wouldn't be any problem. At least not that kind of problem. Why is it a problem? Why do I feel prejudiced? I don't know. I just feel that way. Why is there a green apple? A red apple?"

"How far does this prejudice carry? How does it affect your dealings, your existence with the blacks?" asked Nicholas.

"I won't live in a black neighborhood, if I were still out there in the upper world, understand what I'm saying?"

"Yes, go on."

"I won't let my kids go to a black school, date black kids, marry black kids. But I don't mind working with blacks, being friends with them. In that respect I don't see any difference between blacks and whites."

Nicholas wondered how much of what he just heard from this one white American held true for the rest of white America. He believed every word Edward spoke. The man had no reason to be dishonest about any of it, to hide or disguise anything from anybody.

"Now, tell me about this fight," said Edward next, sucking on the cigarette. "Did anybody get killed?"

"Almost. The black guy finally let it all out on this white guy and just about killed him. And then another white guy got in the fight and the black guy wiped him out too. That's when I stepped in to calm him down."

Nicholas told Edward the essential details and background of the incident, focusing on the racial issue in it and how it affected some of the ideas and beliefs he had about America and its people. After he finished, Edward scowled at him, saying:

"Hey, where've you been? That's America today. That happens everyday. You shouldn't let it rattle you so much. You haven't seen the worst of this racial hatred. But you shouldn't have to. You should just learn to accept it as part of the American society. The same thing with everything else that makes it all up, good and bad: baseball and football, crime, Hollywood, divorce, bums like me, immigrants like you, hot dogs and greasy hamburgers, Disneyland. You follow?"

Nicholas was staring at the homeless man as he listened. He didn't figure to get something like that from the bum. He expected a response that perhaps connected more with Edward McKenny's current personal role or place in society, not such an encompassing pronouncement on the culture and the socio-economic condition of America.

He almost forgot that whatever Edward said and how he said it shouldn't matter all that much. He wasn't supposed to care. He just wanted to open up. Uncork. Now, he realized he couldn't have done it with any white American in the upper world, even some Rhode Scholar out there, and made more sense out of it than it did with Edward.

But now, with what Edward said about America, he must re-evaluate his own view of it. Though he wasn't about to toss out the beliefs he had accumulated through twenty years of living in America, maybe it would be wise to look into them now. Also, give a second thought to many of the things he had written Emil through the years.

Could this street dweller, this materially impoverished man be right about America today? Is racial hatred as much an identity of this country as baseball and Disneyland? Does it remain so?

Is divorce and homelessness as much the way of the American society as hot dogs and mom's apple pie?

Should one take calmly to seeing a black man try to spill a white man's brains out, and vice versa, on any given day in America?

Are these part of that process? A means to an end? Or are these the end? The result of that process?

Hey, where've you been? That's America today!
No!

There will be many more hurts, brutalities and hatreds. And fights. And brain spilling. More bums like you, Edward, on the streets of America. But America will persist. America will survive. Human dignity will...

"You know what I might suggest," Edward said in a measured, knowing voice. "If you want to learn to accept the good and the bad in our society, this American society, and be a part of it, you're going to have to let go of the way things were in the old country. You're not there. You're here, man. That's a different culture over there. A different way of life, you know that. You can't force one way into another." He paused to size up, with his face now partly obscured by the night shadow of the blanket over his head, how Nicholas was taking it. Nicholas had turned up his fur-lined winter coat collar and pulled his head down so that his neck disappeared into his body. He brought the vodka to his lips and emptied the cup in one quick motion. Edward gently offered to pour another round but Nicholas declined. "I guess maybe I better shutup. None of my goddamn business."

"I don't care. Like I said, you can say anything you want." Nicholas felt that Edward was a little straightforward with his suggestion, but he wanted to hear the rest of what the bum had to say to him about his apparent difficulty taking in the present-day American culture.

"I don't mean to butt in to your personal ideas and beliefs. That's your business. But maybe I could point out some things about this good and cruel society we all have to put up with, the culture it has created which I as a native can understand why some people, especially those who weren't born and raised in it, can't quite follow."

"You're saying some people are too dumb to know how to live in America, isn't that right?"

"If you want to put it that way. I might point out - too pure and innocent, instead."

And they don't fit in, Nicholas thought to himself instead of saying to Edward, at the same time thinking of Haj Fujiwara. He wanted to tell Edward about the Japanese-American who was giving up on this good and cruel society, but changed his mind.

Nicholas was suddenly feeling self-conscious that perhaps Edward McKenny could see through him more than he thought the bum did. He even began to suspect, now feeling defensive about it at the same time, that Edward saw things about him that he was not even aware of in himself.

He shifted his rear end to a new position in the bum-bag and jabbed at Edward: "You know, for an ordinary bum, you certainly do a lot of pointing out to people. But, again, I don't give a shit. Go ahead. Do all the pointing out you want."

Edward regarded Nicholas carefully behind the rising smoke as he drew the last three puffs out of the cigarette before flicking it away expertly in a perfect trajectory on to the grass some twenty feet away.

"People who come to live in this country from another have a handful to learn about America," he said with a sureness in his voice that brought Nicholas to a disbelief that after twenty years here, he must now listen to a social derelict about living in America. "First, they must understand that there is a culture that's at work here. An American culture, which resulted mostly from a lifestyle of materialism that developed here and is unique here in America. It is a culture whose only tradition is the process of change it undergoes constantly. But nevertheless it is a culture. One that must be understood and learned for it could either make you rich and happy real quick or it could kill you, if not just destroy your dreams and your precious ideas, just as quick."

"What are you - a social archeologist? If there is such a thing. Or a sociology professor at what - Lafayette Park University?"

"I'll tell you what I am, and this should help your understanding of America," Edward jabbed back, ignoring Nicholas' insult altogether. "I am a part of this culture, a vital part, just as much as you are and everybody else is out there in your upper world. Even those at the top, and especially those at the top. You know why? Because in order to have a top, you must have a bottom. And that is the nature of this culture. It is based upon both success and failure. Somebody has to be poor so that somebody can be rich. We can't all be winners. Somebody has to be a loser. I know that may sound simple enough to understand, but do you?"

"Don't talk to me like I'm stupid. Gimme some of that vodka, please," Nicholas averted his eyes from the shadow under the blanket as he spoke and held out his cup. He resented the idea of backing off, but that was what Edward had him doing. Edward's hand came out of the blanket with the bottle and poured him half a cup which he eagerly sipped in an instant. "Divorce, kids from broken families growing up into adults with fucked up values in their heads," Edward went on with total self-reliance, reciting more than conversing, "selfish people, men and women alike, trying to beat each other out of a position of advantage at home, at work and everywhere else, constantly. Those who get the upper hand rise in power and reap more and more success. Those who lose out sink into destruction or just float and wander aimlessly. Bums or people dressed and living like regular respectable people but living empty, meaningless lives. Pseudo-bums, but bums just the same. Those are what we have in this American culture. It's good, and it's bad. It could be ruthless, and it could be benevolent."

No, you bum, you loser, it's not exactly like that here in America, Nicholas thought to himself still backed off and unable to come forth. The bad part of it is bad, he thought, but it's better than what you're saying.

"The next time you see a white man grind down a black man or a black man clobber a white man, don't be shocked," Edward went on saying. "That's part of the culture. Children who don't give a shit about their parents especially when the parents are old and parents who don't give a shit about their kids even when they run away from home and turn into prostitutes, peddling their bodies on the streets - these are all part of the scene. The family is weak in this culture. So is marriage and every other kind of human relationship.

"On the other hand, the next time you see someone make a few million before the age of thirty, don't be too amazed. But more important, don't think you're a failure if you happened to be over thirty and you're not a millionaire."

That one hit hard on Nicholas somewhat. He remembered the thought he had one time not long ago upon learning of a twenty-two year old star athlete buying his fiancée a two-hundred thousand dollar engagement ring. It's disgusting to know of anyone so young, he had thought, being in a position like that in life while millions of poor slobs like me have to put up with all kinds of shit working in an office for some working class wage day in and day out. It's not only disgusting. It's personally insulting, this unequal distribution of wealth in our society.

He raised his eyes at Edward, finally deciding to pull himself out of his slump and let the bum have a piece of his own mind. Listening to Edward, he decided, one must understand where Edward McKenny was coming from: was he echoing a man's bitterness for his life's misfortunes or was he making a true personal observation of the life and culture of America out of those misfortunes along with his experiences in his other life prior to his descent to the bottom of society?

Nicholas didn't waste a moment to try and find out.

"You said a lot of things which are bad and which are mostly true about this country," he said with an undertone of cunning in his voice. "And I agree to just about all of them."

"You want to hear more?" asked Edward, lighting up another cigarette, illuminating his face under the blanket. He didn't favor Nicholas even with a short glance as he spoke. He was looking at the fire, squinting from the smoke he created, a man sure of himself with the knowledge he possessed and would be kind to share with someone such as a naturalized American to help him understand life in America a little better.

"I'm sure there's plenty more you can tell me. Or *point* out to me," Nicholas shot back. "But there's something you mustn't forget, and especially here in the United States: that there are always at least two sides to everything. And sometimes more. You have your say about this country and its culture. So do I, and so does everyone else. Some of us might have the same ideas about it, and some of us might not. You know what I think? I think you really don't believe a lot of those bad things you said about America. And even if you think they're true, the reason you talked about them was not really just to bad-mouth America but because you wish they wouldn't be true, hoping at the same time that things would get better."

Now it was Edward who shuffled his rear end and Nicholas didn't think it was because the manhole cover he was sitting on was getting too hot. "I'm only trying to help you get adjusted some more to the culture," Edward said, steady as he took a drag on the cigarette, inhaled slow and intense, and blew it out towards Nicholas. "You seemed a little perturbed by what you experienced today."

He did it again - made another hit, thought Nicholas, and the bum didn't even know, hadn't the foggiest idea, of his other experience of the day, at lunch time with Haj Fujiwara. He felt glad he had decided not to tell him about it and particularly the fact that it did perturb him to a degree that for a moment or two during the day he actually tried to justify in his mind his remaining in America, his existence here and conversely, an imagined decision to return to the old country like Haj Fujiwara had decided to do.

But what was he doing allowing Edward to corner him again? He was supposed to be defending his better ideas and beliefs about America against the bitterness that's poisoning the mind, what's left of it, of this one American and causing him to make those dark observations of the country and its culture.

"You are right, Edward," he said in a calculating voice. "I was - I am perturbed by that experience of racial violence I saw today. And you know why? Because I haven't given up on America and the idea behind the *making* of America. I still care and will continue to care what happens to our society. That's where you and I differ, at least for what I've seen of you and heard from you so far. However, I think we really do not - differ. I think you care, like I do. Deep down inside I think you do. You just don't want to admit it to yourself, much less to anybody else. And you even try to make yourself believe you don't give a shit. And you're doing the same thing to me. But you don't fool me."

Edward sucked on his cigarette pensively, eyes intent on Nicholas. "What the hell are you talking about?" he uttered under his breath that was thick with the carcinogenic smoke.

"You know what I'm talking about," chided Nicholas. "Moreover, you really don't want to be out here. At first you might have wanted to. What better way is there to blunt a bad turn in one's life than by giving up on life itself and being free of all cares? But now you see things differently since the pain has subsided. You're still alive... "

"Shutup! You don't know what you're talking about!"

"And life has to go on. Now you want to get out of here and go back to the upper world, but you're too stubborn to admit it, let alone make the effort. You can do it to. I know you can, if you could just get over this stupid grudge against the world. Who hasn't got one? Everybody has one. Some people have more, but even so, when they're down on their luck and down on their ass, they get up somehow, they find a way, and get back up on their feet." Nicholas raised the cup of vodka to his lips and emptied it.

"Maybe I shouldn't have you drinking that stuff," Edward said, peering at Nicholas with a pair of mocking eyes. "You start talking funny, and you can't hear either. You haven't heard one word I said about America."

"I'm cold," Nicholas complained, wrapping his arms around his body. "Shit, how could you live out here? Listen, do yourself a favor as well as me and the rest of society. Give one of your kids in Philadelphia, or Detroit or wherever they are, a call. They'll come and get you out of the streets. They will. I'm sure they will. I know they will."

Edward tensed. He straightened his legs out from under the blanket, leaned towards Nicholas with hands posted on each side of him on the ground ready to spring himself up to his feet.

"You know! You know! What the hell do you know?" he yelled at Nicholas. "You don't know my kids or any of my family. You don't know who they are. What kind of people they are. Being blood relatives don't mean shit anymore. Maybe where you came from. Not here, not in this stinkin' society!" He stood up briskly, revealing the loose overcoat and baggy pants under the blanket. Nicholas imagined the grime and the smell of it on Edward's body. "And I was right. You haven't heard one word I've said about America. I said America has it's own culture and part of it is me and all the other bums you see on the streets of Washington and all over the goddamn country; and broken families and lost children and blood relatives who don't give a damn about one another. That's my culture and the culture of this country, and if you can't accept that, leave it alone. Don't try to change it. Don't force your way upon me!" He turned and stepped away from Nicholas, breathing heavily and turning his head from side to side in a great inner turmoil.

"That's not true and you know so! America is not all like that -" Nicholas was half yelling at Edward and was about to heave himself up to his feet also from his seat in the bum-sack when the string that held it together broke, some of its contents spilling between his legs. Something slid out of the pieces of clothing that came out. It was a small spiral-bound folder about four by six inches. Nicholas picked it up and opened it indiscriminately at about the middle of the half-inch thickness. He saw that it was actually a picture album as he found himself looking at a picture, on the left page, of a man in a suit he recognized immediately as Edward McKenny standing between a younger man and a woman in their mid- to late-twenties, he estimated. Edward's children.

On the right page was the picture of a man with a benevolent and very dignified look in his eyes and a half smile at the corners of his mouth. On the vertical white-edge border at the right side of the picture, Nicholas read 'Matthew McKenny, Philadelphia', followed by the year the picture was taken. Seven years ago. At the bottom, handwritten on the album page was 'Big brother Matt.'

He was very quick to bury the album among the spilled clothing when Edward turned back to him, saying:

"It's easy for you to say that, and even believe it: that it's not all like that here. Because you know another culture. You know different."

"Forget about culture! Forget about society and all that shit!" Nicholas yelled angrily, jumping up to his feet. "People are people no matter where they come from and who they are. We all think, feel, eat, drink, shit and screw. We all do the same things and we all need the same things in life no matter what country you live in, good or bad. But you and I know that America is not all that bad and you didn't listen either to what I said about everything having two sides to it especially here in America. Don't be too one-sided. Look at the good side of America too. It's not that hard to see if you just choose to look at it. You don't even have to look for it. Forget your past if it serves you no useful purpose. Learn what you can from it and let it go, man. Don't let it beat you down to the ground more than it already has. Get off your ass and make yourself part of what's good about this country and not what's bad about it! Are you listening to me?"

"Shutup!" Edward McKenny screamed, half-turning his head over his shoulder towards Nicholas. "Get outa here!"

"I am! I am getting out of here! Out of this cold and discomfort and into my condo in Alexandria and enjoy the comfort and the good life America has to offer which you can have too if you just stop being stupid and stop punishing yourself!" Nicholas began to walk away.

"Get the fuck out of here! Leave me alone!"

Nicholas was already stepping out of the park grounds and on to the street sidewalk heading for his car a block away and he could still hear the homeless man calling out to him: "Go on! Get outa here! I don't need you! I don't need anybody!"

Edward McKenny's voice rose in the winter twilight shaking in mixed emotions of anger, self-pity and supplication. Hearing it, Nicholas knew as he continued to walk away that they hadn't heard the last of one another.

📖 10 📖

OPERATION SUNRISE

He took a long deep breath and sat in the car for a few seconds after pulling in to a space in front of the apartment building. The night had fallen but it wasn't a dark night. There were still streaks of light above and the sky was bright and clear.

Some day this had been, he thought to himself during those seconds he sat in the car, letting his arms and shoulders just hang effortlessly for a while, glad to be out of that Monday evening rush hour too.

But this day wasn't over yet. In fact, the next hour from the moment he opened the mail would begin a succession of events he never imagined he'd be a part of.

He knew something was up the moment he took Emil's letter out of the mail and felt the bulk of it bulging in the envelope. It didn't look like it had been tampered with but even if it had been, he thought, there wouldn't be much sense in speculating on it at the moment. He just wanted to tear it open, dive into it to find out what the situation was with Emil and the old country and then, depending on what Emil had written, do the speculating on what if the letter had been tampered with.

He tore the envelope open and immersed himself in it. A few minutes later, with the last page of the letter still in his hands, he shot to his feet, staring in space but his mind racing to put together pieces of events and information from the most recent time to as far back in the past as seemed relevant to what he just learned from the letter.

His main concern was the safety of everyone in the family and because of this, the first thing he recalled was his conversation with his mother on his last telephone call. Did she know? Did father share his political persuasion with her and if he did, to what extent?

What danger did any of them realistically face now, and how much more would they should the government in the old country and its brutal intelligence service, the NIS, find out?

Next, he thought about those mysterious dead phone calls that started last week. It happened again twice this morning before he left for work. He picked up the phone and after a very short 'hello', he didn't say anything else and just waited for any kind of sound to come from the other end. Absolutely nothing other than the void in the open line until it clicked and the dial tone came on.

A much bigger question in his mind now, bigger than all the others that all of a sudden were crowding inside his skull was how important, how big a figure was his father in the rebellion? In the freedom movement?

He must not waste any more time than he had. He may not be in a position this very moment to lose any time to reach his father. According to Emil in the letter, his father expected him to call as soon as he received the letter, or his father would call instead ten days from the date in the letter. It had been nine days from that date.

It was a few minutes before seven o'clock. Three hours before that, he thought, out there as he listened to his parents' telephone ring in their house in Brentwood Park, California. His father, he knew, usually came home from work a little after four. But there's always a chance that today he might be home a little early.

He was. After the third ring, Domingo Gabriel, a man bearing a physiognomy as near a model Eurasian as anyone can imagine, picked up the telephone in his study. He carried so many strong features beginning with his broad and perfectly horizontal shoulders, then the square Slavic jaws, the thick brown hair and the gold-tan complexion, all belying the fact that he was sixty years of age.

The first thing his son told him over the phone was that he had just read Emil's letter. He said that he understood and before Nicholas could say another thing, he gave Nicholas another number to call five minutes after they hung up, and a password to identify himself with to a switchboard operator who will answer the call. He hung up and immediately opened a safe in the opposite wall of the study to take out another telephone with which he placed a call that went through a private circuit that connected to Langley, Virginia, with the same switchboard through which Nicholas' call would be coming in.

He identified himself to the switchboard and gave the operator Nicholas' password.

Everything had happened so fast in the last four days. But, hopefully, after twenty years of working patiently and oftentimes dangerously with other expatriates against that evil man who occupied the seat of power in the old country, everything that was now happening would finally put an end to that reign of greed and oppression.

Jack Dodson, the latest man - a special field agent from Langley, or should he say his current friend from Virginia (there had been a couple of others assigned over the past year and a half), had finally admitted with permission from his superiors that the CIA had a mole in high place in the NIS. It was this mole, Jack Dodson disclosed, the number one deputy director of the intelligence service, who got the message through to Langley five days ago that NIS agents had been unleashed to go after certain expatriates in the west coast and in Washington after the courier route to Hong Kong was discovered and the last vital dispatch intercepted.

Jack Dodson got in touch with Domingo Gabriel immediately the following day. In less than twenty-four hours, the CIA agent had installed the safe and the telephone line, wired the house and Domingo Gabriel himself and put both under protective surveillance. Another agent was fielded to cover Nicholas in Washington, Jack Dodson assured Domingo Gabriel, together with another man, a former agent recently back from a foreign assignment in the Middle East, who agreed to be re-activated for the job as a temporary assignment.

This potentially catastrophic development revealed by the American intelligence happening at the same time with a number of other events such as the arrival of Cesar Ibarra, the number one opposition leader, from Paris three days ago and the continuing progress of three major arms shipment operations in Europe and the Middle East via central and south America had put Domingo Gabriel's life in a tailspin.

Most of the payments for those arms which were now in boats docked in Costa Rica and Ecuador waiting to be transported to the old country, were halted with the interception of the courier dispatch to Hong Kong. But Domingo Gabriel whose duty it was, among other things he did for the freedom movement, to monitor and coordinate the shipments was informed just two days ago by Daniel de Mesa, the opposition leader in North America, that certain financial sources had covered the loss, funds had been transferred to the opposition accounts in Europe and the Caribbean and that he can go ahead and remit payments for the arms and proceed with shipment schedules. However, there were some adjustments that had to be made not only to the arms shipments but the entire Operation Sunrise.

Sunrise was a plan conceived by the united opposition, finally agreed upon with rebels at home after several years of fund raising and many months of careful research and intelligence works. The operation, with the objective of toppling the government the quickest way possible, was in three stages: first, the rebels would launch beginning a certain date in December simultaneous major assaults, quick hit-and-run sabotage strikes on important government military installations nationwide but mostly within a hundred kilometer radius of the capital; get to their nerves steadily; also, put several of the government-controlled TV and radio stations out of operation and at the same time intensify propaganda warfare over the airwaves and by airdrops at night in the rural areas and as close as possible to the capital region. This was to last a whole week. Thereafter, the second stage would begin with the arrival of the first arms shipment on the west coast of the island country and the second, the same day, on the east coast. The entire rebel forces including the flocks of new citizen recruits would be handed the new arms and trained on them intensively in three days.

This second stage of the operation would be done mostly inside the rebel-held regions in the central west coast and the southeast, an area of the country now totally governed by the rebels and from which they impose economic and ideological dominance throughout all the provinces of the southern half of the country. After the three-day re-armament and training period, the regional commanders would lead their forces out of the woods and the jungles, down from the hills and the mountain ranges and begin the first day of the full scale revolution.

It would be a concerted push northward practically starting right from the 20th Parallel, a line one could almost visualize running across the rich agricultural and dairy lands of the central plains provinces from the Pacific Ocean right through to the Philippine Sea. Then the drive would converge, by most conservative estimates - within a week, around the capital and hold it captive with plenty of men and materiel to spare for as long as it might take the dictator government to decide to surrender.

Hopefully, around the last half of the second stage, many of the government forces would have been persuaded to swing to the rebel side to prevent more bloodshed than was necessary especially among the civilian population. But as a measure to firm up the revolution anyway, the third stage of Operation Sunrise would begin around this time with the arrival of the third arms shipment together with Cesar Ibarra and a contingent of leaders of the provisional government who together with the regional and local leaders of the freedom movement would march to the capital to demand the president's surrender.

Operation Sunrise, in a nutshell. So everyone in the freedom movement at home and abroad had hoped to see happen not only in words and in top secret papers but in history books later on.

As far as Domingo Gabriel could foresee, other than the hazard he and his family and others in the opposition now faced because of the snag with the courier dispatch to Hong Kong, there was only one other way Sunrise may have been jeopardized. And this was in the change of the arms shipment dates. The whole operation might have slid weeks not only because of the undetermined length of delay but because of difficulties in communication with the rebels in the old country. Through data gathered by the government in the dispatch to Hong Kong, rebel communication lines were found and cut off. Fortunately, they were quickly re-established with the installation high in a mountain province controlled by the rebels, of a satellite link to the western hemisphere which became operational three days ago. Through it on its first day of operation the following day, Domingo Gabriel was able to contain the delay in the launching of Operation Sunrise to within two days.

Payment for the arms were remitted, and then within minutes, Domingo Gabriel got on the satellite line to the rebels in the mountains in the old country to tell them of the two-day delay in the launching of the first stage of the operation which would now be on the Wednesday of the week before Christmas.

Two days from now, Domingo Gabriel was thinking as he watched the time on the clock over the wall panel of the study. Nearing four minutes gone since he and Nicholas hung up. A few more seconds, the phone rang.

Aware that Nicholas' head must be overflowing with questions to ask from Emil's letter, Domingo Gabriel decided it would make it easier for both of them if he took the lead in the phone conversation. The first thing he told his son as calmly but as boldly as he could was that the NIS knew everything, that they read Emil's letter which was intercepted together with the courier dispatch to Hong Kong and later re-sealed and put back in the mail.

Next, he told Nicholas about the CIA mole inside the NIS, a man known by the cover name of Bobby Kay because everyone in the intelligence ranks of the freedom movement thought he looked like Robert F. Kennedy, and to whom they and many other people of the opposition in the United States and Canada owed their safety, some quite possibly their lives.

"Listen, Nicholas," Domingo Gabriel pressed on, keeping his calm, when Nicholas tried to interrupt in a voice thick with apprehension, "I know it isn't fair that you and the rest of the family should get caught in all these -"

"Father, forget about that now. And don't worry about me," Nicholas interjected, talking rapidly but very soundly. "I want to know about mother and Melissa and her family."

"They are fine. They're safe, and so am I. We, in the opposition have a security system in operation here together with... the local system. The same thing over there in Washington. There are three men there who know about you, besides those the NIS might have sent out to track you down. Two of them are CIA men. I was told by the one I have here they've been on to you for the last four days. They got you covered and should be making contact with you any time now, if they haven't already tried. But they should be in the clear. The U.S. can not get involved, you understand."

"Yes, I understand."

"The third man is one of the most vital intelligence workers the opposition has in Washington. He's from the old country, not an American. He wouldn't give up his homeland citizenship and plans to go back. He's got himself and one or two other men taking turns keeping an eye on you, he told us, together with the two CIA men. His name is Fausto Cristobal. He's a good man. A trusted friend of mine."

His father then proceeded to tell Nicholas about Operation Sunrise, filling him in on the dates and sequence of events that were to take place through the rest of December and the weeks in January but hopefully, he said, no later than the month of January. Next, he told him about the latest contact via satellite with the rebels and the bit of news from them about Emil going underground with Joseph Livingston and joining the ranks of the armed freedom fighters.

Their conversation decelerated gradually as pressing questions were given more thoughtful answers. Then Nicholas came up with the question that halted the conversation completely for a brief period until his father decided on how to tell him the reason they left the old country, twenty years ago.

"For economic reasons, Nicholas, which your mother agreed with. You can ask her. She wanted to come to America more than I did, as a matter of fact. For my part then, I wanted to leave the old country, more than I wanted to come to America, just as much for political reasons. When Guillermo Tobias Sakai became president, and even before that when he and his party were rising in power, I saw what was happening, and what would happen to the country in the years to come."

"And all these years we've been in America," Nicholas interposed, his mind leaping between his memories of their lives in Michigan, Washington, California. "You've been working with the opposition to bring him down."

"If and when I'm in a position to help, and only after my obligation to my family."

"Did mother know?"

"Yes. She did all along. In fact, she helped too. Son," said Domingo Gabriel, sensing a feeling of uneasiness building up between them, "I realize what you might be thinking about this because I didn't want to complicate your lives with things you don't need to worry about. I wanted you and your sister, the two of you at least, to start a fresh life here in America. I hated the thought of uprooting ourselves from our homeland when I decided to do so but the idea of just leaving, cutting off all ties and not doing anything at all -"

"Father," Nicholas interrupted in a tone of voice that demanded to be listened to, "you don't need to explain yourself, what you've done, to me. I feel proud of what you've done and what you continue to do. I'm proud of you. And you make me feel proud of myself too. You and mother both. But now, if I must have a reason to be really proud of myself, I must become part of what I'm being proud of."

"But you are, Nicholas," Domingo Gabriel said, relieved at the reaction of his son but at the same time concerned about what Nicholas had up next. "You are a part of it. I'm your father."

"I'm going there, father," Nicholas declared, his mind already made up, "to California. You must let me be a part of this."

That was something Domingo Gabriel had not given a moment's thought, and couldn't possibly have in the acceleration of events through the last five days. Delight at his son's approval of his work for the rebellion quickly changed to worry. He couldn't let Nicholas face more risk, deliberately or any other way, than he already did, the same with the rest of the family.

"Son," he said with difficulty, "I don't want anyone else in the family involved in this. I can't afford to risk any more than I already have. I'm under a lot of pressure right now, taking on a lot of responsibilities I had not expected which just fell on me one after another all within the past week. And that's why I hadn't even been able to get in touch with you which I should have done five days ago since this whole thing started building up. Thanks to our supporters over there at Langley, Virginia, though, and Fausto Cristobal, for protecting you. I know they'll make sure you're safe."

"If I'm going to be in a dangerous position here anyway where I would need all these protection, I might as well be in a similar situation where I could be of some use, to you, or to the cause. At least let me be there. Let me be with mother and Melissa."

Domingo Gabriel's mind raced through that for a moment. But what could Nicholas do here? His mother and sister were well protected. The opposition had seen to that. There's no reason to disrupt anyone else's life in the family more than it already had been. Besides, they, the NIS and the government behind it - wouldn't really dare kill any of them. They're all American citizens. They are Americans.

No small country anywhere in the world sends killer agents into the United States and kills Americans and gets away with it. If the old country did, they could - they would - have a war on their hands. The American president would have to take measures which would most likely be supported by the people and the Congress.

The killings of some of the opposition leaders in the past were a different story. The victims were not American citizens. In fact, none of them had any status in America. They were all carrying visitors' visas. No. They wouldn't dare touch any of them. Domingo Gabriel thought it over a few times, each time trying to convince himself that the dispatch Jack Dodson, his CIA guardian, had received from the mole in the NIS was not correctly decoded or not accurately interpreted.

Two people of the opposition in southern California were to be put under control - taken by NIS agents, or kidnapped, according to the CIA interpretation of the dispatch - pumped of as much information as could be had from them and then 'terminated'. A second dispatch from the mole said the same thing about one other opposition member in Washington, D.C. A list of names were provided but, unfortunately, the mole was unable to identify those who were singled out for 'control and termination'.

If those dispatches were saying what they were according to Jack Dodson and the analysts at Langley, he couldn't be one of those in the list who were targeted. So his name, last name only, was in it which possibly referred to him only in southern California and not Nicholas in Washington, D.C. too. They wouldn't do anything to Nicholas. He had absolutely nothing to do with the opposition and the rebellion in the old country other than being a friend of Emil, and being his son. And again, they wouldn't dare touch him. He is an American.

But, and this was one big but in his head that wouldn't go away - did any of that make any difference to those demented officials in the old country, much less to the field agents they had out in the United States and other parts of the world? Indeed, the U.S. president and Congress might send their armed forces out to avenge the killing of their citizens in America. But in the meantime, he and Nicholas and the rest of them could wind up quite dead for good.

"Stay put for a few days," he told his son on the phone, trying to sound as resolute as he could not only to Nicholas but especially to himself. "Don't do anything outside of your daily routine. I will talk to Fausto Cristobal within the hour for an update on their situation there in Washington." He paused quickly to part the drapes slightly and look through the window. They were out there, the two men assigned to protect him, sitting in separate cars parked inconspicuously among a row of others on the other side of the residential street. One was a CIA man who took turns with Jack Dodson, and the other parked four cars away was an opposition man. He let go of the drapes and looked at the wall-clock before speaking again on the phone. "Fausto Cristobal or a Langley man will get in touch with you around eleven o'clock tonight. If not, you can call me back or either one of them any time after at this same number. Two things to put the call through. Take these down."

"Go ahead."

"You need our code names. You'd need one too. Ask for Kingfisher to contact Fausto Cristobal.."

"And the Langley man?"

"Blue Whale. I'm Mount Everest. And you are, from now on, Sparrow."

Domingo Gabriel needed some time to determine what actions would be best for him to take concerning his family. They would depend upon the developments in the next eight or nine days right from this very hour through the launching and duration of the first stage of Operation Sunrise.

Hopefully, sometime during that period, more intelligence would have come in to shed light on the fate of the freedom movement above all, the revolution, and the people of the opposition such as himself and all those many others scattered not only in America but in other parts of the world who had not given up their native citizenship in the hope of being able to go back home someday.

One piece of intelligence everyone was hoping would come in soon related to Bobby Kay's last dispatch which said 'Will try to countermand control-and-terminate order. Will advise, next dispatch'.

"Do it, Bobby," Domingo Gabriel now thought with some desperation, gripping the phone and pressing it hard against his ear. "Call it off. Call off the order to these NIS dogs here in the United States. And please don't get caught. Don't ever get caught, Bobby Kay. You don't know how important you are to a lot of people here in America and back there as well."

Again, before they hung up, he told Nicholas to stay put for a few days and also to listen to whatever Kingfisher and Blue Whale might tell him. "Their words in as far as your welfare is concerned," he said indisputably, "are the same as mine."

One thing he didn't tell Nicholas which he was glad Nicholas didn't think of asking was his plan to go back with Cesar Ibarra together with the rest of the returning leaders of the opposition on the same day the freedom fighters come out of hiding in the second stage of Operation Sunrise to begin the full-scale revolution. They were to arrive there three days later, the same day as the third arms shipment which would mark the beginning of the third stage of Sunrise. And then together with a full complement of the freshly armed rebel forces from the entire southeastern region of the country, they were to march north to the capital for the next seven days to demand the dictatorial government to step down.

A few minutes after he finished talking to Nicholas, the line operator at Langley located Kingfisher for him in a house in Falls Church, Virginia. They talked for over an hour.

☐ 11 ☐

SPARROW AND KINGFISHER

For more than two hours after he talked to his father, Nicholas moved about as if his feet didn't even touch the floor. He felt so disoriented with his new personal life situation he wouldn't know how to identify a point at which he could begin to deal with it.

Somewhere out there on the street right at the moment was a man, maybe two men, within a handgun-shooting range of him, he assumed, staked out in the dark for his protection. The reality of it didn't sink in at once until, slowly, he considered the effort of those who feared enough for his life to give him protection.

The frightening part about it once it had really sunk in was that he could get killed. What if those people who were supposed to be after him got through to him? He wondered what their orders were. Was he to be taken

216

alive or killed? No. Nothing there for anyone to gain - getting him killed. To be held hostage, yes. A hostage to be exchanged for information not from him but from those who cared about him. His father, to be exact, and maybe even those who cared dearly about his father in the ranks of the people working to topple the government in the old country.

He weighed the possibility that perhaps people were over-reacting. He's an American citizen. They wouldn't dare touch him, in America, let alone the fact that outside of being the son of an opposition worker and a close friend of a rebel soldier, he himself had nothing to do with overthrowing the government. This was what made the whole situation so unreal for him and also that, all of a sudden, he was in it. But he understood that those vicious people in the government, ruthless as they had proven themselves to be in the past, would stop at nothing to get to the opposition.

At a quarter of eleven, Fausto Cristobal called. Nicholas picked up the phone and said a 'hello' so mechanically it sounded like a recording at the other end.

"Sparrow?" asked the man.

"Who's calling, please?"

"Kingfisher. How are you, Sparrow? Is everything alright with you?" An unknown voice over a secured telephone line, using code names. It all seemed so strange to Nicholas, and frightful when Fausto Cristobal said further: "If there's anything wrong with your present situation, if you're under duress, just say 'no', quickly."

"I'm doing fine, Kingfisher. There's no one here but me. I'm glad to finally hear from you."

"And I'm delighted to finally get to know you, Nicholas. Please, let me introduce myself properly. I'm

Fausto Cristobal. Your father and I are very good friends."

"Yes. That's what he told me. Would it be possible for us to meet, Mr. Cristobal?"

"I was just getting to that. I talked to your father a little while ago and told him how really sorry I am that I hadn't had the chance to contact you sooner and meet you in person. These last few days had been like a whirlwind for all of us - the opposition workers, here in America as your father probably told you. I realize how anxious you must be since you first learned of what's happening."

"More than you and he can imagine, Mr. Cristobal."

"You may switch to the first name anytime. It's Fausto."

"Thank you... Fausto. Can we get together tonight?"

"I'm afraid not, Nicholas. I can't leave my post at present."

"Tomorrow, then?"

"Yes."

"Name the time and place, at your convenience."

At a few minutes past one in the afternoon the following day, Nicholas drove into the driveway of a split-level brick house in McLean, Virginia, three houses away from Westmoreland Street on a quiet upper-class street with its landscaping and neatly manicured evergreens alongside the concrete sidewalks. Two other cars arrived at the same time, one parking two houses ahead of him on the street, the other two houses back.

Only the man in the back got out of the car and walked up to him quickly after surveying the area routinely for a few seconds.

"Kingfisher Two, sir," the man introduced himself with a courteous smile, extending a hand to Nicholas as they met beside the car on the driveway. He was a tall man, around six-four and very trim in his brown suit, very alert with every move he made especially with his head and hands. He was an American. "K2 for short, sir."

"How do you do. Good to see you, K2." Nicholas made no attempt at all to hide his relief at finally reaching their destination by shaking the man's hand rather vigorously.

Kingfisher Two had called earlier in the morning at work to inform him of their route to the McLean destination for his appointment with Fausto Cristobal. It was a smooth ride throughout except for a couple of times when he imagined a car pulling up alongside of him first on the G.W. Parkway and then again on the Dolley Madison Boulevard, and opening up with a hail of bullets at him.

Inside the house, Fausto Cristobal viewed the men's arrival through the window blinds in the living room. An armed guard stood at the door. He arrived at the house some forty-five minutes earlier.

Fausto Cristobal felt glad to be looking after Nicholas, to be of service personally to Domingo Gabriel, one of the key figures in the events that were about to unfold in the old country. He could not admire that man in California more for the work he had done for the opposition and the quest for freedom in the old country.

Everything Gabriel had done meant something important to a lot of people. But to him, it meant a great deal more. He felt that whatever Gabriel did, if it meant in any way getting back at the tyrants who destroyed his family, murdered his brother who was a duly elected provincial governor, and seized their estates, he would lay his life on the line for the honor of protecting his son Nicholas against any harm.

When he left the country, escaping literally in the dark of night on a bamboo raft that took him to the Batan Islands of the Philippines, he vowed he would go back someday and get even. That was eight years ago. Now in his early fifties, the vow he had made remained part of his daily life, a fire that kept burning within him and will not be extinguished.

As a resident in the United States with a status of a political refugee, he had been working continuously with the opposition movements in New York, Washington and the west coast since he came seven years ago.

"Anybody touches this man does so," he now thought, looking at Nicholas closely just before he left the window to meet him at the door, "over my dead body."

Fausto Cristobal's greeting was happy, enthusiastic, and so was Nicholas', albeit measured. But Fausto understood fully. The poor man was completely innocent of what was going on for which he was now being personally jeopardized. The least anybody could do to be fair to him was answer the few questions he might like answered at present.

Thus, quickly then, he took him to a spacious reading room which opened to a veranda at the back of the house where they had a drink and unwound to each other quickly. Most of what Fausto told Nicholas was about Operation Sunrise which was almost a repeat of what he was told by his father. But Fausto Cristobal had other things to speak of which he was only too glad to share with Nicholas, such as the opposition network and activities in the east coast, from Washington to New York and Boston, his part in it, the Americans' part in it specifically that of the CIA.

"A few hours from now would be daybreak in the old country," Fausto said as he was coming back to face

Nicholas from the liquor cabinet with the refills. "Operation Sunrise begins. I wish I could be there now. Right now. I can't wait. Two more weeks."

"What do you mean two more weeks?" asked Nicholas.

"That's when we land the provisional government. Cesar Ibarra and all the other leaders of the freedom movement from abroad. The third stage of Sunrise. I'll be with them. We leave Monday after next, arriving there three days later. New Year's day, their time. Nothing can stop us now unless somehow the government managed to triple the armed forces and their arms supply. Again, thanks to all the people, such as your father, who have worked for years to make all these coming events finally happen. He's going to stand tall among many others next to our new head of state in the palace once we get there. I hope to be right there with him."

Nicholas rose to his feet gradually, drink in hand and gazing at Fausto meticulously.

"Wait... wait a second," he stammered. "Are you saying my father is going with you? He's going back too?"

"Yes," Fausto replied summarily. "Didn't he tell you?"

"No," Nicholas snapped, causing Fausto to ease back in his seat near the fireplace, looking up uncertainly at Nicholas. "Tell me, what else is going on, Kingfisher?" Nicholas shifted gear suddenly, turning a puzzled look of sarcasm.

Fausto Cristobal - Kingfisher, picked up on it quickly. "Please, listen to me, Nicholas," he said, rising to his feet too, gesturing with one hand to calm Nicholas down. "I had a long talk with your father last night -"

"So did I," Nicholas cut in irascibly. "But apparently not as long as you did. I'd like to talk to him on the phone right now, please."

"Please, listen to me first," Fausto pleaded, cordially, which stayed Nicholas. "First of all, if you're concerned about the safety of your father going back, I have to admit there are some minor risks, but they are no more than the ones we all face here now. It's not going to be like he's going there to fight and get shot at. No. He'll be there with Cesar Ibarra and all the other important opposition leaders as a figurehead, to represent the will of the people. He would be one of the returning heroes of our country."

"Aren't you forgetting something? He's an American citizen. He is an American."

"I know that, Sparrow. And that's exactly what I want to tell you about next. Everything he's done and is about to do are all his own choice. Nobody is asking him, or forcing him, to do anything. If he wants to be one of us, be with us, he's certainly most welcome. As far as I'm concerned, he's still as much a citizen of the homeland as I am or anybody living back there is."

Nicholas stared at Fausto intensely for a few moments, then his eyes turned blank as he slowly turned away and walked toward the glass sliding doors opening to the veranda. Out at the far end of the veranda overlooking part of the street on the side of the house stood dutifully one of Fausto's armed bodyguards.

All these were entirely new to him. It was like knowing his own father over again or for the first time.

Since the night before, he had been putting together this part of his father, piece by piece, and now with the few more pieces he gathered from Fausto Cristobal, he had a better picture of the man. And he also had a better understanding of how different they were from each other in ways that mattered the most as far as the old country was concerned.

His father never left the old country. It had always been his homeland. Not America. He said it himself last night: he hated to uproot them and cut off all ties. He didn't want to leave but he had to because he wanted to give them, his family, a decent and comfortable life in America or possibly anywhere he could do so, materially and in other ways as well, and keep them free from an oppressed society and the limitations it could impose upon the children's lives as they were growing up. That's what he wanted to do, and that's what he had done.

Now his children had lived in America more than they had in the old country. They had become Americans. And now he had grandchildren too who are native-born Americans, true American citizens. His children and grandchildren now had more roots in America than in the old country. And this, Nicholas thought, is how different he and his father are from each other.

But, now Nicholas asked himself, how true is it really that he had less ties to the old country and is less rooted there now than here in America? How does he really feel deep inside?

Does he really feel like an American? Does he feel American more than anything else? More than what he was before he came to America when he was twelve years old?

Once again he thought of Haj Fujiwara and the Filipino man from the Ivy League schools. He also thought of Emil and Emil's family and all the other people he knew and remembered well in the old country from his visit three years ago and even as far back as when he lived there, twenty years ago. He decided that although he now had more roots in America, the old ties to the old country, brief though they may seem in the twelve years of his life there, remained. And when he weighed them against those of his father's, especially those old ties which made up the reason for his father's wanting to go back, he felt a tugging of the old country that would not let go. Yes, he thought to himself, he's an American. But being an American doesn't mean being just an American and nothing else. It could mean being a lot of other things, depending upon one's beginnings, upon how strong the pull is of his native roots on his life in America, on his blood, on his heart.

Yes, they're all Americans. Haj Fujiwara, the Filipino man, Lester Jenkins, Edward McKenny the bum; his father and his two grandchildren. Some of them would want to go back to the ancestral homeland when it's time, some would live and die in America.

Perhaps his father's time to go back had come. But, at the moment, he couldn't just spend time knowing how it came about. He needed to know realistically what happens now. Did his father plan to go back and stay? What if he got hurt? Or killed? Nicholas wasn't really sure if he could trust what Fausto said about landing the provisional government which would simply march to the capital and demand the surrender of the ruling power. That march could very well turn out to be a march of blood and destruction. He felt he needed to know more and decided that he would in any way he could, if it meant going back to the old country himself.

He turned back to Fausto from the glass door, an expression on his face somewhere between anger and pleading.

"What else did my father tell you that he somehow forgot to tell me?" he asked, looking closely at Fausto Cristobal's face.

"We talked about a lot of things that only he and I and a few other people are allowed to know at this time. You must understand this, Nicholas. Right now, communicating information between us in the opposition is a very risky thing. You know very well what happened because of the government interception of that courier dispatch to Hong Kong. I know about that letter you were sent by your friend Emil."

"I'm only asking about what concerns me and my father, and the rest of the family."

Fausto Cristobal fell silent, visibly stung. Seeing this, Nicholas hesitated for a moment and then pulled back a half a step.

"I'm sorry," he apologized. "I didn't mean it that way."

"Not at all," Fausto deprecated.

"Of course I realize how critical everything is right now for everyone. But I just feel that I am not being told enough of what I should know. I'm just as much a part of what's happening as anybody else is in it. I'm just as much at risk now with my own life as you are."

"You're right about that, Nicholas. And it's exactly for that reason your father has asked me personally, which I promised him I would do, to protect you and to try to prevent you from getting involved more that you already are." Fausto fixed a determined eye upon Nicholas, one that spoke of a formidable resolve in the man. "And I intend to keep my promise to your father, if it cost me my own life while I'm here," he added. "The least I could do for all the important contributions he has made for the freedom movement, and for the good of a lot of people including myself and my folks back home."

"Now, there's -" Nicholas stuttered, trying hard not to be intimidated, "there's no reason to be so drastic about this. I most certainly appreciate what you're doing. But could you at least tell me how long is this supposed to go on? And does everybody really expect me to go on with my normal life as if none of this is going on?"

"Yes. You don't do anything. Before you leave here today, you'll know the two men we have out there on the street right now. One of them, K2, you already met. He's the CIA man working the shift today. The other man who drove in front of you coming here is an opposition man. You'll meet him. There's another CIA man working with us. He alternates with K2. You'll meet him probably sometime this week." A furtive smile which baffled Nicholas for a moment fleeted over Fausto's face. "You'll know him when you see him."

Nicholas paced the carpet of the spacious room. Every room in the house was spacious and carpeted, even the split basement rec room below which opened to the thirty-foot pool out back. It never occurred to him to question whose house it was. Probably some sort of a government-run multi-purpose guest house. There was simply no time to spend on such superficiality at the moment.

Nicholas finally halted about a step away from Fausto and looked the man straight in the eye.

He said: "Forget about my father for a minute and what he told you about me."

"I can't do that, Nicholas," Fausto replied firmly. "I just told you a minute ago - I made him a promise."

"Alright, alright, so you did! But will you please listen to what I have to say too? You can't treat me like an object you swore to protect with your life and move about any way you want without expecting any reaction. I'm not an object. I'm a person! Now, let's just you and I talk. I want in."

"What do you mean?"

"I want to be a part of the revolution," he said seriously. "I just decided nothing could be more significant in my life right now than becoming a part of it."

"Stop!" Fausto literally held up a hand as he raised his voice. "You're contradicting yourself. Aren't you forgetting something? You're an American!"

"Dammit, Fausto, quit hedging!"

"Listen to me," Fausto said aloud, "two things you got to understand more than anything else, more than your father, the old country, the revolution. First, there is an NIS order out to kill some people in Los Angeles and here in the D.C. area. Who it is for, we don't know. One of them could be for you or me or for one of the other opposition leaders here. Second, we don't want any implied and certainly not an open involvement of the Americans. You understand that. No complications with any of the superpowers. And this is why we are trying all we could to protect you. If the NIS hit you or any of your family who are all American citizens, the U.S. government is not going to stand for that. Now, the Americans aren't particularly anxious themselves to get involved if they could help it, because if they did, it most certainly means the government of the old country turning to the other powers, China, Russia, for help."

Fausto paused to take a deep breath. He looked tired and showed signs of lack of sleep around his pale eyes and the stress lines on his cheeks.

"And that explains the presence of the CIA," he continued. "They're strictly for preventive measures, not to help us in our efforts to topple the government back home."

Nicholas gave Fausto a ridiculous look. "You really expect anybody to believe that?" he chided. "Including me? C'mon, Kingfisher. What about Bobby Kay back there? What have you got to say about him, and who knows how many other spies they have planted out there?"

"Bobby Kay is not an American. He's an intelligence officer working for the rebels. Look, Nicholas, believe me, we have all the help we need. Do us a favor. Please stay out of it. Just bear with us for the next two or three weeks. Hopefully, by that time we wouldn't have to worry about the NIS any more, and the country's long struggle to depose that dictator government would be coming to a successful end, at not too high a price, let's hope."

📖 12 📖

NIGHTLIGHTS, STARLIGHTS

Three days into the first stage of Operation Sunrise, the number of casualties was coming up much higher than any of the rebel commands had expected in each region. The first stage involved mostly sabotage raids on military supply installations, capturing arms and ammunitions when possible, but avoiding any deliberate engagement with the government forces. The objective was to weaken the government's war resources prior to the all-out revolution to follow shortly.

The rebels succeeded in this with many of their lightning strikes mostly at night and early dawn but not without some cost in human lives. Not just their own but those of the civilian population as well.

Knowing that most of the civilian population particularly those in the rural areas were always ready to

229

come to the aid of the rebels everytime they emerge from the hills and the jungles, the government as usual descended on them with their informers and interrogators and their bribe money. Many rebel sympathizers were turned in and executed immediately. Some rebel raids were not carried out because the military had been informed in advance, and there were some that were carried out anyway in spite of the intelligence leaks, resulting in a terrible devastation on both sides. Those who knew of the coming full-scale revolution, people in the rebel high-commands, hoped it would not come to such an event as a whole, or there might not be anything or anyone left to live for once it's over.

One such person was Commander Juan Vargas Smith of the southeastern regional command. After a number of successful raids he had engineered, he went out himself the night of the second day with a commando party of fifty men on a mission to destroy a training and supply depot located two kilometers from Fort York, a major government foothold which controlled the central plains provinces with several army divisions.

They walked right into a snare where they were immediately surrounded by a whole infantry battalion. A group of well-armed civilian sympathizers from a nearby town showed up to try to help them break out. But it was too late to back out so together, they went ahead with the mission. They destroyed the depot, cut off the power supply line to Fort York, and blew up a large munitions warehouse which lit up the night sky for many kilometers away.

They accomplished what they came for but none of them, save for Commander Juan Vargas Smith and two of his men, managed to escape. All the civilians were killed.

The commander was severely criticized by Gustavo Carreon, the supreme commander of all the rebel forces, who was in the region on his way up north to the capital to coordinate plans with the capital region command, specifically with Commander Utak.

"Your orders do not include taking such high risks," Carreon reprimanded. "The revolution has not begun, yet. It will begin according to plans, and you know what they are. I trust you understand what your orders are, Commander, according to those plans."

When they weren't raiding supply depots or blowing up major transportation roads and railways, the rebels were cutting communication and power lines, at the same time waging a propaganda campaign in small towns and cities by mingling with the population and distributing materials or airing them in mobile radio stations.

By the end of the first week of Operation Sunrise, they had succeeded in putting the government in a state of disarray that practically cut off the capital region from the rest of the country.

The day before the arrival of the first arms shipment on the west coast marking the beginning of the second stage of Operation Sunrise, Commander Utak summoned several of his combat and intelligence officers into his office. This was at the headquarters of the capital region command, in a village within only a hundred kilometers southwest of the capital city limits. For years, the command had enjoyed the advantage of being located inside the capital but since the day Commander Utak had to go underground, it had to be assumed that all command headquarters operations inside the capital had been compromised and must be moved out of the city.

Among those present were Deputy Commander Carlos Yee May, Commander Utak's second in command; Julius

Tanner Ikeda, an intelligence officer, a young man only in his late twenties, one of only a few agents left whose cover had not been blown and was still working on the surface in the capital; and another intelligence officer, one whose cover had been blown, a man even younger - Emilio Stuart Sabater.

Commander Utak held up a piece of paper before him with both hands and read it in silence briefly. The latest satellite transmission on the progress of the arms shipment. Then he said to the men around him at the table: "Everything is on schedule. The first cargo is due at Port Malinaw on the west coast in twelve hours. The convoys just took to sea from Batan Island of the Philippines an hour ago. The second cargo should be arriving at Port Anihan on the east coast three hours later."

Commander Utak turned to Carlos Yee May, his deputy, and Emil, his communication officer, to report on the preparation for the mission the two were to embark upon in a few hours. They were to lead a valued group of munitions specialists, highly paid specialists both domestic and foreign, to the west coast within hours of the arrival of the arms shipment. The group was to conduct the rapid seventy-two hour training of the rebel forces and new civilian recruits on the new arms.

For the third and final time, Carlos Yee May laid out the details of the mission before the commander, on a sketch on the table. The journey was to take them through several provinces, in one of them around Fort Sagrado, the bastion of the government defense stretching from the Malawin Naval Base in the northwest coast of the province to some twenty kilometers inland southeast. Over half of the government's armed forces were fielded and rotated from there. One of the vital objectives of Operation Sunrise, thus, was to contain the bastion, keep it on the defensive early on and later overwhelm it in a major assault from the west, south and the east and force its surrender. There were only two other government defense bases that were of major concern to the revolution: Fort Hiroko, the combined Army and Civil Guard forces which served the dictator government in trying to control the south, and Fort York in the east central part of the country.

Fort Hiroko, as it was at the present stage of Operation Sunrise was almost totally on its own: cut off from the capital and Fort Sagrado, with its land transportation and communication lines disrupted. The rebel leadership were now readying a pitch to the line of command not for a surrender but for a change of sides. Being deep in hostile territory with limited supplies, both sides knew it would be a slow but sure defeat for the military who, given the situation they were in, really had nothing to lose and everything to gain by joining the rebels.

Combined with the military force of Fort Hiroko, the rebel forces which would be those from the entire south and southeast regional commands - newly armed with the second and third arms shipments, would have much less of an undertaking in capturing Fort York on the drive north than they would taking Fort Sagrado.

Satisfied with the details and the contingency plans presented by Carlos Yee May and Emil on their mission, Commander Utak wished them well and turned next to Julius Tanner Ikeda. The undercover agent was just back from the capital to update the commander on the rebel intelligence activities, what's left of it in the city, after Commander Utak went underground.

"The Customs agents and their NIS advisers bought our false lead on the locations of the arms shipments," Julius Ikeda informed his commander. "They're sending navy gunboats and helicopter gunships at least a hundred and fifty kilometers away from the right place."

"Good work. Good work," said the commander, nodding and smiling broadly at the young man, a strong handsome mix of Japanese, northern Chinese, Malay and German blood, one of the common racial compositions of a Silanganese. "Anything on Bobby Kay?"

"Yes, Commander. I received this from him just before I got on the way here today, sir." Julius handed the commander an envelope. In it were two sheets of paper containing information on the progress of the government mobilization in the capital region.

Most of the intelligence report did not contain more than what the rebels had expected in addition to what they already knew. Checkpoints at every major road access to the capital, Civil Guard deployments at every outpost all around the city, armored patrols roving the streets of the suburban areas night and day. A part of the report detailing some of the troop movements from Fort Sagrado out to its field camps in its province and several of the neighboring provinces caused Commander Utak to cast a glance at Emil and Carlos May.

"That much activity we had anticipated, sir," Carlos May told him after he read the report to them. "We have several ways of getting around them."

"We have field guides already waiting for us in every province," Emil explained, "to keep us away from government troops."

"Commander," Julius Ikeda spoke dutifully as he wound up his report a little later, "Bobby Kay also said to inform you that he had succeeded three days ago in transmitting the order to countermand the control-and-terminate order the NIS had on Kingfisher in Washington,

D.C., Mount Everest and Red Eagle, our satellite communication station man in the U.S. west coast."

"And those three were the targets?" asked the commander pensively but with a sigh of relief.

"Yes, sir."

"Thank God. Those are some of our most important people abroad. Without them, we wouldn't be anywhere closer to freedom now than where we were twenty years ago. Mount Everest, especially. I know him only briefly before he left the country. What I wouldn't do to thank that man now for everything he had done for us, for our country."

Over half of the people, just under a hundred of them - armed to their chins with the same deadly weapons of war they specialized in, going on the ten-hour mission to the west coast were foreigners. There were from one of a kind in nationality to as many as over a dozen of a kind. Those of the same nationality spoke to each other in their native tongue, and to others in English. Everybody spoke English in various accents.

This was how Emil initially determined with fairly high accuracy where they came from. The way they communicated with each other. There were at least three men he heard speaking to each other in Portuguese. Brazilians, he knew immediately. The weapons they were carrying as well as a portion of the arms shipment due to arrive, he knew, came from Brazil. There were two he heard distinctly speaking in French and they did tell him they were genuine French from France, the same with the three Englishmen who spoke to him with their genuine British accent.

Most of the other foreigners, he knew with even more certainty, were Americans. There were a couple among them, though, who stepped up to him at one time and made a point of it to identify themselves as Canadians. He smiled at them apologetically and begged their pardon for his inability to distinguish between the two North Americans.

An hour before they were to leave, Emil decided he was ready for the mission and took respite from the long day that it had been with the many activities of preparation for the journey. It was a warm sub-tropical December night with the wind murmuring in the trees, over the grain stalks in the fields and in one's ear with words of what substance one may choose or be inspired in his mind to fill them with.

Standing in a courtyard behind the command headquarters, he was looking directly at the starlit contour of the seven-thousand foot Mount Sibuyas some eight kilometers away. In about an hour and a half, he would be at the foot of that mountain with nearly a hundred other men on their way to play a part in an event that would restore freedom upon the land. This was the substance he put in the words the wind whispered in his ear.

He drank the air which carried the scent of the December harvest-time and cooled his skin as it blew gently. Then a voice came to him from under the acacia tree to his right.

"Beautiful night, isn't it?" it said in a relaxed, easy, almost sleepy tone. One of the Americans, he thought at once and imagined the man stretched in one of the lounge chairs nearby. "I've never seen such a bright night sky. Not anywhere back home, anywhere I've lived in the States. Just look at those stars twinkle... twinkle."

He looked up for a moment to see the near full-moon, a luminous paint of yellow on the southern sky which in turn illuminated a wisp of cloud here and there in between expanses of the field of the quietly pulsating stars in the heavens. When he turned to his right, it wasn't a man sitting in a chair he saw but one perched on the adobe parapet wall surrounding the courtyard, leaning on his back against the acacia tree and smoking a cigarette. The man looked big and strong in his camouflage fatigues, and with a voice so deep and solid and yet so calm and controlled speaking in a regular American accent, Emil thought, like one of those movie actors he was familiar with - Robert Mitchum, Burt Lancaster, the man couldn't be anything but American.

"It's almost like somebody painted it," Emil remarked. "A beautiful picture."

"That's what it is," said the American man, his eyes fixed upon the firmament, one hand keeping the high-powered lightweight submachinegun on his lap, the other busy with the cigarette. He took a drag, inhaled and exhaled contentedly. "I could sit here all night and look at it, be a part of it and not care about anything: if I'm rich or poor, young or old, handsome or ugly. I wish there was a place like this back where I come from."

"Mind if I ask where is that?" Emil turned to the full view of the man who suddenly recognized him.

"Mr. Sabater," he said, leaping to his feet from the top of the parapet wall to direct his full attention to the rebel intelligence officer. "I'm sorry, sir, I didn't recognize you right away -"

"Relax, soldier. Don't worry about it. Tell me, what part of the States are you from?"

"Well, I moved around some, but I'm originally from Pennsylvania."

Emil turned partly to himself, a querulous look on his face. "Let's see," he said, "is that the city or the state?"

The American man thought for a second and then smiled. "That's the state. Philadelphia is the city."

"That's right. I always get those two mixed up."

"Born and raised in a town called Greensburg, not far from Pittsburgh in the southwestern part of the state. Went to high school there and... I've been on the move ever since. Lived in the midwest - Illinois and Indiana. Got married, for a while, divorced later and moved on out west to California."

Emil peered at the man's face in the semi-darkness, only half-turning his head so as not to make it look obvious. Middle-age, he thought, mid- to late-forties. Amazing how a man could describe most of his life in only so many words, he thought. Or is this the way Americans talk in person? And is that a common life story in America?

He forced back into his mind the years of letter-writing between him and Nicholas. The letters from Nicholas, the ones that were the quickest to bring back to mind now because of the many interesting and significant things Nicholas wrote in them about life in America. Those were the closest he ever got to learning about life in America firsthand, talking to an American or someone who would be an American; never a real live native-born American as this war weapons specialist from... Pennsylvania.

He remembered the letters Nicholas had sent him first from Michigan, then Maryland, California and the past few years from Virginia. And, yes, in one of those letters, one he distinctly remembered Nicholas wrote before his family moved from Michigan to Maryland, Nicholas talked about how mobile the American society is and how sad it is in some ways, especially at that time when they themselves were moving, that people don't take roots long enough in a place to make it worthwhile knowing them, let alone becoming close to them.

Emil wondered why is this and could only theorize that that must be a way of life which evolves from a country so large and so rich, with a society that enjoys so much freedom and opportunity even for the most ordinary of its citizens.

As much as he saw how respectful and friendly the man was, he decided that - anxious though he was to learn about the man's life in America especially now that he hadn't heard from Nicholas in a while - he wasn't going to dare the chance of intruding into the man's personal life even if the man might feel obliged to reveal it to him. He wasn't going to ask the man about his family, where they came from.

Were they rich or poor? Were they from the south, maybe, like those people Nicholas wrote him about, who moved to the northern United States for better economic opportunities? Were they immigrants from Europe or first or later generation Americans? And of what descent were they?

It was curious how he fleeted through the telling of his marriage, making it sound as if marriage is just another time segment in one's life (in America, perhaps?) like high school or college. Could it possibly be that way there? He couldn't recall Nicholas ever writing to him about marriage and divorce in America and how such a beginning and end of a time segment in people's lives there actually affect them and the succeeding segments of their lives.

Having lived, having been only in one country and such a small one compared to the United States all his life, he couldn't quite get a handle on the American man's brief description of his life in his country. It would take a considerable amount of time to understand such a life and so he won't ask about it. Should he eventually find his way to America someday, perhaps he would find out for himself. And then maybe he would know if this man's story is a common life story in America, and if so, why?

One thing he could not help asking the man, though, was the question about his present occupation which was what obviously brought him to the country. The man talked about an old friend who was the leader of the American group of the arms specialists going with the training mission.

"Twenty seven years ago, when I was twenty," the man said and Emil was quick to note to himself - the year I was born, "he and I were in an ice hole in Korea and we believed then that that hole was going to be our grave. But we fought our way out of it and made it back with our unit to camp. We re-enlisted when we got back to the States and took up a new military occupational specialty. MOS, we call it. We became combat weapons specialists. I got out of the army before he did. Went to college and majored in math. And that's what I do for a living now - I'm a math teacher at a state college in Orange County in southern California.

"A few years later after his army time, he looked my up and asked if I'd be interested to go in a gun-running adventure with him in Latin America and I said why not. Life was getting too dull. I was newly separated, bored and restless. So I took a hiatus from school and normal life as a whole and got in the business with him."

"And that's what you're here for in our country?" Emil asked. "On a business with your army buddy - as a gun-runner?"

"Not exactly. Not this time," said the American man thoughtfully. They had moved to the edge of the courtyard in slow, leisurely steps while they talked and now they stood at arm's length facing a moonlit view of the land to the west which dipped slowly for two or three kilometers and then leveled somewhat abruptly into a valley that flickered with the night lights of what must be a little town.

"Then, what brought you here to our country?" Emil asked courteously. "I don't imagine you're doing it all as a favor to your friend who should be making a fortune out of this operation."

"No, not at all," said the math teacher curtly. He pointed to the little valley town to Emil and continued: "You see that place down there?"

"Yes. That's where the National Memorial Shrine is located, among several other historical memorial sites. We consider that valley one of the most sacred places in the land. That's where most of our war heroes and patriots going back to the 1920 Revolution are buried."

"So is my grandfather," said the American man, "and one of his sons - my uncle. A younger brother of my father. My father and I came two years ago and we went down there to bring some flowers for my uncle's thirty-fifth death anniversary."

It seemed, for a few seconds, the two of them were held captive by the tranquility of the night. Only the soft wind spoke to their ears as they gazed down at the solitary faint lights of the valley. And the only movement they were aware of were those of the tree branches swaying in the wind, and the sentries keeping watch at the perimeter of the command headquarters.

"You haven't answered my question." Emil was the first to break silence. "Why are you here now?"

"My uncle was born in this country," replied the American from a greater depth than Emil had heard him speak since they found each other in the courtyard. "He was a citizen of this land, and he loved this land. So did my grandfather, I heard. So does my father. My uncle fought and died for it in the Second World War. My grandfather was a diplomat physician of the American colonizers here for many years. But he supported and actually worked for the idea of the country's independence from its colonizers. He died in the 1920 Revolution on the side of the freedom fighters, caring for their sick and wounded.

Emil stared at the American in disbelief. A chill ran up the back of his head from way down his back and he felt goose bumps rise all over.

"Doctor Steven Vincent James?" Emil asked, peering closely at the American. "The famous Doctor James of the Revolution?"

"My grandpa," said the Orange County college teacher. Extending a hand to Emil, he added: "And let me introduce one of his grandsons. My name is Vincent Francis James, sir."

"I'm... I don't know what to say," Emil stuttered as he shook the man's hand. "It's a great honor to know you, Mr. James."

"People call me Frank, or Francis when they're trying to be cute," offered the American man, smiling. "After my uncle who lies down there next to his father."

"And my name is Emilio Stuart Sabater, as you already know. Emil would do, especially among friends. And you may skip the 'sir' too anytime."

After they had shifted gears and got comfortable with the idea of having become personally acquainted, they spoke more freely to each other. Emil hoped there would be other such occasions as this between the two of them during the mission.

"I can say you're right if you think I'm here for sentimental reasons," Frank James said, picking back up on the conversation. "But - sentimental or not, I'm here because of a belief I have for which I'm willing to risk my life like they who rest down there in that valley did."

After a short but reverent silence between them, Emil said: "Your grandfather is considered a folk hero pretty much throughout the country. Children learn about him early at grade school in history books. I did. And the first thing I learned about him was his advocacy of a nation's self-determination, his idea, his belief that a people born upon a land must be born to freedom and all the natural birthrights in that land and not to the control and exploitation of any rule, foreign or native, that suppresses such freedom and birthrights."

"You've done your homework well."

"On the subject of Doctor James, yes, I have. And so have most of my countrymen, except that dictator in the executive palace and his tyrants in the military."

"Now you know what I'm here for: one, to help restore what that belief won for this land and lost to that dictator; two, to put him and his kind out of commission for good in this land." Frank James fell silent for a moment, contemplating their surroundings, the firmament, the mountain, the valley, the fields, and Emil just waited for he saw that the man was burdened with thoughts that he had yet to put into words. Then, the American man said: "I have strong personal feelings for this country, this land. And its people." Emil stole a quick glance at the man and bowed his head slightly. "It's a beautiful country. A good land with a good nation which shows the East can be one with the West, and that people of whatever nationality can live as one people with a common citizenship. I wish America would evolve more towards this kind of a nation. I wish it could quit dragging its feet moving in this direction, to make itself truly the United States of America in every sense. Of one people, one nation, indivisible."

Emil was speechless for a while, muted by the unexpected revelations of his first real-life American acquaintance born and raised in America and who also happened to be a direct descendant of another American man who had earned himself a permanent niche of honor in the nation's history. A thirst, however, to know more about America did not keep him silent for long. Everything Frank James just said about America was new to him.

Nicholas never told him about a divided America. What does Frank mean by what he said?

"I have a friend," Emil said reminiscently, "a very dear friend whom I lost to America exactly twenty years ago. I didn't really lose him in a sense because we've kept in touch. He is now an American citizen. He has written me many letters for years and most of what he said about America never discouraged me in my desire to go there and live there too someday. Soon perhaps." He paused a moment to look Frank directly in the eye and asked: "Isn't America one nation? Aren't Americans one people?"

"I wish I could give you a straight yes or no for an answer, and be truthful about it."

"Why couldn't you?"

"Depending on who you're asking - yes, America is one nation, of one people. That's what the lawyers, the politicians and everybody else in high places in society would say. But not the poor and the underprivileged, the economic underclass, the various minorities - ethnic, religious and racial, like the blacks, the hispanics, the American Indians. To many of them, America is an idea that has yet to find its time. They see it as a country divided in social and economic classes. A good example is Los Angeles, California. East of the city is hispanic, south is black and north and west are mid- to upper-class white and Asians. Another is Chicago. North is white, south is black.

"This is true on the national scale too. The country is divided into economic regions as well. There is the long-depressed Appalachian region, the farm lands and crop-producing regions in the midwest which are going out of business, and most of the southern states where poverty and ignorance are a way of life in many parts. The blacks at one time around the sixties, when racial conflict in the U.S. peaked, proposed that they all move into three or four states in the south to form their own nation and government, their own country and break away from the United States."

"What do you have to say about all that? I want to hear how Frank James, American, see America."

"I sympathize with the underclass," the American replied quickly. "I understand how they feel although I've never really fully experienced poverty and deprivation and hunger with no end in sight. But I know many who have. I know many poor people. I've been with them in the States. In Latin America and here in Asia. I share their feeling, those poor people in the U.S. and that's the way I feel about America. Personally, I have other feelings about America as I got older. A lot of it has to do with the kind of people we Americans have become."

Emil moved a tad closer and remained perfectly silent. Listening to the American talk about America, he was a sponge soaking in water from a gushing tap, an arid field given its first spring shower.

"As a sovereign state, America is still a good country, more so than most others in the world," Frank James continued, drawing a deep breath as he shifted the submachinegun hanging by its strap from his right to his left shoulder. "But it used to be better. People respected each other more, took up more meaningful values, more lasting values and stood by them, defended them more vigorously as much as they could. Today, hardly any of those human characteristics exists. You can see it in how people relate to one another in various forms of human relationship: man and woman, children and parents, teachers and students, people at work.

"My marriage lasted five years. The last two of it we spent apart and trying to get out of it, getting a divorce. I feel sad that I have no child but I also think it's best that there isn't any out of that marriage. God, there are so many of them already: America is raising generation after generation of children out of broken homes, single-parent families, let alone children out of wedlock."

Emil kept his eyes fixed at Frank James, taking in as much of him as he could as if this was the last he would ever see of the man. His perception of the American had undergone a gradual transformation more than once from that of a yankee fortune hunter, adventurer, mercenary when he first found him sitting on the adobe wall carrying his weapon, to that of a would-be patriot like his grandfather or a war hero like his uncle, to that of an honorable schoolteacher, a respected academician and, now, to that of an ordinary citizen of his country taking this opportunity to give vent to some criticism of the society he lived in.

"You can also see it, this lack of human character," Frank James continued, now appearing solemn with a sadness in his eyes that affected Emil so much he could almost feel the same sadness burrow inside him, "in the way people do their work at their jobs and at school. And then they can't understand why American products and services and quality of education have lost their competitiveness. I'm a school teacher, I've been for years, and I saw it happening with the hundreds of young people I've taught, or tried to teach.

"This is one thing about America today, the case with the young people, which I believe is the most tragic setback for the future of the country: their lack of discipline, their mindless upbringing which I hold their parents accountable for. Most of what I've seen of the American youth these past few years is a total waste. Nearly a third of them can't read or write effectively or do simple math. Rock, sex and drugs are all they're interested in and in not too many years, these young generations are going to make up the adult population of America. God help us then.

"That is why when I look at you and other young people I've met here in this country and in Japan, Taiwan, the Philippines, Korea, Malaysia, and see how they respect each other and their parents, how obedient they are, how hard they work, how eager they are to learn, I get the urge to hurry back to the States and whip the ass of every youngster back there, beat their brains out and stuff into them some of those better human qualities which we've lost."

Emil didn't doubt for one moment how serious Frank James was about everything he said of America. Even in the faint wash of the moonlight, Emil could distinguish in the shadows of the man's face some of his emotions, a yearning, a sadness which betrayed some undercurrent of hurt and anger. How lonely this man must be, Emil thought, and he felt so right and so good in himself that he had this opportunity to share some of the man's thoughts, and some of those emotions.

But it was all so new to him. This life, this society Frank James speaks of, in America. Nicholas never talked to him about life in America in this way. Surely, he must have experienced living in that same society. Was Nicholas holding out on him on the true picture of America? At least his own picture of America out of his twenty years of life there?

Perhaps Nicholas was really aware of America as being that way with respect to what Frank James said but didn't concern himself with it because he had a different walk of life from that of Frank James. It could be that the American society is so diverse that one's sensitivities in his corner of it might be lost in another.

He resolved that this he could only answer by himself and so once again, he renewed his promise to himself to go to America, follow in Nicholas' footsteps and understand one such set of sensitivities and one such life as that of Frank James. But for now, he'll have to put all that aside. America must wait.

He must answer a call of duty to country and everything he loved and believed in including his family; Arthur Sabater, his brother, who had been arrested and incarcerated outside the due process of law; and Greg Carson, his friend, who had been imprisoned incommunicado for months now and whose place in the country's struggle for freedom he now held.

He and Frank James, together with all the rest of the freedom fighters, had a job to do. They had missions to accomplish to restore liberty and justice upon the land.

◫ 13 ◫

FACT, CLASSIFIED INFORMATION

The day Bobby Kay sent out the order to rescind the control-and-terminate order in Los Angeles and Washington, D.C., Fausto Cristobal and Nicholas rode out of the District in the back of a car driven by an opposition intelligence security man. Next to the driver was another man, the security lookout for their back seat passengers.

Ahead of them, keeping distance of some four or five car lengths was the lead car occupied only by its driver, another opposition security man. Back of them was another car carrying two CIA men. One was Charles Goodside, the man code-named Blue Whale who occupied the passenger seat, a man in his early forties with an expressionless face behind a gray-streaked mustache, cold brown eyes that mirrored no sensitivities of any kind at all save for one thought: that of staying on the job,

performing the duty he was called upon at the momei
The man at the wheel was one of the two alternates
assigned to him by the Office with whom he took turns
protecting their charge - the two men in the back seat of
the car ahead of them.

"Anyone back there, K3?" Charles Goodside routinely
asked the man at the wheel code-named Kingfisher Three,
as they crossed the Potomac on the Fourteenth Street
bridge over to the Virginia side.

K3 scanned the traffic behind them on the rearview
mirror, carefully, for a few seconds. It was two-thirty in
the afternoon, the time of day with the least traffic on the
road.

"No. Nobody out there, as far as I can see," replied
Kingfisher Three softly, glancing once more at the
rearview mirror.

They were headed to Nicholas' condo in Alexandria
after Fausto Cristobal and Charles Goodside had notified
him earlier at work that they were coming to pick him up
to have a look at some of the pictures they had of certain
individuals his CIA and opposition protectors had spotted
both at his place of work and his residence premises. It
was decided, when Nicholas suggested, that his place
would be best being the closest of all that were
volunteered by the others. Besides, it might prove of
some help to his memory in identifying certain people he'd
seen before, in a place where he was most comfortable.

Earlier, Charles Goodside had shown Fausto Cristobal
a separate set of pictures where Fausto Cristobal identified
a man he had seen on several occasions near his place of
business. When he was shown the set of pictures they
wanted Nicholas to look at now, he identified the same
man plus another he insisted having seen some place else a
few times in the past few days.

The pictures were taken intermittently by K2 and K3 while each was alternately posted to cover Fausto Cristobal and Nicholas. Then they put together the pictures they'd taken at each post. The two men Fausto Cristobal identified showed up in the pictures taken by both.

Not long after they got on the G.W. Parkway, Charles Goodside picked up the transceiver from under the dashboard and checked with the two cars ahead as he had done twice before as they were leaving the District. He hung up as soon as he got the 'okay' message from the driver of the leading car and the 'no problem' response from the middle car, the one directly ahead of them carrying Fausto Cristobal and Nicholas. This response did not hold true for more than one minute though.

The last time K3 looked at the rearview mirror, the only traffic he saw were the two school buses they just passed as they neared the National Airport. A few seconds later, a car, a deep red late model Firebird, barreled down the left lane at about eighty miles an hour past them and caught up with the middle car which was some four car lengths away. Then it held steady with the middle car while a man rose from its back seat, aimed a short-barrel automatic through the window and opened fire directly at Fausto Cristobal.

As soon as Charles Goodside saw what was happening, he literally leaped to the back seat, screaming at K3 to get closer to the rear of the Firebird while rolling down the window at the same time. He hoped the driver of the middle car would not panic but pick up speed instead and try to get away. And he did, but not by much. Ten fifteen feet at most. But that was all K3 needed to get close enough for Charles Goodside to explode the right rear wheel of the Firebird with a high-power service pistol he fired while leaning out of the car window.

The Firebird careened violently for a moment as it slowed down and they passed it. And then it rolled several times over on the parkway median like a smoking tin can. The last Charles Goodside saw of it in the next couple of seconds as they sped away and he moved quickly back to the front seat was a large orange flame giving off a thick black shaft of smoke, from the burning oil and gas, twisting rapidly up to the sky.

Quickly, he picked up the transceiver and checked with the occupants of the middle car.

"How bad?" he asked as calmly as he could sound.

"We're okay, Blue Whale," replied the driver. "No serious damage."

"Put on Kingfisher, please."

"Everything is fine, Blue Whale," said Fausto Cristobal bravely, though obviously still coming out of a shock with the slight tremor in his voice. "Just a small flesh wound on my left arm. Nothing that can't be fixed with a first-aid kit."

"And Sparrow?"

"Not a scratch."

The first hail of bullets battered the high-tempered shatterproof window glass which didn't give right away, allowing Fausto Cristobal time to duck below the sill level. One round caught his arm though when he raised it instinctively to shield his face just as the glass finally broke. The next burst was aimed at the bulletproof door which trapped each round completely in its high-tensile double steel plate linings.

Charles Goodside next instructed the driver of the lead car who had kept pace with the action all along to keep going, proceed on course. Then he relayed the incident to

Langley and asked for a report back on the occupants of the Firebird as soon as the local authorities got through with their jobs at the scene.

Nicholas saw everything as it happened in all its suddenness from the moment the Firebird appeared on the side of their car. He was practically looking down the barrel of their attacker's gun at no more than twelve feet away while he was talking to Fausto Cristobal from his end of the back seat. He might have actually saved Fausto's life because within two seconds of the first burst, just before the window glass disintegrated, he had pulled Fausto by the neck down to the floor with him. In the process, a few bullets went within an inch past his head.

Although terrified as he had never been before, he was able to contain the shock and didn't lose mental control. Who were they after? He had asked himself during the few long seconds the attack lasted. But no sooner had he asked this than he was jolted by the realization that what was happening was actually happening and that he was in it; that he was no longer just imagining it as he did only a few days ago when his protectors escorted him to his first meeting with Fausto Cristobal.

He had never met Blue Whale and Kingfisher Three in person so that he felt thrilled when Fausto Cristobal told him that today he will finally know who these CIA men were, what they looked like. He had never met a CIA man. Not to his knowledge.

As they entered Old Town, Alexandria from the parkway just now which put them within a mile and a half of his place, he couldn't wait for them to get there and shake their hands and thank them for their services. He felt the same way for the other men, the opposition security men in the car with them who held their ground during the crisis and kept their presence of mind. The security man in the front passenger seat was actually able to fire a few rounds from his .38 revolver at the gunman and, even at a difficult angle leaning back to the rear side of the car, one of them pierced the gunman's forehead, killing him instantly even before the Firebird turned over.

But getting to his place didn't turn out to be any easier from there on as he thought it would be. At the parking lot in front of the condo building, the passengers in the last two cars got out and walked in pairs up the concrete pavement leading to the front entrance of the three-story garden apartment building. Nicholas up front with the opposition security man beside him and Fausto Cristobal with Charles Goodside behind them.

K3, the driver of the third car stayed back in the parking lot while the other two drivers were posted on the street a short but inconspicuous distance from each other near the building. All three remained in the cars.

There weren't many other cars parked in the area. In the parking spaces in front of the building nextdoor, two cars, a Chrysler Dodge sedan and a Nissan Z, were parked next to each other. In the sedan which was parked in the space with a clear view of the approaches to the other building, a man's head rose from below the steering wheel to watch the four men walk to the front door. Very quickly, he brought a two-way radio microphone close to his lips and repeatedly uttered a few frantic words to it.

Inside Nicholas' apartment, the words were heard in the radio carried by three NIS agents who for the past fifteen minutes had been ransacking the apartment. One of them, apparently the leader, immediately motioned to the other two to head out to the balcony quietly. It was too late for any evasive action for all of them other than taking the escape route through the balcony which was actually only a short one-and-a-half story leap to the ground. The only other way out was the way they came in which was through the apartment door that opened to the stairwell around which the condo units were clustered at each floor. The leader of the intruders took no time in deciding to leave the same way he came in, shutting Nicholas' apartment door quietly and as quickly as he could when he saw the four men through the entrance glazing below almost at the front door. He made it to the second floor level in two big leaps down the stair and a short bounce to the top of the last half flight of steps leading down to the foyer before the front entrance. There he stood for a second to calm himself down and fix his tie before stepping down to the door.

Nicholas saw the man coming out as he was pulling the door open. The man stepped out of the doorway between Fausto Cristobal and Charles Goodside on one side of him and Nicholas and the opposition security man on the other. Fausto Cristobal had a good look at him, and so did Charles Goodside as they returned the man's pleasant 'hello' in passing.

Fausto Cristobal and Charles Goodside exchanged looks in an instant, acknowledging with their widened eyes and bobbing heads that they both recognized the man. Nicholas watched them intently, not sure of what was going on until Fausto Cristobal drew out a .38 from under his suit coat and aimed it rigidly at the man as if to fire right at that instant.

"Hold it!" he ordered softly. The man stopped at about ten feet away on the concrete walk and half-turned. At this, the opposition security man beside Nicholas moved toward the NIS agent. On his way, one of the NIS agents who had been lying low up in the balcony fell on him, the other on Fausto Cristobal.

Fausto Cristobal's gun discharged as he crashed to the ground with most of the NIS agent's weight on his back, knocking him out senseless. The NIS man was up quickly on his feet but just as he was making a running start in the direction of the Dodge sedan at the other building, Nicholas in a lightning hop was standing in front of him and was packing a powerful roundhouse kick which caught the man straight on the bridge of his nose and sent him doubling back on the ground. He staggered back up to his feet, dazed and in pain and angry. This time, instead of running away, he faced Nicholas and, to Nicholas' surprise, charged forward not like a mad animal but a trained fighter.

Nicholas fended off the man's first two kicks and even landed a solid punch on the man's ribs. The man countered swiftly with a round hook-kick which Nicholas never saw coming and landed on the back of his head, making his brain feel like a handball bouncing inside his skull. From then on, he was completely in his opponent's mercy.

He had to be a black belt, the thought flashed to Nicholas' mind as he endured the punishment the NIS agent proceeded to deliver to his front, side and back with a combination of kicks and handknife chops. Then, just before he crumbled semi-conscious to the ground, he saw the NIS agent turn away from him. Somebody had come to his rescue by attracting the attention of the murderous brute with a loud yell followed by a flying sidekick to the back of the NIS agent.

In his semi-consciousness, Nicholas could not be sure of the face he saw of his rescuer, but in his mind he knew it was the face of Brian Cooper, no doubt about it. But where in the world did he come from? And how did he get into this? Then, when he fell on his back with a bleeding face which turned to the side where the street was, he saw the car where Kingfisher Three, the CIA man, was supposed to be posted. The car was empty, and its door wide open as if someone who was in it bolted out in a hurry - to rescue someone, a friend, from a black belt Karate expert perhaps. Then he remembered that puzzling smile on Fausto Cristobal's face when Fausto first told him about their CIA protectors. Now he knew what it was for. K3, one of them, is Brian Cooper.

While K3 battled the NIS black belt, the other part of the ensuing violence culminated rapidly into a fatal conclusion. The opposition security man had clung on to the NIS agent who fell on him it seemed from outer space, and would not let go. They struggled on the ground with beastly ferocity for a few moments until the NIS agent succeeded in bloodying his face with a solid heel-kick. The NIS agent pulled out a gun as he broke loose. The opposition man was just as quick in doing so even as his face bled.

Two shots rang out almost simultaneously and the two men fell back on the ground, their lives snuffed out like a pair of candlelight in a sudden windstorm with the NIS agent taking a bullet on the right temple and the opposition man on the left chest.

Brian Cooper, who was a two-stripe red belt in Tae Kwon Do, quickly found out he was no match to the NIS black belt either. He valued his belt ranking and took pride in having achieved it so that now, to be so expertly handled and outfought by a real opponent humiliated more than hurt him physically even though half of his face was already swollen black and he was licking his own blood.

Upon hearing the gunshots, the NIS man glanced around quickly and seeing how suddenly the area had become unpopulated, he gave Brian Cooper one last turn on today's lesson in marshal arts by delivering a bastard of a flying sidekick to the unswollen half of Brian's Cooper's face. Then he bounded head over heels toward the street where he was picked up by the Dodge sedan following in the smoking tail of the Nissan Z driven by the escaping NIS leader.

Throughout the quick but deadly encounter, Charles Goodside kept busy trying to allay his fear that Fausto Cristobal might have been seriously injured by dragging him into the building and trying to revive him. Fausto Cristobal had come to just in time to hear the fatal gunshots and see through the glass of the front entrance the two men expire.

Now he got up telling Charles Goodside he was fine as he saw Nicholas coming through the door with Brian Cooper hanging by his side. As soon as they went through the doorway, two other figures appeared in it - the other opposition security men, the drivers, who were posted a certain distance away in their cars. They looked frantically from one face to another, taking an extra moment to register shock when they turned to Brian Cooper who now looked as if he just finished a fifteen-round lopsided boxing match where he was the underdog, instead of the two minute real karate fight that humbled his spirits.

Nicholas didn't look any much better. His face was raised from his upper lip to almost the entire upper right half of it. His right ear wouldn't quit buzzing and his left rib cage where he took some savage blows ached like hell.

Fausto Cristobal instructed the men at the door to stay outside with the bodies and keep anybody in the area from coming close. As soon as they were in the apartment, phone calls were made immediately, first by Charles Goodside, and then by Fausto Cristobal. Shortly after, two ambulances arrived followed by a half a dozen unmarked cars from which emerged men with expressionless faces similar to that of Charles Goodside. Not a single sign on any of them or their vehicles indicated the presence of the local authorities. No police cars showed up at all.

The bodies were picked up while Charles Goodside conferred with one of the men. Two medics went up, at Charles Goodside's request, to treat the three men in the apartment. The bullet wound on Fausto Cristobal's arm from the attack at the parkway was more bothersome than he thought, he and one of the medics found out, that his arm had to be put in a flexible cast on a sling around his neck. Nicholas and Brian Cooper were given painkillers and dry-ice packs to dab on their swollen faces. They swore in their minds to track down the assumed black belt NIS agent, at an appropriate time in their lives such as perhaps when they'd reached the rank of black belt themselves, and get even with the savage bastard. All three men were urged to go to the hospital for a more thorough check and treatment but they all refused. There were more pressing matters to take care of at the moment than licking their wounds.

And pressing they were indeed, especially for Nicholas and Fausto. First, Nicholas determined how the NIS agents operated in his apartment. Neat. That was how they intended to leave the place after they were through, at least make it look like they were never there. But, apparently, in their hurry, they didn't have time to put back in place the picture album one of them was looking at. Nor did they bother to close the drawer containing Emil's letters through the years. His telephone and address book which he kept next to the telephone was definitely missing.

Next, Fausto Cristobal, Charles Goodside and Brian Cooper finally had him look at the pictures. He, too, like

Fausto Cristobal, identified two faces in a number of the
pictures, with both of them showing up in the ones taken
by Brian Cooper and the ones taken by K2, the other CIA
man. Nicholas turned cold when Charles Goodside noted
that one of those men he identified was the NIS agent who
was killed. The other was the one who came out through
the door. Looking at the two sets of pictures, Fausto
Cristobal said, and memorizing the man's face was how he
was able to identify the man as he went by them.

The atmosphere in the apartment soon came to a level
of calm where one sat quietly for a moment and collected
himself, then looked at another to recall certain segments
of the events that occurred during the short but deadly trip
from Washington. Nicholas at last had the presence of
mind to serve the refreshments. Later, he ushered Brian
Cooper to a seat in the balcony to peel the CIA agent's
cover. Fausto Cristobal was busy on the phone while
Charles Goodside was occupied with a colleague who had
stayed behind from the bunch earlier.

"Now, you're going to tell me the rest of the story,"
Nicholas said to Brian Cooper, sinking in one of the iron
chairs of the lounge set with a bottle of soda in one hand.

"What story?" replied Kingfisher Three innocently.

"Start with what you left out of the adventure story you
told me about the Saudi Arabia job, and continue on to
what you've been doing since you came back."

"Sonofabitch has got to be at least a second black belt,"
Brian Cooper said as if he didn't hear Nicholas at all. He
held the ice pack to the dark lumpy area which was the
cheekbone on the right side of his face. "Maybe even a
third or fourth black."

They were looking directly down at the two opposition
security men posted at the entrance below. Over at the
street curb at the start of the concrete walk to the building

were two other men who were among those who arrived after Charles Goodside made his phone calls. The rest of them had left with the ambulance as quickly as they had come. The whole operation took between ten to fifteen minutes: picking up the bodies, scrubbing the area clean, the brief conference between Fausto Cristobal, Charles Goodside and a couple of those men who came.

"C'mon, Brian," Nicholas urged. "This is no time to bullshit anybody. Were you in the Middle East as a CIA man?"

"What? Of course not!"

"Yes, you were. Don't lie to me. I'm your friend!"

"I wouldn't put it quite as lying," Brian protested.

"Alright, then, let's say you're an - agent in place? Or what is called in intelligence work - a mole?"

"You've been reading too many spy novels, my friend. No. I'm not that at all. I did have a contract job with a consulting engineering firm doing some projects in Saudi Arabia, fact. While I was there, I was approached by the... office -"

"What office?" interrupted Nicholas.

"The Agency."

"You mean the Central Intelligence Agency."

Brian Cooper nodded reluctantly and continued. "And I was asked to do some work, gather some information, fact. Purely technical information which I wouldn't classify as out of line of the work I do for a living anyway as a civil engineer, fact."

"Nicely put, my friend," Nicholas snickered. "You should get a job on the Hill or at the White House. Maybe run for public office, if you could talk like that."

Brian Cooper smiled at him acquiescently and with mischief in his eyes.

"I understand you couldn't go around telling even your closest relative about it. So I wouldn't dig into the details, too much. Only where it concerns me, though. So tell me, when did you start following me around? And what did you discover of my private personal life? My habits, and things you didn't know about me?"

"Tell you the truth," Brian Cooper replied with mischief still in his eyes and a half-smile on one side of his swollen mouth, "not much that I didn't already know. I was re-activated only last week and was fielded right the following day."

"Re-activated? Fielded? And you say I read too many spy novels?"

"Listen, I shouldn't be talking to anybody about any of these at all. Yes, Nicholas, including you. And especially you for reasons you know darn well why."

"I know, I know, so they told me, including my father. No open CIA involvement. Nothing to invite participation of any of the superpowers. Just look at that." Nicholas pointed to the ground below with his nose. "Who'd ever think two men lost their lives on that ground a while ago? That some foreign agent who was unmistakably a black belt was beating our balls off and spilling our blood on that grass area down there? Those guys are very efficient. They clean up a mess really fast."

Brian Cooper shook his head and laughed. "But they're right about this whole thing with your old country, you know that too. It's non-aligned foreign policy," he said.

"Yes, I know," Nicholas replied, sinking into deep thought for one moment. "So tell me, what else did you find out about me all the time you were spying on me?"

"Everything. Down to how often you change underwears."

"You lousy prick."

Brian Cooper laughed but in the process of tossing his head back stopped himself when a pain shot through a sore muscle on his neck.

"Good. I hope it's broke," Nicholas said as he watched Brian wince and rub his neck tenderly, "if not I'd be glad to do it -"

"Look, lover boy," Brian interrupted, "you're an American just like me and any other. And I couldn't care less where the hell you came from or what and who you are. Any foreign agent attacks you, it's the same thing as attacking me or some U.S. congressman from Pocatello, Idaho. It's an attack against the United States is what I'm saying. And knowing you face exactly such a danger, the government is taking it on itself to prevent it from happening because of the consequences it would entail which we just said we both understand. So we got to protect you, and your family, hoping they wouldn't be mad enough to draw us into an open confrontation."

"Well, they did today. They certainly did today for sure. So what do you guys do next?"

"We'll know shortly, I expect," Brian replied, glancing into the living room at the three men inside. Fausto Cristobal was talking to the third man, Charles Goodside's colleague, while Charles Goodside was on the phone. "It's up to them," Brian Cooper added, nodding in the direction of the people inside. "They make the decisions. I'm just a common patriotic peon."

The phone had rung twice and each time Charles Goodside picked it up after getting a hand signal the first time from Nicholas in the balcony to 'go ahead, whatever you have to do in there'. Both calls were for Charles Goodside. The first was from a colleague reporting on the G.W. Parkway attack. Both the driver and the gunman were confirmed NIS agents. And both were dead at the site. The driver from the fatal 'accident', fact. The gunman from a bullet in his head, classified information.

The second call was from the office, informing him that Bobby Kay's order for the NIS to cancel the control and termination order for the targeted opposition people was out. He was also told that Fausto Cristobal was the target in Washington and Domingo Gabriel one of the two in southern California. The question, however, which nobody knew the answer to was - had the NIS people in the U.S. received the order already and if so, were they honoring it?

The way things stand - a coordinated attack and intrusion in broad daylight, four people dead, I'll be damned if any of the bad guys knew it or if they did, had any intention of honoring it, thought Charles Goodside as he listened to his superior on the phone. And sure enough, he was ordered to maintain their post over their charge in full alert. The news of Bobby Kay's order was a welcome relief but it's one they couldn't risk enjoying.

"Come to think of it," Nicholas was saying to Brian in the balcony, pulling his back out of the hollow of the lounge chair, "glad you mentioned my family, I got to talk to my father."

"Sit back and relax for a few," Brian suggested before taking the beer can to the working side of his mouth for a sip. "Everything will be taken care of and you'll get to that shortly."

Another phone call had come in soon after Charles Goodside hung up. Fausto Cristobal had picked it up and it turned out it was for him. The caller was his counterpart in the opposition in southern California calling from the Gabriel home in Brentwood Park.

Fausto Cristobal tensed up the first minute of the conversation during which he listened more than talked.

He glanced furtively at Nicholas through the glass door to the balcony about every five seconds throughout.

The call lasted about five minutes after which he replaced the phone on its rack, real slow, as if it weighed a few pounds, turned and walked gradually towards the balcony.

The other men in the living room couldn't help noticing.

"What's up, Kingfisher?" Charles Goodside inquired.

"It's Domingo Gabriel," Fausto muttered, turning halfway back to the two CIA men. "They hit him too, this morning, in Santa Monica. Two opposition men killed."

"What about Mr. Gabriel?"

"He survived the attack, but he's in a coma in a hospital. They said it doesn't look good for him right now."

Fausto Cristobal had told Brentwood Park that Alexandria would be returning the call in a few minutes, just as soon as he had broken the news to Nicholas. Other than tensing up for a minute as he tried to get a hold of himself, Nicholas took it with calm. Quickly, then, he was on the phone and in a matter of seconds was talking, through a line via the Langley operator, to his sister who had just arrived at their parents' house.

She gave it to him in a succession of one major detail after another: it was a quick-strike ambush early this morning, no more than ten minutes after he left the house on his way to work; his two bodyguards, opposition intelligence men, fatally shot during the close range gunbattle; the attackers, three men one of whom believed to be also a fatality, was fought off by Jack Dodson, the CIA man, who took father to the hospital; mother is in there now and won't leave him for a minute; he's stable now although still in critical condition and in deep coma;

shot twice - one just below the back of the head, another at the back barely missing the spine.

They listened to Nicholas tell his sister about a possible flight within twenty-four hours, direct from Washington to Los Angeles. After he hung up, he stood by the telephone with his back to everyone for almost a whole minute, his head low between his shoulders. Everyone kept quiet. Brian Cooper stood the closest to him.

They were expecting a distraught appearance when he turned around but he had instead a placid, thoughtful expression on his face. No emotion of anger or grief. All these he controlled, packed underneath, they found out as they heard in his voice when he spoke.

"I am going with you, Kingfisher," he declared bluntly, his eyes riveted at Fausto Cristobal. "I want to personally see those tyrants and murderers brought down from power. I want to make them pay for what they've done to their victims all these years. I want to see them, every goddamn one of them go down."

📖 14 📖

SUSPENDED LIFE

"Sit down, gentlemen," said the section chief, motioning Charles Goodside and Brian Cooper to the chairs in front of his desk. He was standing by the window away from them, sucking on a pipe while viewing the landscape around the headquarters building and the lush green of this part of McLean, Virginia. He had a pleasant and very accommodating smile when he stepped up the desk. "I realize you've had a long day. I won't keep you long. We've received all the reports on what happened, here and in California. But we have local procedures at the end of the day."

"I understand, sir," Charles Goodside followed up quickly in his desire to get on with the closing of the day's business, according to procedure.

And procedure was to come home or roost after what headquarters classifies as a high-hazard day such as this one had been. The requirement was to substantiate in person what had been filed from the field. Give a rehash of what happened out there was what it boils down to, Charles Goodside always thought as he had on many other high-hazard days he'd seen in his years with the agency. This and the problem Brian Cooper had been giving him since they left Alexandria were the reason they were now sitting in the boss' office at headquarters.

And the problem Brian Cooper had created was his persistence to go with Nicholas, not only to California but all the way to Nicholas' troubled country of origin should things get that far with him. He threatened that if he can't go in the service of the agency, he'd resign his part-time sleuthing for them and go anyway on his own.

So, rehash the day's events, they did to the section chief of local area operations first, then Charles Goodside brought up the case of the recalcitrant part-time agent, anxious to see how the office would handle this one.

"But wouldn't that amount to you taking a full time job with the agency?" said the boss to Brian Cooper after listening to both of them, feeling some uneasiness everytime he looked at the swollen black and blue on Brian Cooper's face. "And what does that do to your personal life? Your job. You're an engineer as I understand. You got other things to do, don't you?"

"Begging your pardon, sir, but that's my personal decision. My personal choice. I go either as your man or as my own man on the side of the opposition."

Charles Goodside stiffened in his seat. He had never talked that way to the chief even in the worst mood he had ever brought into the office.

"You're not giving us any choice at all?" queried the section chief. He wasn't upset nor the least bit offended as Charles Goodside was worried about. He understood this young man pretty much, he thought: what's a year or two out of the many ahead of him assuming he survives this daring adventure he's itching to be a part of? He certainly doesn't look like any regular eight-hour-a-day big-city commuter from the suburbs, not right now anyway. "You go one way or another," he added.

"Yes, sir. Of that I'm sure. And, yes, you do have a choice: I'm willing to work for the agency, operate at its direction, either part-time or full-time."

The section chief and Charles Goodside exchanged secret glances under the hood of their eyebrows. They knew their thoughts about the matter connected. But as though to confirm them, Charles Goodside sounded them out when he told Brian: "Saudi Arabia was a different story. I wouldn't classify that as a hazard assignment. That was mostly academic technical research you did for the agency back there... "

"Technical espionage," corrected Brian Cooper.

"Non-political, non-military. What you want to get into now is an entirely different situation in which you have no applicable experience that we know of."

"A major change is in the process of taking place there now," the section chief threw in, rising from behind the desk and sucking on the pipe assiduously. "A shooting war with a potential for an extremely high casualty on both sides. One reason why we're trying to stay out of it as much as we could, for now. See how it goes first."

"That I can do while I'm there," Brian suggested confidently.

"Do what?" asked Charles Goodside.

"See how it goes," replied Brian quickly, "during and after... the revolution. And I'm not too proud to admit I could use the salary, even a part-time one. So, you see, gentlemen, we'd be helping each other out. And speaking of applicable experience, I don't know what else anybody in the agency would call the activities of the past few days, including today."

The boss shot a fleeting eye at Charles Goodside before sauntering to the window, leaving a trail of aromatic smoke behind him. He had his back to them for a good thirty seconds before he pivoted back to his desk, grabbed a pad, told them to stay put for a while and went into the glass enclosed inner office a few feet away from them where they saw him pick up a phone and engage in a ten-minute conversation with someone at the other end.

"I like the way you put it," said the section chief when he came back behind his desk. "But that doesn't mean I endorse the idea of any young American professional man throwing himself in the middle of a turmoil in some remote island country in the Far East for any reason. Now you understand, I'm sure, the decision is not up to me. I don't field agents outside of my jurisdiction, especially for a foreign assignment."

Brian Cooper hovered at every word the section chief was saying. It would be a nice break if they hired him; to be traveling - with pay.

The chief continued: "That was one of the station dispatchers for East Asia I had on the phone. He likes the idea too. He said they could really use some help for some of the extra legwork they need done in there."

Brian Cooper let out a long breath he'd been holding in for a few seconds. He caught Charles Goodside giving him a smart up and down.

Next thing, the section chief tore off the top sheet of the pad he had in his hand and gave it to Brian.

"Report to that room number at seven tomorrow morning. Ask for that person's name and give them that code number," the chief instructed. "They'll be expecting you. They know who you are, from Saudi Arabia."

Nicholas went into the office of Harold Forker, his boss, during the ten o'clock break the following day. The first thing Harold Forker noticed was his face. Harold Forker simply raised a hand, palm up, toward the lumpy side of Nicholas' face, slowly dropped his jaw till his mouth was partly open but didn't say a word.

"Accident," Nicholas said passively. "I stepped on a patch of ice and fell on my face." It got cold in the area later during the evening the day before and there was icing on the ground.

Harold Forker asked if there was anything he can do and Nicholas thanked him properly and assured his boss that he was fine. Just a slight bump and a couple of surface bruises. But the more important thing he came to talk about was his father in Los Angeles who had a stroke early yesterday morning and is now in a coma. He needed to fly out there immediately to give his mother some support and must therefore ask for a leave of absence for a week to start with. He'd be leaving at ten in the morning the next day on a non-stop flight to the west coast. He would call later to give a definite date when he could return to work.

Harold Forker expressed hope that his father would make it and that his family would be alright. He wished him a good trip.

In his second call to Brentwood Park later in the evening the day before, his sister's assurances that everything was well with her family, and mother, and that it was understandable if he can not travel immediately the following day to the coast, put him at ease and allowed him time to collect his thoughts. There was nothing anybody can do at this time more than the hospital was doing and the security the opposition was providing with the help of the U.S. government. The comfort it would give his mother to see him, he decided she could be without for just one more day. This to give him a day's time to work out the details of suspending his life in Washington before he goes away to be with his family, to be pulled back, in a true sense, from America by his origins, to take part in the freedom movement, perhaps even liberate the old country from the grips of tyranny.

Fausto Cristobal, along with the Americans, continued to disagree with Nicholas' insistence to take the place of his father. But Fausto Cristobal was not as forceful this time with his objection to Nicholas getting directly involved in the opposition. The matter was left to be resolved, they had agreed in so many words, when they reach Los Angeles at the opposition headquarters there. Fausto Cristobal decided then to scrap his scheduled departure later the following week and take the trip with Nicholas as it had now become more important for him to be in the west coast than in Washington in preparing for the return to the old country, not to mention his own personal concern for the life of Domingo Gabriel.

It took Nicholas most of the rest of the morning turning his workload over to Harold Forker who would in turn re-assign them temporarily to another engineer. In the afternoon, he got busy cleaning up at his desk and making phone calls to people he needed to notify of his leave of absence.

At home, it was close to midnight when he finally got to start packing, pulling out about a third of his wardrobe from the closet, most of his spring and summer wear, and stuffing them into two medium-sized suitcases. He spent time in the study room taking care of bills due shortly and writing instructions for Gail on looking after the place and the car, taking care of the mail and the other bills due soon. He signed her a three-thousand dollar check for all that and any expenses she might incur on his account.

In the process, he had four telephone conversations. The first one was with Fausto Cristobal who called to confirm their departure schedule at ten in the morning. They'll pick him up at eight. The second was with his sister whom he called to inform about his arrival and to inquire about their parents. She said father had started to show some encouraging signs, according to the doctors. He has improved and they expect him to wake up soon.

Then Lester Jenkins called and everything that had happened during the entire week and cast his personal life into a whirlwind, came to a standstill. He re-acquired a sense of his normal life in America.

California, the old country, the opposition, the struggle for freedom, were temporarily pushed aside. He was back in America.

Lester said he had taken leave for the rest of the week since the day he 'came loose', as he now put it to Nicholas. He had called Nicholas in the office yesterday afternoon but was told he was out the rest of the day. One reason he called was to ask to use Nicholas for one of his personal references in his resume which he said he was shooting out to several firms who were interviewing to staff some big projects.

When Nicholas said he himself had taken leave but that it was for a longer one, he gave Lester the same explanation he gave their boss. He wished the black man all the best in his job search. After that, he just sat by the telephone in the living room for a time and let his thoughts and feelings of the moment linger on and take their course.

One after another, the people who had recently touched his life and evoked certain strong feelings in him about life in America now and his twenty years in the country came to mind. First came the people he had known through work: Haj Fujiwara, Norman Tilley, Harvey Dugan, Gary Clemens, Lester Jenkins.

Next came some of those who peopled his private life: Gail Phillips, Brian Cooper, even the owner-cashier at the small neighborhood foodstore he went to occasionally in Old Town, a neighbor downstairs - a woman whose son is a relief pitcher in the major leagues and, perhaps more significantly than all the others, the homeless man - Edward McKenny.

Remembering Edward McKenny was actually brought on by something, a piece of paper sticking out of the phone book next to the telephone, which he just happened to be looking at presently. He had put it there the night he came home after seeing the bum at Lafayette Park. On it, he had written 'Brother Matthew McKenny, Philadelphia'. And now he remembered, too, what he did that for.

He got on the phone and called Philadelphia information. There were two Matthew Mckenny's and two M. McKenny's. It was the second Matthew he talked to who turned out to be Edward's brother.

After they established the identity and kinship of the brothers, Nicholas spoke of Edward's situation in Washington, carefully, not knowing how Matthew would take it. He spoke hesitantly when he said "Yes, he is one of those. He is a homeless man. He lives on the streets of Washington, sleeps in the parks, on the grates."

Matthew's response was immediate, preceded only by a short pause and Nicholas felt triumphant as if a heavy burden was lifted off his head when Edward's brother said mournfully: "My God... I... I didn't know... I never thought it could go this bad with him. Poor Ed. My poor kid brother..." His voice trailed off into empty space, full of pity, full of pain, reminiscing, remembering the life they had together perhaps, Nicholas thought, when they were younger, when they were kids, little boys at home with their parents in the old neighborhood. "Please, Mr. Gabriel, tell me where I could find my brother."

꠱ 15 ꠱

THE MAN IN
A FAULTLESS PINSTRIPE SUIT

The big jet plane became airborne slowly, as if weightless, its sleek body sparkling in the bright morning sun over Dulles International. Inside the spacious DC10 in a window seat, Nicholas looked out at the ground below, the runways and the man-made structures in the area as they got smaller and smaller while the 8:50 direct flight to Los Angeles climbed higher and higher toward the clouds.

There had been other plane trips, many others headed in the same direction, but none of them like this one. He had never looked out the porthole without knowing when he might be back, his personal life suspended indefinitely. He had never looked at the airport, the cities, the land, as he rode to the clouds inside the jumbo jet and got the feeling that he was looking at the entire country, at America, with

276

better than two-thirds of his whole life he was leaving behind while he was being pulled back to his origins. Back to his family, to his people, to Emil and the old country.

Thinking of Emil and remembering certain parts of the last letter filled him with aspirations and hope for his boyhood friend.

'I had no idea at all how the course of my life would change, and how much more it would differ from yours,' he recalled from the lengthy letter. 'I still hope... to go to America, experience life there and know for myself the origin of part of our heritage.'

Suddenly, he felt anxious to get to wherever this one journey of his life might take him, most specifically to the old country. And to be exact, in the company of the rebels and Emil. The sympathy he felt for Emil, the course Emil had chosen to take in his young life brought on some sense of guilt. Everything Emil did at the moment was as meaningful as anything could be in his life back there not only for himself but for others, many others. And he, Nicholas thought of himself, could have chosen to do the same. He felt the same way thinking of his father, the same burden of sympathy. But with it also came anger.

Anger, sympathy and guilt. These were the burden he now bore inside him while on his way to bring comfort and whatever assurance he could to his mother and the rest of the family. He felt the guilt part of it the most and the only thing he had at the moment to soothe it a little was his admiration for what his father had done, and what Emil was doing in the service of their country.

He ached to talk to Emil and tell him that. He had many other things he must tell him: more about America, life in America as he had never written Emil before, from the point of view of a homeless man, a black man, a Japanese-American, a poor family from West Virginia, among others.

But even more than this was his desire to share in the challenge, the undertakings Emil had assumed, risking his life, and his dream of America, to help bring freedom and justice to the old country. He swore that he would find his boyhood friend and join him, fight with him and win or die for freedom with him. This was the only real way to fully appease his sense of guilt and to calm his anger at the thought of his father lying with bullet wounds in the hospital.

A few minutes after the takeoff, as he was about to turn away from the porthole, a man deposited himself in the vacant seat next to him. He guessed it was one of the opposition security men who were traveling with him and Fausto Cristobal sitting directly in front of him.

"Good morning," said Brian Cooper, looking at his face with scrutiny. "Well, well, you certainly look a lot better than the last time I saw you."

"Brian! What are you doing here?" Nicholas asked, surprised but not really so in that he sounded as if Brian's appearance had been a real possibility.

"The same thing you and everybody else here is doing," Brian replied, "flying out to Los Angeles. Isn't that where this big baby is going?"

"Nobody told me you were coming."

"You're not supposed to know. Not until you have a need to know."

"Now you're talking like a model Washington bureaucrat. I thought you have a regular eight-hour-a-day job back there. What happened to it? Never mind -" Nicholas held up a hand to help retract his question. "I don't know if I could believe anything you tell me now."

"Alright, listen," Brian said, shuffling in his seat rather earnestly. "I realize I've created a crisis of confidence here which I must now overcome. No problem. It's all part of the job."

"What job?"

"Uh-h, government job. You know - with the Agency."

It took Brian Cooper a little time explaining himself, picking words Nicholas would understand without compromising the position, put plainly, the full-time job he had taken with the... Agency. This meant of course, in answer to Nicholas Gabriel's question, quitting his job as an engineer in the private industry.

His mission, as detailed to him at headquarters by his dispatcher the day before, was to travel with Nicholas and the opposition, on his own; as a private citizen. In the process, he was to continue to help render protection to Nicholas, Fausto Cristobal and to other opposition figures he might be called upon to do so. At the same time, he was to pay attention to everything that would be happening, everything that would be said and done by anybody who's anybody in the opposition so the Americans might have a heads up on the advanced profile of the potential future government of the island country. He was to report periodically through channels, other agents already in place, in the west coast and in the Far East.

From him to Nicholas, it didn't come out too differently. With some slight omissions, he believed he said enough to restore his credibility to a workable level.

"I thought it over, hard," he told Nicholas with a serious expression on his face that still bore the same marks as Nicholas had, left there by the same person. "Believe me, and finally I decided to do it. Do it full-time. That way I get to travel, with pay. I get to go places and get out of the eight-hour-day rut which I had complained to you about not long ago, remember?"

Nicholas looked penetratingly at Brian, studied the still half-swollen face and found himself believing what Brian had told him. He remembered that day, only last week as a matter of fact, when the poor fellow complained about not knowing what to do with the rest of his life and he, Nicholas, gave him a minor lecture on picking up the ball and playing the challenges of life. Get married and settle down was what he practically suggested to the man although he didn't think that was any solution to Brian's sense of aimlessness.

Well, maybe the man had a point in this after all. Maybe this was the job that was tailor-made for him.

A short time later, when they had finally become accustomed to the role each played in their journey, Brian turned smartly to Nicholas and asked:

"By the way, I've been meaning to ask you, what's with the bum at the park?"

Nicholas felt amused enough to chuckle at the unexpected question.

"You really do well at that job, don't you?" he said.

"I do okay for an amateur. So what was the action out there? For the life of me I can't place it."

"That was strictly personal. Nothing to do with politics, foreign or domestic. Nothing to do at all with the opposition. Someday, maybe I'll introduce you to him. Interesting fellow." Nicholas went on to tell Brian the background of his association with Edward McKenny.

"The man is either a pathological liar or a mental case," remarked Brian afterwards.

Nicholas shook his head. "No. Not a liar. A mental case, maybe, and I mean that only in a facetious way. Actually, he's quite intelligent. Has a lot to say about... many things. Even more than most regular wage-earner, tax-paying people I know."

"Many things like what?" asked Brian cynically.

"Like - social issues," replied Nicholas after a moment's thought. "Things similar to what you said to me recently about what you learned in the Middle East; about how it isn't right for one people to force its way, its culture, upon another. Something like not shoving a Big Mac on a guy's face instead if he wanted to eat raw meat or monkey brains?"

Brian was silent for a few seconds while he recalled the occasion from which Nicholas had quoted him. Then, when it all came back, a smile broke on his face and he started bobbing his head at Nicholas.

"You're right," he said curiously, "maybe I'd like to meet this fellow someday."

***

The minute he emerged from the arrival gate beside Fausto Cristobal to be greeted by a half a dozen men who moved quickly to cordon them off from the crowd, he began to acquire more of that sense of a total departure from his normal life. He never landed at an airport to have so many people, strangers he never saw before, fuss about and pay such careful attention to him. But this was hardly anything at all compared to what lay ahead of him from this day, at the hospital where his father had finally come out of coma, through the next three weeks of his life.

One of the men stepped up to Fausto Cristobal in a hurry. They spoke in whispers for a moment then turned to Nicholas, the man tall, formidable-looking, about the same age as Fausto Cristobal, saying: "Good morning, Mr. Gabriel, sir."

"Good morning," replied Nicholas.

"This is Victor de Alba, my counterpart here in Los Angeles, as best I could put it." Fausto Cristobal explained, speaking in a low voice. Everybody seemed to be in the habit of speaking in a low voice to each other, Nicholas noticed.

"Exactly," confirmed Victor de Alba, shaking hands with Nicholas. He then asked the newly-arrived to follow him and another man who joined him at his side, down one side of the corridor where two more pairs of men walked ahead of them, making sure the way was clear. Bringing up the rear were Brian Cooper and the three opposition security men they came with.

They went out through an exit door to a small parking lot and with the direction of Fausto Cristobal and Victor de Alba hurriedly boarded four cars.

At the hospital, there were more men waiting for them. They were taken to the fourth floor where someone else took over and ushered them through a corridor that led to a private ward. Other men looking like the one next to Victor de Alba stood guard at four-yard intervals on each side of the corridor.

A few yards outside the door, Victor de Alba waved all the men away, leaving the man beside him along with Fausto Cristobal, Nicholas and Brian. The man next to Victor de Alba who was introduced to everyone as Jack Dodson stepped back to Brian and said 'Concord'. Upon hearing this, Brian perked up and replied 'Kingfisher Three', shaking hands with the man.

"I got the message from Langley about your coming, late last night. Glad to see you make it," said Jack Dodson, a man of light build but solid, very trim in his gray suit which made him look more like a company vice-president than a CIA field man. He was not much older than Brian but since the shooting two days ago where he shot a man dead and saved another - the man all these people from Washington and everyone else had come to visit - he felt a much older man. He looked close at Brian's face with a frown and said: "Good heavens, are you well enough?"

"Yes, I'm just fine," Brian assured, casting a glance at Nicholas.

"We were told what happened in D.C. the same day we were hit here, but they didn't give us a lot of details." Jack Dodson turned to Nicholas and surveyed his face too, then to Fausto Cristobal to cast a pathetic look at the arm in the sling. He then motioned Brian to move with him up front and to pull out his government ID.

"Gentlemen," he said formally, "we have a couple of unexpected visitors in there right now, and they would like to meet every one of you, so I've just been informed. Please follow us."

He and Brian led the way to the door which was held open for them by one of the two U.S. Secret Service men after they flashed their CIA ID's to the other. No one had ventured to guess who the visitors might be, assuming only that they were some of the people high up in the ranks of the opposition.

One of them, in fact, was high up there, one holding the highest rank in the opposition: Cesar Ibarra himself, the man who would be the next head of state of the Republic of Silangan. For the second time, he had come to visit the man he had long regarded as a major part of the backbone of the opposition, as soon as he learned that Domingo Gabriel had come out of coma. He occupied one end of the couch in the lounge area nearest the patient's bed.

The other visitor was an American. He occupied the other end of the couch talking to Ibarra and looking very suave in a faultless pinstripe suit as only the current Secretary of State of the United States could look.

An aide came up to the newly arrived, very diligently, to greet every one of them, his smile as officially warm and friendly as his handshake. Then, as he led them to the lounge area, Nicholas broke away from the group and hurried to his mother as soon as he saw her.

They spoke in whispers except for a brief moment when his mother had a first close look at his face and let out a gasp. He quickly calmed her down, assuring her that he was alright and kissed her on the cheek. She hugged him a second time then they turned and stood close to his father in bed.

Domingo Gabriel managed only a faint smile to greet his son. He had not yet regained his speech and his mobility was restricted to the movement of his right limbs with which he communicated by squeezing with his hand or tapping with its fingers.

The people from Washington were informed that the Secretary's visit was a quick deviation from the day's schedule in the west coast, prompted by the opportunity to meet with Cesar Ibarra as well as Domingo Gabriel and his family. His head of entourage explained that the newly arrived were conducted to the lounge area first instead of the patient's bed because the Secretary wanted to meet each one of them right away but, unfortunately, had very limited time.

While he conversed with Cesar Ibarra and the leadership of the opposition, the scene at the bedside did not entirely escape the Secretary's attention. Instead of asking for Nicholas then to be presented to him in his last few minutes in the room, he walked over to the bedside with Cesar Ibarra. Fausto Cristobal did the introductions. The U.S. Secretary of State then spoke to Nicholas of how important his father's contributions had been not only to the legitimate opposition to the present regime in the old country but to the people back there and those living abroad particularly in America. And with a sincere expression on his face, he worded his feelings of regret to Nicholas for what happened to his father, and also to him.

Before he left, he turned to Domingo Gabriel and held the patient's right hand in both his, shook hands with Nicholas and his mother once again and instead of saying 'goodbye', told them 'till we meet again, soon.'

***

It wasn't till the fourth day since he arrived that Nicholas Gabriel began to feel the ground under his feet and to have some time to be with his thoughts. He had been with Fausto Cristobal and Victor de Alba just about everywhere they've been the past two days: at Victor de Alba's home in Torrance for a dinner party where he was one of the honored guests and introduced to the high leadership of the opposition; at the opposition headquarters in Long Beach where plans for the departure of the provisional government five days away, the following Sunday, were being finalized; at the central communication station in Newport Beach where transmissions on news about Operation Sunrise originating from several rebel regional headquarters were being received and decoded daily; and at the hospital where they met not only to visit his father but to consult with him on his work involving Operation Sunrise.

Many in the leadership including Victor de Alba and Daniel de Mesa, the head of the opposition throughout the U.S. and Canada, had assumed Nicholas would be going with them in his father's place. But he still had a job of persuading his father to let him go. It was no easier getting it past his mother either. It was tough seeing her worry about him. He decided to bring it up later and let it rest for a day or two.

Shortly before noon, Brian Cooper had called and proposed lunch. It was a welcome proposition, Nicholas felt; a nice break from all the events that were building up fast in his new life although he was fully aware that Brian Cooper was just as much a part of all those events. But at least Brian was not one from the old country.

"They really move fast, don't they?" Nicholas remarked while they ate shrimps and lobsters in a restaurant on La Cienega Boulevard talking about the surprise meeting with the Secretary of State. "Those government foreign relations people. They get to you right when you're most vulnerable."

"The art of diplomacy," quipped Brian Cooper. "You got to get there first, before somebody else does, with whatever protocol you could devise. Anything handy at the time. That drop-in at the hospital was perfect. There couldn't have been a better opportunity."

"You said the world we live in is a two-party system," Nicholas said philosophically, quoting Brian from that coffee-and-pastry conversation they had one morning back in Washington. "So what do you suggest the Russian might be doing about this one foreign affair?"

"I think they know that they should be keeping their hands to themselves, and they pretty much do with this one. Silangan is not Cuba or Vietnam or Central America. Not even the Philippines. There is no communist insurgency in the country. Communism does not exist there. Ideologically, it's a neutral country, so far. And we want to keep it that way. The least we, the Americans, could hope for."

"A neutral country, so far," Nicholas repeated, recalling the U.S. Secretary of State leaning over his father in bed, the warm handshakes and all the gestures of assurances at their moment of parting.

After lunch, Brian invited Nicholas to a martial arts gym he said he found in Westwood Village near the U.C.L.A. campus. Again, it was a welcome proposition for Nicholas who, since the day of the attack, had had an urge not unlike that of a vengeful instinct to unleash some energy, burn some; let some natural aggression out and relieve the pressure.

This, the two of them accomplished by donning rented *doboks* and doing light body contact sparring and practicing their *poomse's* for an hour.

▥ 16 ▥

REVOLUTION

Going into the second stage of Operation Sunrise, more news had been received from the regional commands, and all of them positive. Except for the unexpected high civilian casualty figures in the first stage, the operation had been considered a success so far. Its early objective to debilitate the government war resources to the measure planned was accomplished, the propaganda war for the hearts and minds of both the rural and the urban populace went on practically unopposed and in many areas undetected.

The people were uniting and beginning to move in one direction. A rebel intelligence analysis suggested that a civilian non-violent uprising would now most likely do just as well as an armed revolution to topple the government.

But the rebel leadership as well as the opposition would not soften up their buildup of force and take any chance against the tyrants in government with the civilian population.

Operation Sunrise continued as planned.

Rebel-controlled areas mostly in the southeastern and western regions had grown, eaten up more real estate - agricultural, dairy-producing and forest lands, from government territories. The number of defections from the regular army and the Civil Guards, mostly those stationed in towns and cities in provinces with major transportation and communication lines cut off, had been increasing. Whole platoons on patrol duties had been reported to turn themselves in and join rebel camps.

News of the successful landing of the first and second arms shipment was received at the Newport Beach station within forty-eight hours. Two days later, one day before the launching of the full-scale revolution and the departure of the future provisional government from America, another major news item was received at the station: the government had re-opened several of those old colonial-time concentration camps with torture chambers and killing dungeons in them and begun herding people into them like cattle, by the hundreds, the thousands; people rounded up, at the direction of the NIS and the DIC, who were suspected of having had any direct or indirect association with the rebels. The news item also told of rapid national mobilization of the armed forces and emplacement of major fortifications from just above the 20th Parallel all the way north to around the outskirts of the capital metro area. Fort Sagrado and Fort York had opened their gates and were pouring out troops into the countryside to hunt for rebels and rebel-sympathizers to throw in the concentration camps.

The beginning of the days of freedom as many in the rebel forces had nurtured in the back of their minds, thus, could not have come any sooner the following day. At dawn, just before the first gleam of sunlight pierced the eastern sky over the mountains, fifty thousand rebelling native citizens of the land determined to defeat by force of arms the dictatorship government that had oppressed them for the past two decades emerged from the hills and the jungles in the west. Another thirty thousand came out of the hinterlands, the small towns and villages of the southern provinces. Forty thousand more descended from the mountains and the high farmlands of the southeast. And there were more, thousands and tens of thousands more waiting their turn to fight for freedom should the first wave not be enough to overcome the enemy.

Two hours earlier across the Pacific Ocean on the west coast of America, a chartered airplane carrying Cesar Ibarra and the rest of the united opposition leadership took to the air for the long journey to the island country. Twelve hours later, on the other side of the International Date Line, they landed at an air base in the Philippines in the middle of the afternoon of the following day without having been in the dark of night. There, to their surprise, they were greeted by hundreds of their exiled fellow countrymen and women, young and old, cheering excitedly with joy and the hope, the anticipation, as everyone coming out of the airplane had sensed, of soon going back to the homeland.

The night was slow in passing as they rested before starting on the final part of their journey the next day. There were phantoms that came in the long hours before daybreak, visions of the people not by the hundreds but thousands, millions, cheering the coming of the days of freedom and justice, the end of tyranny and oppression throughout the land. But with these came also an apparition of terror, of blood, of pain and killing and destruction.

At eleven o'clock in the morning, they were again airborne. The rest of the journey was only an hour long, less than a thousand kilometers, but to everyone in the plane, it felt much longer, every kilometer and every minute of it.

Shortly before takeoff, they had received messages from two sources in Silangan. The first one was from Tala, the capital of the southeastern province of Dumagit in the heart of the rebel-controlled region where they were to land by the middle of the day. It was a brief report on the progress of the revolution emphasizing the taking of Fort Hiroko in the south after a twelve-hour battle. The military surrendered after a short parley with the rebel regional commander and joined ranks with the rebels. Casualties counting both sides were in the low hundreds, much lower than estimated by the rebel analysts. With the fall of Fort Hiroko, the government's foothold in the south, everything below the 20th Parallel - nearly half the country, was practically lost to the rebels. The message reported also on the arrival of the third arms shipment as scheduled, thanks to Domingo Gabriel, it acknowledged, and closed with an advanced greeting to the arriving provisional government.

The second message came from the capital region and was sent by the popular Commander Utak. The commander reported all operations in his region in progress and advancing steadily. He closed with a 'long live the revolution' and 'we await you'.

After the plane glided to a flawless landing and decelerated to a taxiing speed on the runway, the terminal buildings of the Tala Provincial Airport slowly came to view. For a while, Nicholas strained his eyes looking through the porthole trying to make out what seemed at first to be a gigantic pulsating movement on the ground at a distance near the buildings. Then, as they got to within a quarter of a mile and closer, he saw that the movement was that of a multitude of people, a mass of humanity which was reported later by the local and foreign media who were finally allowed by the rebels to begin coverage of the events, to be at least a half a million people.

When the plane finally came to a stop near the terminal gate, it was quickly surrounded by armed men in uniforms many passengers in the plane recognized as those of the Civil Aviation Security and the Civil Guards. It didn't look as if the men, as close as a half an arm-length with their guns leveled horizontally before them, could hold off the initial surge of the welcoming crowd but they did. As thousands upon thousands pressed closer to get near, the noise grew louder and louder until it sounded as if the whole of humanity had joined in a triumphant chorus of echoing one single but never-ending note. Then, a large band which had quickly assembled on the observation deck above the arrival terminal began playing a march.

Everyone was stunned particularly Cesar Ibarra, but none more so than Nicholas not just by the size and enthusiasm of the crowd but by the sudden awareness that his father and the work he'd done with Cesar Ibarra and the rest of the opposition leadership could mean this much - to so many. And this was not all, he thought. This crowd was just a small fraction out of the country's population of twenty-five million people.

They went out of the plane two at a time. Each time a pair did, the crowd let out a roar. At the bottom of the steps, a contingent of the rebel high command headed by Gustavo Jones Carreon, the supreme commander and Juan Vargas Smith, commander of the southeastern region, welcomed each one of them into their open arms.

Nicholas had paired with Fausto Cristobal to be among the first group to go but when they headed out the door, Cesar Ibarra held them and said he wanted them to go out together with him. They were the last to appear to the masses. Most of the opposition leaders who went before them were well-known figures in the country but none as popular and revered as Cesar Ibarra. Once he emerged from the plane, the multitude burst into a thunderous applause that was yet the most deafening. Each time he waved at a certain direction in the crowd, the din intensified. He was clearly in command.

There were people, young and old, men and women, who were overcome with emotions and were crying. Fausto Cristobal and Nicholas who stood on each side of the leader felt the same way and were close to tears themselves. Nicholas regretted it so profoundly that his father could not be present. He was glad, though, that his persistence to take his father's place overcame his parents' reluctance, especially his mother's. He had had to seek the help of Cesar Ibarra himself, just two days before their departure during an afternoon visit at the hospital, in assuring them that there won't be any more danger to his life than he faced in America. Cesar Ibarra vouched for this and even said that he wanted Nicholas to be traveling in close company with him to represent his father in the ranks of the future new government's leadership.

For two days, the people who had masterminded Operation Sunrise and who now formed the provisional government for better than half the country met to analyze the progress of the operation, make any changes that had become necessary and strengthen their resolve to push north as fast as they could do it. Bring the totalitarian regime, what's left of it, to its end with the least amount of bloodshed and ruin to the country.

The third day, they began the five-hundred kilometer march to the capital. Fort York which was less than a hundred kilometers away along the route had been under siege for the last twenty-four hours. The revolutionary leaders had attempted to negotiate a ceasefire so a peace talk could begin, but the military declined. It, instead, tried to break the siege by mounting an offensive of two regiments which did punch a hole through the rebel encirclement and drove back the rebel forces by two kilometers. The freedom fighters quickly reinforced and the fighting intensified.

The provisional government traveled with a revolutionary force equivalent to the armed strength and number of two regular army divisions. And they were freshly armed and equipped from the third arms shipment a few days before. It was proposed that Cesar Ibarra himself attempt a ceasefire talk and peace negotiation with the military when they reach the field headquarters in the battle zones around Fort York. It turned out that that wasn't necessary. An hour before they arrived, news came that the Fort commander had agreed to a truce and that the peace talk had followed immediately right after. It was rumored that the commander, upon hearing of Cesar Ibarra, not to mention the force behind him, quickly heeded the repeated offer for the ceasefire; also, that the commander wanted no quarrel with the leader, a former schoolteacher who was partly responsible for his military career and where he was now, save for the difference of his political and ideological leanings from those of the respected leader.

Cesar Ibarra learned of this, remembering the commander from one of the young students he had taught in junior college years back, and had wanted to meet with him even briefly. But time was short, according to the Sunrise plan of operation as well as the fresh reports from the capital and the northwest regions. There were many accounts of brutal torture and mass execution inside those concentration camps as well as outside; in public squares and town plazas in the capital region. The revolutionaries, Cesar Ibarra told the leadership, are just as responsible for such inhumanities as those actually committing them. We must hurry, he said, and end all conflicts as quickly as possible. We must get there immediately.

But before they head for the capital, another mission equally important, in fact pivotal to the success of the revolution, must be accomplished. Fort Sagrado in the northwest, the last formidable defense of the regime outside the capital region must be taken. There, they hoped they would be as fortunate as they were with Fort York, that the military would see immediately how senseless it would be to prolong the war and for fellow citizens to continue to be killing each other, using up time and resources that otherwise could be used to start re-building everyone's life and the country's economy.

The provisional government and its forces, thus, moved on past Fort York while the ceasefire was in effect. But they were not to clear the battle zones without a near disastrous incident involving some of the leaders. The officers of one of the military battalions which had been deployed in the battle zone area near the access to the Fort decided they would not be part of any peace negotiation with the rebels, being extreme loyalists that they were as was learned later, and opened fire at a passing group of revolutionary troops.

They barely missed Cesar Ibarra in the company of several other top revolutionary leaders riding in an armored car. They hit, instead, the convoys behind them with rocket grenades, blowing up two truckloads of rebel soldiers and killing most of them. One other vehicle, another armored car, carrying among several other revolutionary leaders Nicholas Gabriel, Brian Cooper and Fausto Cristobal, was hit indirectly. The explosion hit the car so powerfully at the bottom that it tossed a few feet in the air, spilling its passengers in every direction. Nobody was seriously hurt but the attack continued with automatic gunfire and everybody had to scramble for cover back behind the upended armored vehicle.

Everyone was able to take safe cover except Brian Cooper who landed the farthest and had to run in the opposite direction, when the gunfire erupted, to make it behind a tree fifteen yards away. Several groups of the passing revolutionary forces as well as some who were part of the contingent that had laid siege to the Fort came to their rescue and took positions to return the fire of the loyalist battalion.

"We got to get to him," Nicholas said to a young revolutionary officer who was leading him and the others away from the line of fire and into another armored car. "We got to get him out of there."

"Yes, sir," said the officer dutifully. "Please, go! Go now! Keep moving!"

Everyone got in the car and was quickly driven away to catch up with the rest. Nicholas waved and hollered at Brian who was pinned stiff behind the tree but was still able to wave and holler back: "Get down! I'll catch up with you!"

The bullets flew continuously for minutes and he could hear them piercing into the front of the tree when they hit. He began to worry after a while longer that they might start going through. Then he heard a whistle over to his right farther away from the route of the passing revolutionary forces and deeper into the battle zone.

It repeated several times, each time louder. He turned to his right and saw that it was coming from a foxhole. A hand stuck out of it, then a head, two, three heads, each under a camouflage beret. The hand waved at him. It was waving him over.

"Over here!" somebody called.

It was at least a twenty-yard sprint. Or he could drop and crawl, hoping the six-inch deep grass would cover him visually long enough.

There was a lull in the shooting during which he was tempted to do the sprint. And he did. Five yards to the foxhole, the bullets came again. He dropped and scrambled on all fours like a squirrel the rest of the way.

Looking up from the middle of the four-foot deep hollow, he saw three rebel soldiers in camouflage uniforms, their young faces covered with dirt, looking tired and thirsty. Not a word was spoken between them, for no sooner had he dropped in than something else did, hitting just inches below the rim of the foxhole and rolling down at their feet, smoking like a newly lit cigar.

"Grenade!" yelled one of the rebel soldiers.

Everyone jumped or clawed his way out of the hole in an instant. Brian Cooper whose adrenaline had not had time to settle down was the first to spring out of the foxhole as fast as he went in. The explosion rocked the ground so violently Brian felt the earth was slipping from underneath him as he tried to hug it. He had no thought of fear, or injury or death. He just lay as flat on his stomach as he could.

He wasn't wounded. Not that he could tell or feel at the moment. Better yet, he wasn't dead! But someone else was, he realized when he turned his head sideways to look back at the foxhole. One of the rebel soldiers didn't make it out of the hole. The other two got out but he could see that one of them was dead too. The body was sprawled on its back only an arm's length away from him and he could see blood still gushing out of a back head-wound where a chunk of shrapnel had apparently entered and ripped through the soldier's brain.

Ten feet farther away, he saw the other crawling away towards another foxhole.

"This way," the rebel soldier called out to him.

They fell on their backs after they slipped into the hole and just looked up at the sky while catching their breaths. They stayed that way for two or three minutes listening, too, to the continuing exchange of gunfires between the other freedom fighters in the other foxholes and other positions in the battle zone, and the government forces.

"Bastards!" the rebel soldier finally spoke. "I hate those military bastards!"

"I thought there's a ceasefire on," Brian Cooper said, still looking up at the cloudless early afternoon sky.

"Yes, but you can't trust those bastards. I want to kill everyone of them!"

Brian took his eyes off the sky to look at his company across the hole. There was something peculiar about the way the rebel soldier sounded.

"Thank you for helping me -" he began to say and then held himself back when he finally had a good look at the freedom fighter and saw hair, long reddish brown hair fallen out from under the camouflage beret. "Hey, you're a... " he stuttered in astonishment.

"What?" the rebel soldier asked and then caught on in an instant. "Oh, yes, that's right. I'm a girl. Why, don't look so shocked. Haven't you seen one before?"

"Excuse me. I didn't mean to look shocked. I'm just - surprised."

"Well, don't look so surprised either. I can kill just as easily as any soldier man can." She inched up on her back against the wall of earth behind her, clutching her submachinegun across her body.

And what a beautiful body, Brian thought. Beautiful face. What an attractive... woman. But how could one so endowed throw herself into this grimy scene of death and destruction?

"Thank you again for helping me," he repeated.

"Not exactly the way I meant it to turn out when I called you over from behind that tree. I almost had you killed."

"But you didn't. I'm sorry about your partners."

"So am I. They were good kids. They weren't even twenty years old," she said with grieving eyes.

"How about you? Are you alright?"

"Yes. I'm all in one piece. And you?" she asked and eyed him swiftly up and down. "You're wounded," she said, looking at his left arm which he just now noticed as soaking his shirt sleeve red. "How bad?"

He rolled up his sleeve and after seeing the flesh wound - a horizontal cut at least two inches long - for the first time, he began to feel its pain.

"I got something for that. Hold on." She unzipped a side-leg pocket, took out a small first aid kit and proceeded to clean the wound and the area around it with alcohol before applying an antiseptic powder on the cut. While she was dressing the wound, she looked up at him several times, then said: "You don't look like you belong here. You don't sound like you're from here."

"You're right, both times."

"You're an American, aren't you?"

"Right again."

She finished up with his arm and pulled back to her side of the foxhole.

"Great!" she snapped at him, looking very disconcerted. "You're just the type of people we need to see around here now. What - you're coming back to colonize the country again?"

"Wait a minute," he complained. Mighty feisty freedom fighter the country has in this one, he thought, and real pretty too especially when she's reacting.

"Who are you?" she asked before he had a chance to speak further, the submachinegun back in her hands in front of her. "Why are you here?"

"I came with the provisional government at the personal approval of Cesar Ibarra." Brian noticed how she perked up at the mention of the leader's name. "Incidentally, he just went by a while ago and narrowly escaped getting hit too. Anyway, I'm a personal friend of Nicholas Gabriel, the son of Domingo Gabriel who is one of Cesar Ibarra's important supporters in America. Domingo Gabriel did not make the trip back with the provisional government because of an assassination attempt by the NIS that put him in the hospital."

"We know who Domingo Gabriel is. We know what happened."

"I got to get out of here," Brian said, now taking lead in the conversation to steer it away from where he didn't want her to take it. "I got to catch up with them."

Before either one could say another word, an explosion blasted a hole in the ground about the size of the one they're in not far from them. It was followed by a burst of machinegun fires that sent bullets whistling by over the foxhole.

"I'd like to get out of here too and rejoin my unit," she said as they inched their heads back up from the dirt. "You go ahead. Maybe you can show me how."

Brian looked around and surveyed their position the best way he could without sticking his head out too far. He pointed at the direction opposite of where the gunfires were coming from but she was shaking her head at him before he could suggest anything.

"That's mined," she said. "Forget that. We'll get us out of here. Just relax for a while. This Nicholas Gabriel - was that him that got back in the other car with the rest?"

"Yes. They're headed north by northwest to Fort Sagrado."

"I know. We're supposed to join up with them as soon as we get done with the job down here. He's an American too, isn't he?"

"Yes. He's an American citizen. But he was born here. What do you have against Americans? What's so bad about being an American?"

"What's so bad about being a Russian, a Japanese or a Chinese?" she countered. "What's so bad about capitalism, communism, democracy or tyranny?"

"Well, c'mon, let's have an answer. I asked the question first."

"I'm saying just stay out of our country. We'll solve the differences among ourselves, by ourselves. Here we are trying to come out of an oppressive rule which some of us - and I mean these tyrants we're trying to overthrow right now - inherited from our former colonizers, and no sooner than we're about to win our hard-fought freedom than you show up! Again! That's what's so bad about you and the rest!"

"Beautiful. That's beautiful. I like that. I understand -"

"We won't have any north or south, or east or west here like Vietnam, Korea, Germany. This is one country. we are one people and we will stay that way."

"Listen, this is one American who couldn't agree with you more on that. If things could only be as simple as that."

"Well, why the hell not? Why couldn't people mind their own business?"

"Sure, we could do that. We could clam up and don't give a damn about what sort of oppression is going on in the world, what kind of inhumanity whether coming from within a country or from outside of it. Sure, we can get the hell out and stay out."

"Then why don't you?" she yelled at him.

"Because there are people who believe in the same things we do, things like freedom and justice and human dignity which they're deprived of and they look to us for help; we're their big hope and we can't turn our back on them because if we did it's the same thing as turning our back on many of our own people, fellow Americans who went through the same deprivations, the same hardships, the same beginnings, the same shit. The idea of America is not just in America. It's all over the world. Can you understand that?"

"Aren't you taking on a little too much upon yourselves?" she asked irately in the manner that caused Brian Cooper to imagine smoke shooting out of both of her ears under the beret. "We don't need you or anybody to tell us what to believe in and how to pursue those beliefs. And of course we believe in freedom and justice and human dignity. Why do you think I'm in this ditch trying to kill those bastards shooting at us? Don't make it sound like they were discovered in America. We will have them on our own terms, to fit our society and our way of life, not that of any foreign power or their culture or ideology. Can you understand that?"

"I have no quarrel with that, lady," said Brian with zeal, "only, tell me one time in all the history of the world when there wasn't one country whose people weren't divided in their beliefs and ideologies, where there were no oppressors and no one being oppressed. Tell me one period in history when there wasn't a single Vietnam or Nicaragua, or Afghanistan, Hungary, Philippines, Cambodia, Poland, Chile. And right here in your country, look at what you've been through for twenty years."

"That's our business, dammit, and I'll say this again and you listen up: we will settle our differences among ourselves, by ourselves, if we end up beating each other's brains out or brainwashing each other or killing each other."

"Aren't you taking on a little too much upon yourself, talking like that?" Brian shot back, gazing smartly at her. "There are twenty five million people in this country. I hardly think you're speaking for every one of them. And how do you know, how do we or anybody know what's being done to you is not dictated from the outside, or that a way of life, an ideology is being forced upon you against your will? Look at Vietnam. It's now one country. But not everyone there accepts the way of life they now have to live with. Many are risking their lives to get out but can't. How would you like to be one of those people who have no one to turn to for help?

"Put yourself in their place. How would you like it if the opposition hadn't been able to do anything - get support, yes, from the outside, raise money to buy arms including that piece you're holding and everything else, and you're faced with the prospect of continuing to live under this present regime, you and your family and your descendants, for the rest of your lives?"

She glared at him like a threatened animal, rearing, as she sank deeper in her nook of the foxhole. Brian saw that he couldn't have said anything more loathsome to her, more distasteful to say the least, as it sank into her mind like a big headache, and in to her heart like a thorn.

Not a sound passed between them for a whole minute except the staccato of a machinegun at a distance, the sporadic gunfires and occasional explosions on either side of the battle zone. They could still see part of the passing revolutionary forces down on the other side of the country road, the last of them, on their way to Fort Sagrado with the provisional government.

Brian eyed his company surreptitiously for a good first-time look. Mid-twenties, he surmised, college-educated, no doubt. He didn't want to admit it to himself, but he was attracted to her even as part of her face was literally hidden in a *real* mud pack. He felt good being alone with her in this war hole. He would have felt good being alone with her in any hole, thought he.

Finally, he said: "We don't want to interfere. We just want to know if our help is needed, and asked for. Also, we want to make sure nobody else does - interfere, either."

Her expression changed gradually to a friendlier one, that in which she had to hold back a bashful smile with a little teeth and eyes batting, not quite successfully, though.

"You're bleeding again," she said suddenly, looking at the big patch of red that had invaded the gauze around his left arm. "Must be a ruptured blood vessel you got."

She went over to him and started undoing the dressing. He didn't feel concerned. He felt happy.

"We got to put you in a tourniquet," she said, working on his arm with a serious look on her face, "and then we got to start working our way out of here."

Not much later after she said that, a ceasefire bugle call pierced the battlefields from one of the three watchtowers of Fort York, and then another from the second, and another from the third.

One by one, the guns died down.

📖 17 📖

THE LAST LETTER

Massive government forces from Fort Sagrado had been beating the rebels back into their territory for four days and had regained control of some western towns and cities. On a major thrust in the first two days of the revolution, the military came out well-equipped and strong on land and in the air, to their enemy's surprise. They met the rebel advances head on with devastating firepower which quickly put them on the offensive. Casualties were in the thousands, sustained mostly by the rebels who had to pull back fast, leaving many of their wounded to be taken prisoner.

Many more freedom fighters, hundreds of them, in advanced positions on separate missions were routed and captured. One group of several hundred brave men stood up against an infantry company supported by a half a dozen demolition tanks and air firepower from a squadron of fighter bomber jets and several helicopter gunships. More than half of them were slaughtered, the rest surrendered and taken prisoner though only after downing three helicopters and blowing up four of the tanks. Among those captured was Emil Sabater.

They were taken to a small farm town not far from the wall fences of Fort Sagrado, where they were herded into a ranch that had been converted into a prison camp together with hundreds of other captured rebels. There, two days later, he found Frank James, the gunrunner, who had gone on a separate mission with another group several days before and was immediately captured the next day.

Frank James was badly battered after going through three sessions of interrogation and torture. They exchanged information quickly for they didn't have much time. Some of the prisoners who had been called in for questioning by the army intelligence had not come back out of the guardhouse since the day before. Most of them were rebel officers and many believed they had been executed, or did not survive the torture.

Emil informed Frank James of the status of the revolution: the western regional forces were re-grouping in preparation for a maneuver which would not engage the currently superior major government forces but take them around past the enemy line and place them at a position between Fort Sagrado and all its field deployments. There they were to dig in, hold their positions while the revolutionary forces from the southeast moving in with the provisional government converge around Fort Sagrado. The forces from the south which matched the government forces more squarely were to engage the enemy, force them back up north and the western forces holding their position were to squeeze them back down, at the same time cutting their supply line from Fort Sagrado. The forces with the provisional government would aim at Fort Sagrado, then a ceasefire and peace negotiation would be offered by Cesar Ibarra to the military command.

Before Emil was called in for questioning, Frank James hurriedly tried to work out an escape plan. He was afraid Emil might not come back out and, also, he believed neither of them would ever be let out of the prison camp alive in any case.

There wasn't enough time, though. The only chance anyone had to accomplish anything was when a pair of soldiers called out Emil's name and began marching towards him after he raised his hand. Quickly, before they got to him and escorted him to the guardhouse, he handed Frank James a letter he remembered, lucky he did, he had written for Nicholas Gabriel the night before.

Emil knew of Nicholas' coming with the provisional government and told Frank this. They understood, and each assumed it in each other, that this moment of parting could very well be their last. But neither of them had a word of farewell to say to the other. Only a deep, searing look of hope and determination as the guards took Emil away.

Six hours later, he was hauled back out to the prison yard, his shoes hanging down by their shoelaces around his neck, his bare feet with burn marks on their soles dragging behind him, drawing a bloody line on the dirt. He was bloody all over and turned out to be even more battered than Frank James as Frank and several of the men from each of their captive groups found out when they worked to repair him.

During the next two days, Frank and Emil masterminded a breakout plan together with their two captive groups. The plan was to be executed two nights later but it never happened. The following day, a rebel force the size of two battalions mounted a rescue attack on the prison camp.

The camp commander, upon realizing inevitable defeat, took the gun to the prisoners' heads to create a mass hostage situation but changed his mind and pulled the trigger. Not all of the guards obeyed the order to fire at will and this gave many of the prisoners a chance to run for their lives.

Many in the two groups who had planned the breakout found it easy to save themselves as they already had several pre-determined escape routes through locations in the fences already cut and camouflaged. Emil was among those but amid the mad scramble to the fences, he had the mind to go after one of the guards who refused to fire and take the guard's gun with which he silenced the machinegun atop one of the three watchtowers. The massacre continued with the hapless prisoners caught in the middle of the open prison yards falling like flies.

Emil turned to another target, a guard who was emptying his submachinegun on a group of scampering prisoners, and blew the guard's head off in one second. He turned to Frank James who had been staying close behind him, tossed him his gun and ran out to take the gun of the guard he had shot.

Frank took out the other watchtower and for a moment watched two bodies plummet to the ground from it. Then he quickly aimed at one target after another and true to his MOS of combat weapons specialist when he was in active service, did not miss any of them. Between him and Emil, it was difficult to place the number of lives that were spared from the heinous act of the military in the prison camp. Easily, in the hundreds.

Unfortunately, Emilio Stuart Sabater's life, twenty seven years of age, was not to be one of them.

The gunner in the third watchtower finally spotted Emil and for a moment turned the gun on him from the rebel forces outside that were pressing fast around the prison camp. Two rounds struck Emil on the chest and felled him instantly. Seeing this, Frank took no time in putting out the menace of the last watchtower, using up his ammunition in the process. He picked up another gun from one of the dead soldiers and shot his way to Emil. About the same time he got to him, the rebel forces broke through, pouring in in every direction. They shot up the whole camp, apparently intent at not giving the enemy any chance to resist, so savagely that when the shooting ceased later, every man-made structure in the farm-ranch prison was leveled and the survivors moved about in a daze like ghosts lost in the haze and smoke of the ruins.

Frank James barely heard Emil's last few words as he cradled the brave young man's head in his arms:

"Thank you... my friend... my American... friend..."

His voice, though no more than a feeble whisper of his last breath as he expired, hung in the air and came to Frank's ears over and over again, each time a little louder and a little more grateful, beating down on his American heart with all the sadness, all the sorrow he never felt before in his whole life.

The rebel maneuver worked as planned. The forces from the south, altogether seven divisions strong including the two regular army from Fort Hiroko, now on the rebel side, engaged the outnumbered but more heavily equipped government deployment of four divisions.

The battle raged continuously for days. The western forces which had secured a position that now effectively allowed them to isolate Fort Sagrado from the field by blocking all the supply routes to its forces even tried harassing the enemy from the rear with sporadic commando strikes to let them know what a precarious situation they got themselves in. The rebels hoped this might help soften up the enemy's fighting spirit during the peace negotiations, should there be one.

Meanwhile, the provisional government and its forces had arrived and taken up positions around the Fort, at the north and the southeast, and were now spreading west to link up with the western forces. Shortly after they were encamped, Fort Sagrado sent out a few companies of combat troops for a light engagement to test the enemy strength. This was also aimed at preventing the link-up with the western forces which they knew would completely surround them.

A battle occurred immediately, one which came to a shooting standoff over several square kilometers of dairy land and stretches of newly harvested and dry rice paddies. The government forces found out quickly enough how formidable and equally ruthless the enemy was. The standoff lasted only as long as the light of day. Not only did they fail to prevent the link-up of the revolutionary forces but they were decidedly outfought and easily driven back into the Fort, leaving behind to be captured nearly half of what they came out with in men and materiel.

It was the same contingent of freedom fighters that rescued the prisoners in the ranch-prison camp which repulsed the government soldiers. This time, though, its number had grown by a few hundred of the survivors from the prison including Frank James, who were only too eager to take up arms again and continue fighting to bring down the government.

When the link-up finally happened and the revolutionary forces surrounded Fort Sagrado completely, in effect putting it in a state of siege, it was as if they had won the war instead of just having beaten back a few companies of soldiers. Even as everyone was aware of the major battle that was going on not more than ten kilometers to the south, the rebels could not resist enjoying themselves and celebrating their partial victories.

The next day, the provisional government was escorted by the rebel commanders out for a field review of the forces. Frank James got his group into formation and gloriously saluted the men who would be the new leaders of the land as Cesar Ibarra and the others passed in their slow moving jeeps and personnel carriers.

Later, as the leaders mingled and talked to the troop, Frank overheard the introduction of Nicholas Harrison Gabriel to a rebel soldier. The man could not have been anyone else, Frank James thought as he moved closer and listened to Nicholas' standard eastern American accent. Ohio? Michigan? Maybe even southern Pennsylvania, or Maryland.

He felt the letter in his chest pocket and hesitated a moment before stepping forward to meet the man Emil had spoken about many times. The friend he said he lost to America since they were very young.

Nicholas appeared to be too preoccupied with their surrounding, his eyes wandering through the clusters of people coming and going, searching eagerly for someone, even as Frank James shook his hand and introduced himself. Frank James didn't want to make it any more difficult for either one of them, thus, he very apologetically led Nicholas away a short distance from everyone and explained his action.

When he spoke Emil's name, he finally got Nicholas'
undivided attention

A letter for you, from a friend, he said first, and
Nicholas' face brightened up in anticipation. Then a
moment after Frank James said the name in a voice that
did not ring with the kind of festive air around but instead
with a look that spoke of an inner anguish, Nicholas froze.
When Frank handed him the letter, Nicholas felt as if he
was being presented with the whole lifetime of friendship
between him and Emil and all the other letters they'd
written each other containing their separate views of the
two worlds they'd known, their aspirations in life,
especially Emil's dream of someday going to America.

Everyone at this time had heard of the massacre and
rescue incident at the ranch-prison camp but not enough
people had been told of an act of heroism of one brave
young freedom fighter which saved the lives of hundreds
of others, at the cost of his own life. With an unfailing
voice driven by his own deep sense of loss and sorrow,
Frank James thus told Nicholas what Emil did and how he
did it so valiantly before he died. Then he excused himself
meekly and turned away so that Nicholas may have the
sanctity of silence as he bore his own sorrow and grieved
the death of a dear friend, a hero.

The letter was written in a hurry and with some physical
difficulty as he could tell from the irregular handwriting.
Probably in the dimness of twilight or early light of dawn
to avoid being noticed by the prison guards.

Dear Nicky,
        I know about your coming with the
provisional government as I know what
happened to your father, and even to you in
Washington. I'm glad your father survived, and

I hope he recovers quickly. I'm glad too that you did not suffer any serious injury.

I'm writing this here in the prison camp not knowing what chance there is I or anyone may have of getting it to you. We received the good news when you arrived in Tala and I know that you're on your way north by northwest and are now approaching the besieged Fort York, if not already there.

The Revolution had suffered a temporary setback on this side of the country resulting from our underestimation of the military firepower. The western forces had to pull back and regroup. The southern forces which we hope could cancel the imbalance of power are on their way up, fully equipped and mobilized.

I was assigned to lead an intelligence mission to go around the entire enemy positions, penetrate into their rear and gather information on their supply and reserve activities. We ran into a mobile artillery company with high-speed tanks and helicopter gunships. I lost more than half of my group and the rest of us are taken prisoner.

For the past several weeks since Operation Sunrise began, I have learned more about our country, our people, and myself above all, than I have in my entire life. In my work for the freedom movement, traveling with the rebel leaders, I've had the opportunity I never had before to see most of the country.

This is a beautiful country we live in, a good land for growing life and sustaining it. Now I realize how much we have at stake together with the peace and freedom we are fighting for. And the people - I never realized how truly universal our citizenry is. In our campaign throughout the land to unite the population against this oppressive government, I saw hundreds of thousands of people band together as one, people of different faces and complexions as though they all came from just about every country on earth not a hundred years ago but only now. And they're all together, we're all together struggling to be free, fighting for the right to live a decent and productive life in this bountiful country.

Tell me, could this be the same thing that makes America strong? The unity of the people and their common resolve?

Most of my life I've lived only under this present government. When we have finally won the Revolution and all the fighting is over, and it will be soon, it would be like being born to a new world, starting a new life, for me and millions of others.

Then perhaps we could have a country similar to America. A country with freedom and justice for everyone of whatever ancestry, one nation united, indivisible.

We await your arrival at Fort Sagrado and I look forward to seeing you soon.

For the Revolution -

Your friend,

Emil

What Emil's experiences as a freedom fighter taught him about the country and its nation, Nicholas saw in one overwhelming scene four days later when the gates of Fort Sagrado finally opened after its Commanding General and staff council resolved to turn their allegiance to the provisional government. It took the revolutionary leaders forty-eight hours to get them to the conference table while they - the military leaders - as they revealed later, were pressured by the capital to hold the Fort at all cost. The president himself in the palace in Cotamaru got on the line and ordered the Commanding General to do so.

But after the rebel leaders, with the more-than-willing participation of the world media, gave them a documented summarization of the armed conflict and political-ideological situation in better then three-quarters of the land, they knew better than to continue to back up the regime that had already lost most of the country and the heart and mind of the people, even those who had supported it for many years.

The order to end the shooting and all hostile actions went out twenty-four hours later to the troops of both sides in the battlefields.

At sunrise the following day, there was a different feeling in the air, a sense of tranquility, of peace one was so unaccustomed to it was almost scary. There was not the occasional muffled explosion at a distance, the sound of guns ripping through the air from afar or the ominous vibrations caused by some war-machine pounding upon the earth.

There was only silence as the morning light lifted the dark of night. Then, as everyone awakened to the new day and remembered the events of yesterday, that strange feeling in the air was quickly replaced with joy and cheering. And when three divisions of soldiers came pouring out of the gates, the cheering escalated into a celebration several kilometers long around the Fort.

The former enemies, fellow citizens, reconciled. Tens of thousands of them laid down their arms to greet each other. A few hours later, fifty thousand more citizens with their war machines and weapons of destruction appeared in the southern horizon. Former opposing forces, now together in their quest for peace and national unity.

And there were more. Thousands upon thousands of the population from nearby towns and cities, at last free of fear of harm and persecution, massed with the revolutionary and military forces and joined the celebration.

Men, women and children of different ages. People of different faces and complexions, of different roots and walks of life, joined together as a nation.

In this one overwhelming scene, Nicholas saw what Emil wrote in his last letter. He felt what it must have been impossible for Emil not to feel. And, finally, he understood what Emil had willingly and courageously died for.

Yes, he thought as he prepared to march north to the nation's capital with this multitude of tens of thousands of liberated citizens, he could have told him this is the same thing that makes America strong, the same thing that would make any nation strong. The unity of the people. Their togetherness and their common resolve.

During the march, he toyed with the idea, off and on for hours, of coming back to stay permanently. But his mind would not be trapped by all these human events of the moment. He was no more inclined to become a part of this evolving process of a nation than he was to see it suffer for years and now go through the bloodletting of an armed revolution.

He would much rather just see it from the outside. Because all along, he believed that these human events are events of the world's past, not of the present. It must not happen again and again and therefore he can not be and does not want to be a part of it.

What he wanted to be a part of is the world beyond that evolving process. And that world is now where his life belongs and where it had belonged - though temporarily suspended at present - for the last twenty years.

He hoped that this would be the last on earth to go through this turmoil and upheaval. But he knew, as did the world, that it would not be. There would be another, with a similar set of players through the whole cycle of events.

There would be another Guillermo Tobias Sakai and Cesar Tiu Ibarra somewhere else on earth and yes, another Emilio Stuart Sabater, Domingo Gabriel and other opposition leaders and maybe even a Nicholas Harrison Gabriel. And for sure there would also be a Frank James and a Brian Cooper.

Before the march began, he had asked that Frank James' special missions group bring up the rear of the provisional government where he and Fausto Cristobal and other high-ranking leaders of the opposition were, just behind Cesar Ibarra and Gustavo Carreon, the supreme leader of the armed revolutionary forces. Then Brian Cooper appeared from the thick of the troop formations, tired and rugged from a long journey to catch up but happily excited as he stepped up leading a young rebel girl by the hand.

"My brave rescuer and protector, Anna Parisi," Brian Cooper said. The girl was suddenly overwhelmed at having come this close to the future new leaders of the country, first to Cesar Ibarra, Fausto Cristobal, Nicholas Gabriel and then to several of the other leaders of the provisional government close at hand. The two recounted their experience during the siege of Fort York and its eventual capitulation. The forces there had been given a go-ahead by the supreme commander to march separately to the capital, Brian said, so they came by themselves. They then took a place with Frank James' group behind Nicholas in the historic march to Cotamaru.

Yes, Nicholas thought to himself again as he looked at the people around him when they were within four hours to the capital metro area, there would be a similar set of players, each to fill in the role everyone does now. And they would all go through the whole cycle of events in this evolving process of the nation at their appointed time and place in it, in life and in death.

But he, Nicholas Harrison Gabriel, he would simply go back to America, back to his life in that world beyond this evolving process which he chooses not to be a part of any more than he had been. And from there, as if looking back from the future, he would view the birthing of a new world, the start of a new life for those who survived the revolution and those for whom such brave men like Emil died.

There were numerous skirmishes starting from the rural outskirts of the capital area, mostly on the main roads and access highways into the city. Many were quick moving gunbattles between the rebel advance recon forces and the outpost troops of the mostly loyalist Civil Guards, and some army regulars. These government defense forces were easily overrun and either deserted their posts or surrendered.

The fighting intensified as the revolutionary forces secured a foothold in the suburban areas. There were tank battles and artillery exchanges. Whole buildings burned and lit up entire city blocks as the fighting went on through the night and into the second day.

Casualties were heavy on both sides. Many civilians were caught in the crossfire and added to the count, to the horror, as usual, of the world outside who witnessed everything as it was happening just as close as the media crews did while they televised it from the freedom fighters' side.

At noon, the revolutionary forces scaled down their assault throughout the capital and, with the help of the international press corps similar to what they did at Fort Sagrado, made an attempt to reach the presidential palace by radio. The revolutionary front proposed a dialog between Cesar Ibarra and the president but the latter, through a palace spokesman, declined and instead vowed to defend the Republic against its foreign-backed enemies.

The full-scale assault was resumed from all sides of the city. Droves of rebel soldiers and former government troops pressed in a concerted drive into the city limits as fast as they could shoot and kill the enemy or talk them into surrendering.

The turning point in the conflict came when Commander Utak and his capital region forces broke through the government defenses in the northwest and laid siege to the capital garrison less than five kilometers from the palace. In the process, they attacked and destroyed three of those re-opened concentration camps on that side of the city and freed thousands of imprisoned citizens.

Several more of those concentration camps in other parts of the city were taken by the freedom fighters as they advanced. The images of these atrocities and human suffering and emancipation again found their way via satellite television transmissions into the homes of other people in other countries all over the world.

The thousands who were at last freed poured out into the city streets in confusion, happy that they were liberated but at the same time frightened by the continuing battles. Finally, the surrender of the city garrison was announced by the capital region military command.

Gradually, the shooting tapered off. As it did, the people began coming out of their hiding places in their homes, in office buildings, shops and other work places. Soon, a million people were on the streets of Cotamaru cheering the revolutionary forces as they marched the last few kilometers to the main gate of the executive palace.

Riding in a convoy of armored personnel carriers behind a column of tanks, the provisional government headed its troops in their approach to the palace on the six-lane main avenue that dead-ended outside the front-lawn gate. About the same time the flag of the Republic, on its pole on the roof of the palace, became visible to them, three helicopters rose to the air from behind the palace building and vanished into the northern sky.

It was reported later on that the fallen dictator was granted temporary political asylum by Taiwan after being refused by Japan, Australia, Indonesia, the Philippines and other countries of the Far East.

📖 18 📖

A NEW BEGINNING

Coming back to his life in America wasn't any problem at all. He was anxious to return to it as soon as he got back first to Los Angeles where he stayed for a week before flying back to Washington, D.C.

The problem was putting those five weeks he lived in the old country behind him, leaving them there - the events, the cast, so he could get back to where he left off. From the time he arrived at his parents' house two weeks after the revolution, he began wondering how much further the events in the old country - past, present and future, would affect the life of every one of them in the family.

It became clear right away that they would for a lot longer than those five weeks he experienced, as he saw what was happening. People were in and out of the house all day long for his father and the man hadn't been out of the hospital more than a week: people from the newly-installed government of Cesar Ibarra keeping in close contact, making sure he was well on his way to being ready for his trip home and a big hero's welcome back there; people from the media, local and national and some from abroad including the old country; and people from the U.S. government as well as some from other countries mostly of the Far East.

Two full-time clerk-secretaries had to be employed to help keep the order of business through the day. Evenings, there were social gatherings for the viewing of the video tapes people had taken of the various media coverage of the revolution starting from the arrival of the provisional government where Nicholas was seen raising one of Cesar Ibarra's arms in triumph to the multitude at the airport, at Fort Sagrado among the rebel and opposition leaders in battle uniforms, and again at the palace balcony next to Cesar Ibarra as they waved at the multitudes in the city squares and streets below them.

In Washington, D.C. starting the following week, he gradually re-acquired a sense of his return to the routine, at home, and later at work the week after. As he re-adjusted, he found it interesting how eager one gets to fall back into the mold of his lifestyle, how happy it makes him to again be able to do even the most ordinary things of the day. To get back to living and, in his particular case, to be back in America.

One's enthusiasm is enhanced by the many possibilities of this one day of his life or those of the next. It is like coming to a new beginning, finding a refuge, a sanctuary where one discovers new values or finally recognizes some old ones he was not able to see before.

He was happy to be back in America. And he was right about his reason for coming back. In a sense, America is a refuge not just in the way that she had been for those huddled masses who had come to her shores but also for those who have the will and the spirit to overcome a certain misfortune in life, as well as for those who prefer to live beyond a certain evolving process of human society.

We are all refugees in life, he thought, after getting more settled in his third day back at work. Everyone seeks a new beginning at one time or another:

Lester Jenkins, who told him of the new job with an internationally known professional engineering firm in Georgetown where the black man was hired as an associate engineer;

Gary Clemens, the architect he admired so much whose threat of abandoning his profession and depriving it of his creativity and imagination was thwarted by an AE firm owned by an east coast real estate developer, with an offer of a position as a chief design architect.

Even some of those who have lost the will and the spirit to rise above their misfortunes and allowed their lives to reduce to a street existence, a day comes when they see life's other possibilities and decide to make it a day of renewal, a day to stand up and be counted.

Coming back to the office in the afternoon from a jobsite trip, Nicholas found a phone message on his desk from Edward McKenny. It consisted of two words: The Ellipse.

It was a couple of minutes before five in the evening when he got there. He got out of the car carrying a plastic grocery bag containing two packs of Marlboro, a pint of vodka, a quarter-pound burger and a ham-and-egg sandwich from the office vending machine. It was a mild winter day in early February although the ground was half-covered with snow from a moderate three-inch fall two days ago.

Perhaps because he was still in the process of coming back in touch with the realities of life, his life, in America, here in Washington, D.C. to be exact, he was particularly anxious to see the homeless man again and listen to whatever he may have to say for himself this time. And he wanted to know, primarily, how the stubborn street man got himself to call again after the inconclusive tongue-lashing they gave each other the last time they got together.

He had gone three quarters of the way around the egg-shaped park, stepping close to several benches and peering at the empty faces of their occupants when, finally, he stopped walking to glimpse a man walking behind him about six yards back to his right and seemed to be picking up on every step he made. He half-turned, pretending to fix his overcoat collar, to look at the man through the corners of his eyes.

The man kept walking towards him without slowing down as he did before. The evening was still light enough for him to make out details of the man. He was clean-shaven, his hair neatly trimmed and well combed in place, and he held his head erect with a touch of arrogance to the world before him. He wore a matched shirt and tie under an expensive winter coat that looked like it just came off the rack of Macy's men's store at the Pentagon City Fashion Centre.

Some six feet away, the man stopped and looked at him directly. He must be a government secret service man, Nicholas thought as he prepared to make a full turn and face him. A new president was still in the process of moving in to the house across the park and it wouldn't be a surprise to find out the area was under extra security and carefully watched.

What did he have in the plastic bag? What was he surveying the area for? Who was he with?

"Looking for somebody, mister?" the man asked instead as Nicholas turned around, all worked up.

He looked close at the man for three or four seconds until he was staring and then a surprised smile broke on his face as he realized he was looking at Edward McKenny.

"Why, I'll be -" he gasped and blinked and stared some more. "I'll be damned! It's you! What are you doing dressed like that? Bums aren't supposed to dress like that."

"The hell they don't," Edward retorted. This is America. Anybody can dress any way they want. But I'll tell you why I'm dressed like this: because I retired from the business."

"What business?"

"The business of being a bum."

"Since when?"

"A few weeks ago. I tried to get in touch a couple times but they told me you went on vacation."

"Yes, that's right," Nicholas said promptly, still trying to get over his surprise. Then he remembered how distressed Matthew McKenny's voice sounded over the phone from Philadelphia, full of pity and anguish, as he told him about his brother in the streets of Washington. "So how've you been since - you got out of the business?" he asked.

"I'm doing okay, Thanks." Edward McKenny spoke with his head now slightly bowed in a sullen expression as they started to walk beside each other.

Big brother Matthew had come down from the City of Brotherhood two days after Nicholas had called and found him in a bench at Farragut Square. There were a lot of tongue-lashing and browbeating not unlike that between

Edward and Nicholas except that they were more biting and lasted longer. Matthew succeeded to get him off the street and into a hotel the second day. Then there were more talks. Matthew didn't let up until his kid brother was once again the kid brother who listened to what he says because he is Big Brother Matthew.

Then Edward finally let go of his apathy in life and slowly let some sense back into his head. Matthew put him up in the hotel for a week until he found him a place to stay in Arlington at the house of a trusted friend who even offered Edward a job to get back on track with the fast food supply company where the man worked as a district manager.

They were silent for a little while, looking at the pavement as they continued to walk slowly as if counting their steps around the Ellipse.

Edward broke the silence first, saying: "I want you to know that I've thought a lot about ... about some of the things you've told me."

"Oh, yeah?" said Nicholas coyly.

"Yeah."

"Things like what?"

"Things like... being an American." Another stretch of silence. Then their conversation began to flow. "I thought about that over and over for a long time," Edward continued. "I still do and probably will for the rest of my life. It made me run out of excuses for running away from life."

"People don't know these things unless they've seen and lived a different life in a different place, like I have. People have to be told, so I can't say that anybody can blame you either."

"People are just too lazy to use their heads sometimes. I mean, you don't need to be born in Mexico or some Third

World country and then come to America for a share of the crumbs of the American life to know the difference. It happens everyday. You see it even if you were born and raised here, how different life could be for the worse. All you got to do is open your eyes to it. Then you learn to appreciate what you already have, the opportunities open to you still, the value of already being here."

"You had me fooled there for a while," remarked Nicholas.

"I had me fooled too," added Edward. "I actually started hating you for what you were doing to yourself."

"I don't blame you." Edward shot a quick glance at Nicholas. At present, he didn't think he could look the man straight in the eye. It would have to take some time to get to that. "Listen, I'd like to apologize for the way I treated you especially the last time -"

"Skip it."

"Please, let me -"

"I said skip it. If you're going to do something for which you're going to be sorry, then don't do it. But once you did it anyway -"

At that point, they turned to each other, smiling.

"Alright, alright," said Edward. "God, you got a long memory."

But Nicholas wanted to finish the quote and went on:

"- don't apologize for it. Stick to it. If you made an ass of yourself, then be an ass." And they broke out laughing.

A moment later, Edward said: "I would like you to meet Matthew. He wants to see you. He asked me to bring you over for a visit as soon as I get a hold of you."

"Who's Matthew?" Nicholas fibbed. "I don't know any Matthew."

"The hell you don't. You're going to come with me to Philadelphia to meet my big brother and his family if I have to drag you there hand and foot."

"Can I bring my girlfriend?"

"Bring anybody you want."

They stopped walking when they came near a steaming grate occupied by a homeless man who had surrounded himself with several bundles of his belongings to shield himself against the cold. Edward turned his attention to the plastic bag Nicholas was carrying.

"Is that for me?" he asked.

"Yes. There's a pint of vodka in there, some cigarettes and a couple of sandwiches."

"Well, are you going to give it to me or what?"

"If you want it."

"Sure, I want it."

Edward took the bag and thanked Nicholas for it. Then he excused himself and went over to the bundles on the grate. Nicholas watched him as he looked inside the plastic bag and then bent down to shake the man on the grate.

"Hey, wake up, you bum!" Nicholas heard the ex-bum say. "I have something for you. Food! Food!"

📖